# THE FALL OF MARS

**AMALIA COȚOVAN**

This book is a work of fiction. Names, characters, places and incidents are either the product of the author's imagination or are used fictitiously, and any resemblance to actual persons, living or dead, business establishments, events, or locales is entirely coincidental.

No part of this publication may be reproduced, stored in a retrieval system, or transmitted in any form or by any means, electronic, mechanical, photocopying, recording, or otherwise, without written permission of the publisher.

ISBN: 978-1-4709-8871-5

Copyright (C) 2022 by Amalia Coțovan. All rights reserved.

Cover artwork: Diana Coțovan
Cover design: Cristian Coțovan

## CONTENTS

## IMITATION — 5

| | |
|---|---|
| The Sacrifice | 11 |
| Flavours | 15 |
| Dreamless Sleep | 23 |
| Horace | 49 |
| Smelling of Blood | 71 |
| Forget Everything | 89 |

## OLIVER — 97

| | |
|---|---|
| A secret everyone keeps | 99 |
| Mentor, friend, memory | 115 |
| Losing | 131 |
| There are no bad guys | 137 |
| Just Drive | 153 |
| Name and a Face | 161 |
| Calling Home | 165 |

## SERENITY — 179

| | |
|---|---|
| Any means necessary | 181 |
| Last thread | 191 |
| The Brightest Sunrise Yet | 197 |
| Still Burning? | 209 |

# PART 1

# IMITATION

## 1976

The one thing she would be leaving behind was her little canary, Lemon. In a chorus, she could have been the Prima donna. Her song could be recognised anywhere, even in the whistle of the wind or the giggle of glass chimes, but it took Layla only an afternoon to forget it. The memory of its melody expired, and just two years since she entered the ground in a shoebox.

The sun had risen and set since Layla entered the garden, and yet, she didn't find a single champion, not one contestant that could come close to Lemon's song. An entire orchestra could be made from all the birdsongs in her recorder - none to match hers in harmony, or elegance.

She had to have been a special one. Perhaps her song came from her black tongue. Layla was sure normal canaries didn't have tongues black as soot, and neither did these birds.

Laying on the damp earth in the centre of the garden, she gave up, screwing her eyes in frustration. The glass door across the grass slid open, and Layla couldn't help but smile in the dark. "Oh, no," sarcasm greeted the guest.

"I've been discovered."

"Last I checked, you don't stargaze with your eyes closed." Despite the late hours, the kind elderly voice was full of humour that succeeded in brightening her night, refreshing it after a full day of disappointing melodies.

"There'll be enough stars to gaze at where we're going."

The door slid closed, and a pair of footsteps neared her. "But will they be the same?"

"No more riddles, dude! I'm grieving." But she gave thought to the question, allowing a momentary distraction. There was some intrigue in it: the light they saw on Mars would have to pass through a different atmosphere, go a longer distance, hit the eye at different angles. Same stars, different view. Even more reason to think this day wasted. At least he came now, reminding her to open her eyes as she lay on her back.

She owed so much to Horace. Outside this place, they had been strangers, but this strange old man soon became her only friend in the compound these last few years. At first the jet lag, paired with the good old homesickness, made sleep almost impossible. Nobody noticed but Horace, who took it upon himself to ensure she got the rest she needed. It was he who acquainted her with the garden, meant to be some kind of inspiration for the "oasis" they planned to recreate on Mars.

This place really was an oasis. But it only let them forget about the mission, and about the war. The sweet songs of the birds and the perfume in the cool air lulled Layla to sleep better than any lullaby. This was her place, and it pained her to think it was the last time she would see it, for goodness knows how long? Tonight was the last night.

"Can you help me with something?"

Horace circled her and was busy photographing a rose. "Me? I'm sure a genius like yourself can solve any problem better than me." Layla laughed at his flattery.

"It's not work. I just want a second opinion."

"Okay, shoot." He snapped a photo, and the flash made her jump. "Sorry." He turned the flash off. "It's better without it anyway." Layla forgot her question momentarily. Getting up, she changed the subject.

"Why didn't you come earlier? The flowers look better in the sun, and I was the only one here, I wouldn't have bothered you."

"I'm here at the perfect time. Plus, I wouldn't interrupt your grieving." He snapped another photo. "Right now, the flowers are still open," He traced a petal with the pad of his thumb. "But, the dew has already set in, and with the moon out, what does that remind you of?"

"I don't know. Ice, I guess?"

"Exactly. Ice!" He giggled like a child, forcing Layla's smile. "You'd never find real ice on a rose in full bloom. Sometimes, imitations of impossible things are better."

"You don't make any sense, man."

"Good, I'd hate to be upfront about everything. Speaking of... What did you need help with?"

Layla laid back down in the grass. "I'll figure it out." Horace insisted. "I guess I just feel a bit of regret."

"How so?" She heard the shutter of the camera again. "Having second thoughts about the mission?" She shrugged. "Doubt, not regret, then."

"Do you think you're gonna miss any of it?" Horace knew what she meant immediately. "Like... Do you think you can be homesick, but want to get away at the same time? Heh. I'm the one not making sense now, sorry." She pocketed her recorder, knowing she had wasted her last day on earth. "It's confusing, 'cause I have nothing to miss here, so why do I feel like this?"

"I don't blame you, kid. It's hard to think of anything good to miss. War strips the world of beauty. Trust me, I've seen enough of war to know. The desire to be free of fear, while taking home along with you." She pondered over this until the snapping ended. "The time's passed. They've gone to sleep. "As if a rose should close and be a bud again. Is that what Blake said? You should go to sleep, too." He made his way back to the door, offering Layla a hand, but she waved him off.

"It was Keats." She lifted her head just enough to catch sight of his tall body, turned away but looking up at the sky. "Been getting into poetry, buddy?"

For a minute he just stood there, looking around, whatever cogs were turning in the old man's head, she wouldn't know. He never answered her question, but she knew already. It was all she ever talked about, and the compound had a vast library they frequented. It was only time before she infected him with the poetic virus.

"Done any exploring yet?" Layla shook her head, but she could sense he knew that wasn't true. She'd stolen a key from one of the agents who had awkwardly put an arm around her when she pretended to be crying of homesickness. Before the realisation about Lemon had struck her, all that was on her mind was the lexicon of strange symbols she saw in the first room the key opened.

Rows and rows, like a juvenile alphabet poster in a school. She tried recreating it on paper when she got back, but could only remember a few, before she heard footsteps and escaped through the open window into the courtyard. One word lingered in her mind, like a puzzle piece she couldn't find a box for.

Explosive.

She couldn't remember which symbol matched with it, thought, and now that Horace's gaze turned down to her, on the damp ground, the word returned to haunt her.

Before turning the light off inside, he tapped his watch, passive-aggressively, and disappeared into the darkness of the compound.

Layla smiled. Yeah. At least she'll be going with a friend. She'll have more friends on a strange planet than she ever had on earth – who could have guessed? The dew had started seeping through to her back, and she rolled up her sleeves, digging her fingers into the wet grass as it started to rain. Here's one more thing she'll miss, or at least look forward to returning to.

NV002 to OD001 comms request 030486 failed. Message: Col. Denver make contact with WA001 ASAP. Important developments.

NV002 to OD001 comms request 040486 failed. Message: Col. Denver contact any station ASAP. Pres. will not wait for approval to terminate the mission otherwise.

WA001 to ALL comms request 040586 failed. Message: Mission termination as of 040686. Evacuation imminent.

Chapter 1

# THE SACRIFICE

1986

The Colonel sits at his desk. In his dry and aged hands he holds with utmost delicacy a letter. He eyes the watermark. Washington.

The directions came in with the shuttle, the first one in nine years, empty except for a dozen seats, one for each of the Ambassadors, and himself. He is going home.

First, he clears his throat, but it makes no difference. His thirst hasn't been quenched in a decade. The water here is just too pure, too plain. It has no flavour, no sweetness, no temperature, you can hardly feel it going down your throat. Artificial.

He smooths the letter on the desk after the third reading, and gets ready to record the speech. Within hours, it will be played on every radio on earth, and he will be on his way home. All he has to do is lie. Could it be this hard after all these years of practice? It fails to comfort him that the words he is about to read aren't his own.

Suppress it.

He straightens his tie, then his mask. The heavy oxygen tank rests on the ground, giving his back a much-needed break. When he sits upright, his back cracks in several places, and it's the only sound that accompanies the feedback from the microphone.

He begins to talk and it's an apology that drains him of his breath, but he takes a moment to catch it, ducking into the silicone mask momentarily before signing off, hesitating on the goodbye, knowing he will be one of the very few to ever see the blue planet again. By now, the rest of them must have seen the rocket entering the atmosphere, and started to flock from wherever they had wandered, all migrating towards the beacon, the ride home. They will never hear the apology, but their friends and family, thinking corpses of them, will.

None of them will reach it in time. One could have, but his constant – nay, incessant – meddling sealed his fate. Such a shame that Oliver never learned his place in the game. Maybe, one day, he could have had the honour of being the one in front of the microphone. He's eager, and he's young. Both are his own fault, and both reasons that his dream would never come true. However, he was next to nobody before he came here, and that was best for everyone.

He shut the power off four days ago, thinking the rocket would have arrived sooner. People had come and gone since then, suspecting nothing.

The Colonel plays the recording back and heaves the tank up, leaning it against his desk. Even now, he can't remember if the Martian environment had weakened him, or if he's just getting old. His greying hair doesn't stand out among his peers, but in the stagnation, everyone aged poorly.

Not that he'd been in contact with any of them. No, since the final resource shuttle arrived eight years ago there was no point to sticking around except to refill their oxygen tanks every few weeks, only to flee as soon as possible. And here he is now, alone in an empty building in a ghost town on a barren planet.

"- a project that has been my personal pride and joy this past decade and long before, and my sentiments are surely shared by the multitudes of people, both here and on earth-" The Colonel stands up, pushing the chair away, and the harsh scraping drowns out his voice. He'd never had his lies played back to him before. It's a brutal and refreshing experience that stings like looking at yourself through a broken mirror.

"- and after ten prosperous years, the project must come to an abrupt end. Through no fault of our own, the natural balance of the Martian environment has become suddenly incapable to sustain us. We at the Embassy were kept safe inside the city, but those who failed to conform and co-operate were sadly lost, and we will do our best to keep their memory alive when we return to our native-"

He lets his mind wander as he peers through his window at the top of the Embassy, facing the glittering dome - the pride and joy of Odyssey: the orchard. Beside it, breaking the horizon, stands the rocket, a demanding and looming monolith, yet shorter than most of the skyscrapers that still stand, sparsely spread throughout the grey city of imitations. He can see the top of it, pointed to the sky, reminiscent of a certain statue. Another imitation - artificial pride.

Maybe he would stay. The ambassador plays around with the idea, then his mind clears and remembers the plan. Once that rocket lifts off, there won't be anything to stay for. Not that there's much keeping him here anyway. But the people-

What have they ever done for him? Only get in the way. How can he win the game if the pawns don't appreciate the rules? Without them, maybe he would already be home. He'll forget. Soon enough, he will forget, or he will die, and he'll have bigger things to worry about.

"-don't let this... inconvenience discourage or discredit the supremacy of our strong nation, for it has never been greater! And our ten year experiment is only a stepping stone and a worthy example of the full capability of our country. I look forward to seeing the faces of the American people, the glorious skyscrapers and our beautiful culture once more."

Even from the window he can hear the distant clicking of the powerful wind hurling pebbles and sand at the glass dome, peppering it with white scuff marks. If he squinted, he could see the cracked glass tile where the woman's head hit as she fell dead eight years ago. If he can't forget that, then there's no chance he'll live this down.

Before, he liked to imagine that he was part of something bigger, above everyone else. (Maybe she did, too.) He was the connection, the link between here and home, but he accepted that he was yet a player in the game, and his turn had finished long ago.

The statement had been made. The show was over, and now it's time to move on to other things, like winning the war. What part would he play in this new game? At least he would play it on a board that wasn't constantly obscured by a thin sheet of red dust. He parts himself from the window, and ends the tinny drone of the feedback from the microphone.

He makes his way to the rocket.

Chapter 2

# FLAVOURS

1987

Horace straightened the fluttering map over the hood of the truck, smoothing the incomplete diagram down and pinning against the wind with the ball of his wrists. He turned the map around, making sure he was facing the right way. A trip this long in the wrong direction would surely mean losing a day's worth of resources.

Layla was securing the rest of their stash in a cave they had discovered just days ago. In mapping this side of the planet, she and Horace had made discoveries that, in any other circumstances, would have secured Nobel prizes for them both.

Craters dotted around the city provided sufficient resources to bring them at least another year's worth of comfortable survival. Each crater hid valuable metal in the form of scraps, even parts of engines, and, their most proud find, a functioning truck, with suitable room to carry all their necessary items along with the oxygen supply, although they usually hid that in a cavern when they went out exploring.

They probably could have found much more treasure if they searched the city, but they had put as much distance between themselves and that place for a reason.

With no obligations and an abundance of oxygen between them, boredom came too easily, and soon became their deadliest enemy.

So, they started to make maps. Horace's real role in Odyssey was more akin to an architect, but he titled himself after his real passion.

He'd been working on the map of Odyssey and the surrounding caves and craters for almost a year, beginning it only as a means to fill the time, but one day, when he was close to giving up, mind scattered and at wits' end, Layla asked to have a look, and almost immediately discovered a pattern between the craters. Since then, she hadn't made a single wrong prediction about a new crater, each one being more and more rewarding. These expeditions were key to their survival, and – if luck would grace them – salvation.

That was how their supplies remained stocked, though what had shocked everyone, not just them, upon settling here, was the lack of appetite. They joked that it was their work that kept their stomachs full, but both watched each-other's hollow cheeks with a sense of guilt. They occasionally had meals, if they could be called that, but most of their time was still consumed by work, which Layla had begun to show a significant interest in due to the significant drought of wiring to be done in the Martian desert. And poetry didn't do much to keep the hands busy as much as the mind.

Horace produced two small, blocky white packages from his coat, and watched the sun rise from behind the rippling dunes. He imagined that it was the sun's heat that made the vision tremble, and not his failing eyesight. "All done. Did you mark down the co-ordinates?" He looked back to the mouth of the cave, seeing the figure emerge from the shadow, and wipe the sweat from her brow, despite the cold morning air.

He used the two objects to weigh down the corners of the map as he scribbled down some numbers beside a red cross, the mark for this cave, and the number 17 beside it. "If we find nothing, we'll be back by sunset."

"There won't be nothing," Layla assured him, "but we shouldn't stay too long anyway. We should go back in a few days."

"Why?"

"Don't like the look of those clouds." She pointed to the west, where, sure enough, a storm was gathering. "We should wait it out, really, but I'm no cave-woman." This stretching landscape, however monotonous, was infinitely better than an existence in damp darkness. So, whatever they found would have to wait.

Horace sighed, heaving his tank to the ground and stretching. His ill-fitting uniform didn't stretch with his tall body, pulling down his sleeves to expose his thin wrists, which were hit by a cold breeze, and he dropped them. Layla was studying the map when he handed her one of the packets, and she scowled, but opened it when he pointed silently to her eyes, knowing that he'd noticed the deep crevasses below them, that she'd forgotten to try to hide.

She crumbled the contents of the packet with her fists, before taking off her mask and tipping half of them into her mouth. "Flavour?" She held up one finger, pinching the air, and chewing with feigned concentration complete with distant gaze and furrowed brows. In the sun, it was almost impossible to miss the white streaks peppering her jet-black curls. She inspected the wrapper and brought a small notebook from her inner pocket.

"The pink - raspberry and coffee. Interesting blend, but..." She scribbled down a note and put her mask back on. "Dry as a..." She caught herself, knowing Horace didn't care for her crude jokes, but he was occupied with his own meagre meal.

He eyed the cream-coloured bar, turning it over in his hands. "What actually is this supposed to be?" He squeezed his fist and the paper crumpled with a satisfying crackle.

"No clue, man, but I like it."

"Of course you would like it, you like everything with coffee in it."

She sighed. "Oh, what I'd give for a good coffee right now. Or any hot drink... Dude! Hot chocolate." She made another note in the notebook and pushed herself off the truck but soon lost her balance and clutched the door to get her footing. Horace didn't mention it, or the fact that she had been pretending to shield her eyes from the sun. He changed the topic quickly, tucking the map away.

"I noticed you, uh... re-drew my commissioned piece." She drained the last crumbs from her packet and nodded. "Sweden was one of my biggest projects. I had to consult many government officials for the job."

"Mhm," She pushed her oxygen tank behind the driver's seat. "But that was like half a century ago, the map's probably very outdated."

"It took me seven weeks to draw that." He swept some crumbs from his thin beard. "Wait – are you calling me old?"

How she loved to rile him up. "Took me three days, but I was just copying."

"Three days and how many nights?"

She didn't answer. He'd successfully caught her off guard. He would have been proud of it a few months ago, but it was becoming too easy… worryingly easy. "How many nights?" He knew that she knew what he was really asking.

"My recorder ran out of battery. I didn't want to take any from your stuff." The recorder she used to record the birdsongs on her last day on earth. The recorder she plugged her headphones into every night. The recorder which was the one thing that could send her to sleep better than a knock over the head.

"When did it run out?"

"Last week." Her cheeks took on a rosy glow, or was that the sun? Fever? "But I do sleep–"

"Passing out for half an hour at a time is not sleeping! You think I don't notice, but I do. You should have told me - I'm not even using most of that junk, Layla." Layla. The kid was gone. At the mention of her name, her face visibly hardened. "This isn't normal."

"Normal? Look around. What about any of this is normal?"

"I mean… You've come so far and you're content to… to die of exhaustion? My ultimate goal is to get home." Neither of them had ever said it out loud. "And I'm not leaving without you - that's a promise."

Layla threw her head back and smiled, letting out a deep sigh that shook her whole body. Her hands went up defensively. "Okay. Fine, I'm sorry. I should have told you sooner. Let's go, we're wasting daylight." They both knew this wouldn't be the end of it, but were content to let it sit. For now.

"Ahem." Horace folded his arms as Layla placed her hands on the steering wheel.

"What?"

"Shift over, kid. I'm driving." His matter-of-fact tone was almost commanding. Horace never gave orders, and he never drove, not even on earth, but when Layla took up the driving responsibility, with not a single minute of lessons behind her, it was time for him to get back behind the wheel. Here he was again, ten and two. At least the landscape was a comfort, just flat and red, no obstacles, no other drivers. It was peaceful in its boredom,

Layla dragged her oxygen tank behind the passenger seat, slumping down heavily. Before placing his hands on the wheel, Horace flexed all his fingers, cracking his knuckles like a maestro beginning a performance.

"Don't kill us." Layla joked, and he rolled his eyes behind his thick white eyebrows. "What? Don't you want to get me home in one piece?"

"Oh, hush." Their safety really relied on the truck's lingering lifespan. Like Horace, it was on its way out, but also like him, it wouldn't go without a good fight. The occasional dune would threaten its aged engine, and instead of conquering it, they resorted to circling it instead. A rare occurrence, but a sign of the impending end nonetheless.

The engine trembled to life, and the rhythmic whirring immediately began to soothe Layla's fatigued body. She slid back, closing her eyes against the sun, and let herself drift. She still missed the sound of her canary's singing, but that was eleven years ago. Life was different, and she wouldn't let herself be defeated by lack of sleep. It would be too easy, and that wasn't her style.

Eleven years was long enough to settle into some sort of routine. Once she managed to fall into it, sleep was one thing she could control, or at least, let it control her. She could pretend for a few hours at a time that everything had gone well, that someone had saved them, or someone had stopped them leaving. She was yet to decide which was more ideal. To be saved, or to be shielded?

She was never warm, but never cold enough lull her senses. She would lay in the lukewarm air, the added weight over her nose having become part of herself instead of an extension. Rooted to the ground by the heavy tank, she let herself drift out of the current existence. The birdsong would fade, and so would she, shrinking into herself. Shrinking, and shrinking even further into a concave existence, until she was nothing, and she could go anywhere, travelling while stationery over an invisible grid of her memory.

Then she could open her eyes and be anywhere, mobile in space but not in time. That was the catch, she could see anything she wanted but not participate even in the memory. All she was allowed was the memory of a memory and fragments of the past.

Her favourite destinations would flash before her, swirl around her, tie themselves up in her hair and freeze there, choking and draining the time out of her, always on the crest of motion, of movement, of delivering a blow of nostalgia and thawing the sounds, the colours and lights from her frozen memories. She used to wish for stillness, now she longed for motion, for signs of life.

She could stay as long as she wanted in one place, but never chose to do so. Wherever she was taken, she took in what she was given. Still light that never dimmed, silence reminiscent of the space between words and sentences spoken once, somewhere. But the smells... The smells she could enjoy.

Fresh tarmac drying under summer sun. The black tar that would stain her new white shoes. The expensive shampoo her mother would import from Togo, and the glue and brown tape that her aunts had stuck down on the boxes.

Security.

The chemical, burning smell when she first used her flat iron, waking up early before school. The smell of rain that seeped through her uniform, warm May rain that blended with the summer sweat on her brow, walking to the bus stop as her hair escaped its tight, straight stretch. She could stay here forever with her curls.

She never did. Every memory she would return to would fade like a tattoo. It would always be there, but never the same, always overcome by the subtle stench of smoke. Subtle at first, then overbearing, dizzying. It would wake her up. She would gasp for air, lips parted, then clamp a hand over her mouth.

Her favourite memory to return to was the one she never spent too long on. Indulging in mere minutes before the smoke came, she couldn't afford to lose this one.

She might have been eleven. It was the end of the day, and she had recited her lines all morning and afternoon break. From the freeze-frame memory Layla didn't need to deduce anything, the day unravelled before her like the hair spilling out from her studded headband (not in the uniform, but nobody said anything.)

The pedestal was hers. The spotlight, though this was only in her imagination, on her also. A hundred eyes brimmed with pride, awe and envy that would follow her into the next five or six years Maybe it was still there, deep below the resentment. In her thin fingers she gripped the delicate paper, artificial light shining through it. Within minutes the clapping would come, directed by the headmistress, whose repulsive perfume still lingered past the smoke. The past hour of PE lessons still hadn't lost its familiar trace of sweat from the room, and the thin layer of grime from lunch time not yet cleared away by the looming shadow of smoke.

She forced herself awake.

Chapter 3

## DREAMLESS SLEEP

The reality of everything came into perspective at night. Even though nothing had even a semblance of normality, it was hard to ignore every single intrusive thought. She was bored, and whatever she did to chase away that feeling only worked until it ended. The worst truth was the one she remembered whenever she had to look across the vast expanse, the red earthen landscapes surrounding and entrapping them in every direction: they had been abandoned.

But the night came, and the truth hung in the sky where the moon should have been. The night came, and it was painted on the sky, connect the dots and it's there, written in the stars.

Layla, Horace, and every other person given this "opportunity" would only be remembered by the selfishness of those who sacrificed them to save themselves. Made them into martyrs: poor sods with nothing to do but rot away.

They spread far and wide after the bloodbath that followed. However, it wasn't that rare of an occurrence that, while searching for a new crater, they spotted a dark shadow on the horizon. This was a shadow of another soul, condemned by the same evils, and suffering the same boredom.

1978

Layla had managed to evade boredom for the first two years of the expedition, distracting herself from the monotony of Mars with her commission. The first year was spent in a collective effort to build the orchards, which became the pride and joy of all who contributed, and the beacon of hope that would be reported on back to earth, while their communications were still working. Occasional "presidential reports" would be read aloud, but it wasn't hard to see the watermark on the letters were from the Colonel's own stationery, and didn't match that which was seared into the vision of all who stared too long at their invitation letters. They stared for validation if they found nothing else there.

Validation was all they were offered. With the orchard being finished, the next project was the city, with the orchards as its predecessor, yet the plaque outside the city would say otherwise. When the city was finished and the war was still raging, most were left to wander the empty streets. Layla's work truly began then.

Layla would give Odyssey the gift of light. She passed the plaque every day, venturing alone into the city while everyone mingled in the orchard, occupying themselves with wondering how the trees took to the Martian soil so quickly. They grew fast, but seemed to linger between life and death at any time.

It had been only seventeen weeks since the orchard's completion, but the city was already in its final stages. Layla's heart dropped every morning when she returned to the city, only to see a skyscraper double in height every day. Horace hardly concealed his own concerns.

When she'd finished wiring the light in the embassy, she was presented with her first fraction of the commission. The rest of the workers were gathered and lined up outside the ambassador's office and each handed another letter with the presidential watermark, allegedly having arrived that day, though nobody could see how, since the shuttles with supplies had ceased when the orchard was completed.

Along with this, they received a variety of luxuries from earth, a chocolate bar, some ground filter coffee, and a goose down pillow. Each of these letters were thrown away almost immediately. Layla gave her pillow to Horace, who'd been burdened by neck pain since they arrived. She used her letter as a coffee filter, which wasn't provided. The first sip of coffee almost made her retch. Clearly the water here was not made for brewing. She joined the others in donating their coffee grounds for fertilizer.

Horace kept his distance from the city. Nobody knew what his commission was, but his remarks about the city's plan being unsustainable, modelled after the car-persuaded New York City, were openly expressed. He avoided even looking in the city's vicinity and winced at Layla's reports from within. It was only with the first nightfall after the city's completion he agreed to give it a proper look, though admittedly it was Layla's pride at her own work that convinced him to this.

When he first glanced at the city, once the sky had become a void of light, the city itself was almost invisible against the black backdrop.

Maybe that was for the better. What he could see were the little squares of light, the patchwork of candle fires in neat rows blending into the realm of the stars, distinguished only by the boundary where the scattered lights glowed ordered rows, equal distances apart. Layla gleamed with pride watching them fall into place.

The night was spent in the dome.

When morning came and the real stars faded, the artificial ones burned out and the rough and jutting structures stamped their presence into the sky. Their forms in straight grey lines fixed on the expansive canvas. No fragment of horizon escaped into the city, not past those watchful guards. The darkened windows stared down into the empty streets, sentinels protecting their territory from the rogue, foreign warmth.

Layla stayed with him, always in earshot, but stealing a glance at the sapling she had fostered. Horace found her attachment to it endearing, but a shame she could not make any friends other than him. Neither could he, but he thought it might have been easier to leave her side if he knew she had someone else to go to if he did. Maybe it was him that refused to leave her, maybe he was holding her back.

"Isn't it amazing?" Her prideful eyes hadn't wandered from the scene since fluttering awake.

"The lights are off now."

"No, the rest of it! Aren't you proud of it all?"

"This city won't last a month." He scoffed, and Layla's heart dropped to her stomach. "It's such a shame, all your work was put to waste."

"Don't say that." He immediately regretted it when the corners of her lips curled downward. "You might not like it, and maybe I wasn't paid as much as you think I deserve, but this isn't a waste." Her hands tightened into a fist, knuckles staining white.

"Please, let me explain." He held up one hand, as if expecting to have to hold her back.

"Why would I listen to your explanation?" Only seconds before, the mouth that had gleamed brighter that the lights of the city had tightened and began quivering, her bottom lip curled in defence, preparing to spit a string of insults.

"Because you think I'm insulting you."

"You are."

"Not at all. I think your work is divine. It is a shame your best work had to be here." Layla looked back and forth from him to the grey cuboids touching the sky, withholding the sunrise from her. "It won't last. It's an insult to put something beautiful onto something that won't last."

"How do you know it won't last?"

His grim gaze momentarily broke into a smile. "Surely you know... Surely you've guessed by now."

She folded her arms. "Guessed what? Guessed you're just a judgemental old man who has nothing else to do but criticise other people's fine work?"

"Your work is more than fine, kid. It's splendid. But you should be insulted it had to be plastered on top of my work."

*****

At night, though, he still caught her gazing in awe at the lights. She could pretend that she had hung those stars up all by herself. She was a God among these astronauts, who may have been a lost cause, but she could see her legacy whenever the sun set, and brought to life her own constellations.

They orbited the city and the orchard, finding petty work to pass the time, but Horace's prediction came true only a week and a half later. Their camp in the orchard was joined by two others in one night, who found it less convenient to make the trip to the orchards from the city just to refill their tanks. Every night, less and less lights turned on in the city as more realised this.

By the end of the month, almost everyone had left the city, one by one, leaving the city full of empty rooms and quiet streets, like it started. The embassy became the sole inhabited building. The only light in the dark city, but none looked to it for hope or home anymore.

"Is this technically a rebellion?" Layla asked to nobody in particular. Horace had fallen asleep, and she was chewing absent-mindedly at a nutrition bar, cringing at the rich honey flavour she despised.

"It's a strike." Layla spun around. The response came from a woman perhaps in her late fifties, which said nothing for her energy, but wore an unapproachable glare that reminded Layla of her mother, adding an odd trace of familiarity to this unwelcoming place. The sapling she had just relocated seemed to glow in her presence, like her very touch had brought out life in its limp leaves. "I've seen a few in my time."

When she turned, the face the woman made it seemed like she nearly regretted opening her mouth. She struck Layla as the kind of woman that spoke little, but said a lot in a few words, and what use would it be to waste words on a child?

"Have we spoken before?" Layla pried, desperate for conversation while Horace slept.

She wiped her brow with the back of her glove, leaving a smear of reddish earth on her forehead. "I doubt it. In my field. There were very few people at the compound that tolerated me. I might have guessed."

"Why wouldn't they tolerate you?" The woman seemed to give up on the possibility of escaping this conversation. She drove the spade into the earth and walked forward, giving Layla a hand, which she shook.

"By day: Botanist. By night..." She exaggerated looking left and right. "Agricultural Journalism," she whispered through cupped hands, and gave low bow before returning to her spade's side. "People don't like I report on their dirty laundry. They don't see I'm yelling with them, not against them."

"People in your field... they got things to complain about too?"

"You'd be surprised. Industrial gardens are where rebellion ripens. It's more than that... Rainforests, taigas, soil purity and – Hell, you should read up on gluten of all things." Her foot slipped, scattering a spade-full of soil onto her boots. She balanced on one foot and shook the redness off. "I'm shocked they even invited me here. I've been giving the FDA hell about insecticides since the 60's." She planted both feet firmly in the ground. "Yeah, I think I can safely say nobody here likes me. I'm too..." She held up two gloved hands, dusted with the scarlet soil of Mars. "Red."

"Oh. I understand." A cloud was gathering above, and a deep rumble erupted in the sky. Layla hadn't witnessed thunder on Mars yet, and could hardly contain her excitement, and also her worry at their only shelter being a glass dome. She talked to distract herself. "So you're a hippie reporter on a government expedition? Isn't that sort of counter-productive?"

"I wouldn't say that."

"What would you say?" She stopped shovelling.

"Whatever you do in this world, your actions will have two reactions. The forward and backward. My forward reaction is that I'm currently planting trees on Mars of all places. The backward... well, my shovel has a government emblem on it, and I'm using the same fertilisers I wrote culms condemning. I'm not proud of it, but hey..." She started shovelling again. "And I'm not a hippie. I have a job; in case you couldn't tell." She shook the shovel sarcastically.

"So... Why not go work for the enemy?"

She shrugged. "Got a fancier letter."

Horace's eyes snapped open. "Something is happening. Help me up." Layla took his hand, but he almost dragged her to the ground while pulling himself up. His eyes darted wildly around, unable to focus on a single thing. "Do you feel that?"

"What?" Layla held his shoulder, but the woman came to her side.

"He's right." She knelt to the ground, placing her palm on the damp earth. Soon, she was joined by everyone, stirred from boredom by the tremor running beneath them, and above them the glass panes began to rattle.

Layla noticed Horace had taken her hand, and was squeezing it comfortingly. She didn't know if it was for herself, or if it was Horace who needed comfort now, but it grounded her for a moment, at least.

The rattling grew louder, grittier, and encompassed them. It was as if the air itself was in a tremor, pulsing and pushing against the glass like a barrier, the wind forcing itself through the cracks in the panes, widening and stretching the white lines until the fragments fell, letting the air inside with a violent whistle. Shards began to fly, lodging themselves in tree trunks like bullets.

The whistle of rushing air was drowned out by yells and screams, the clanging of oxygen tanks and shuffling of feet to get out of the way of the glass bullets. Horace, holding Layla's hand, almost dragged her outside, completely forgetting his oxygen tank.

Once outside, he gasped for air, inhaling the cloud of dust that began to grow, spitting red powder into the air and into his lungs. The dryness he had coped with for over a year was nothing compared to this. His throat felt like it was closing up, contracting and relaxing uncontrollably, either inviting plumes of dust into his lungs or paralysing them entirely. He choked on nothing, his vision blurring, dark shadows swimming in his eyes.

Something covered his mouth, a warm hand, as a silicone mask was placed over his nose. "Breathe." A desperate whisper pleaded in his ear. His eyes had welled up with tears, but he controlled himself for long enough to take short, shallow breaths. The tremor hadn't ceased, it grew stronger and more violent. It was louder now – rhythmic – or was it his heartbeat, mocking his irregular breaths by rising to his throat?

Breaths slowed consciously, deepened, the heartbeat slowly descending, silencing. Yet his bones still shook with the trembling of the engines of the rocket that had just landed, a mere twenty feet from him, which sent flaming hot air hurtling towards him. Layla returned; her hands busy with another tank and she overlooked the searing heat burning at her flesh as the ground ceased moving. She drew the shaking creature away, toward the crowd that had relocated to a safe distance to watch the thing in awe.

The Colonel cleared his throat, appearing out of thin air, obscured by the red cloud than hung around him on the far side of the crowd. He came from the city. From the Embassy.

He was a smallish man. Slightly taller than Horace, but nearer to him in age than Layla, who glared at the approaching figure. She cradled the oxygen tank in one hand, and held up Horace with the other, but hey eyes followed the Colonel's path. It looked like he was floating. The dust too thick around his feet to see them. He cast her a sideways glance before settling right in front of the rocket, that had fallen silent, but the cooling engine clunked and groaned occasionally, enticing Layla to crawl inside, to get her hands on its innards, but she resisted.

"Your new project has arrived. Begin work immediately." This was addressed to Layla personally. She would get new toys after all.

Turning to everyone else, he motioned to the shattered glass done, and announced, "The reparations will begin immediately." He didn't even look at the Orchard, which was one wrong glance away from collapse. Piles of glass littered the red earth, and the trees themselves were bare of leaves, stripped of their greenery by the violent storm. Layla spotted the woman she'd been talking to among the glass, that glinted in the sunset like flaming snow, shifting it into piles with the toes of her boots. Perhaps she cried. Layla wouldn't know. She looked over to the shuttle – her new project had just begun.

*****

Two days. The monstrosities Layla assembled were born out of two days' panic and it showed. Layla muttered to herself while wrenching wires out of the giant blocky stations. Each one was a cube of unnecessary material, wasted potential and insults, both to her, the orchard they had built, and the field of electrical engineering in general.

These new oxygen stations were supposed to "increase productivity" and "encourage patriotism in the struggling community," but it was clear that they were trying to keep people in the city. With a whole new planet to explore, why keep everyone in the earthliest place?

Horace was drawing in the dust by his feet, avoiding looking at anything but the ground, but leaned against the side of a building. He listened to Layla's mumbling with a tremorous soul. She should have been a poet. The flaming insults escaping her lips in that moment warranted to be written down and organised into neat verses, perhaps sung out loud. He would have listened were it not for the fact that it hurt to think. A poet he used to know could curse him out in his sleep.

"I should be over there."

He raised his head.

"He's just gonna walk back into that big tower and act as if it's not their own fault that we were all almost doomed. Scumbags, the lot of them."

"The mouth on you, kid."

"I'm allowed to be angry." She sighed deeply, and it shook him to the core, hearing her inhale the pure Martian air. Never again will he open his mouth if avoidable. He could still feel the dust coating his throat. He was thinking too much, too far back. He distracted himself by talking to her. Her. She could always make him feel better, and even watching her furrowed brow and curled lip, he was distracted by her passion. She reminded him of someone. It couldn't be himself.

"You are. You have a way with words."

"It's just..." Her elbows straightened as she made a jabbing motion into the machine. "I'm here, doing this. And – and he's there. In that big tower – that I made sure had light. And I never asked for much. I never asked to live in that big tower."

"Would you?"

"Hell no! But they didn't even ask, that's what hurts. It's like they don't think I even want anything in return except for a pat on the back and coffee that's undrinkable. But I would hate the view from up there. Honestly, I hate every view around here."

"Good. We're leaving this place."

She didn't even look up from her work. "And where would we go, buddy? Ouch!" A sharp zap made her retract her hand and she sucked on her fingertip for a moment. "It's all just sand." She closed up the control panel. "All sand and dust and sky. All red."

"How is that different to here?"

"There are people here. People that need me." She scoffed. "I am making a difference." The falsetto slogan of the mission brought Horace back to a time riddled with similar posters.

"Is that why you're complying?" He pointed to the row of Oxygen stations lined up one beside the other in a row, running down the side of the street.

"I'm no revolutionary."

"On the contrary...Poetry is-"

"Don't." She held up her hands. "I'm not a poet here. I just want to get my work finished. At least this way I'm having fun."

"You don't sound very entertained."

"Being entertained and having fun are two veeery separate concepts." She smirked, opening up the control panel of the next station. "This-" She pointed to the open panel, a mess of wires, tangles and twisted around each-other. She took a fistful and put her foot up to the wall for extra power pulling with all her force until she held the wires in her hands, and the panel was barren. "This is fun."

Her eyes sparkled when she did this, like the electrical sparks being emitted from the open panel, tiny flecks of gold. She faked a long whiff through the silicone mask and threw up an 'okay' sign. "Like a new car." She slammed the panel closed, walking back to the first station. "Now, let's see if these things actually work, or if we just wasted a couple billion in taxpayer dollars."

She took her mask off with such little care as to make Horace flinch, but Layla took no notice. She stuffed the wires into her already overflowing pockets and kneeled down, plugging the oxygen tank into the opening and pulling a stiff switch.

A silent fizzing sound could be heard, after which the sound reduced to a hiss, and the red bar on the side of the tank rose from half full to completely full, after which the sound ceased, and the tank was ejected. She nodded with satisfaction, putting the mask back on.

"Guess it works. Yours is getting pretty low." She made a grab for Horace's tank, but he flinched away, his eyes wild with fear. "We need to fill it up, you're almost out."

"It's not." He held it closer to his chest, putting his knees up and wiping away the lines in the dust. "It's fine." The air felt ten times hotter every time she reached her hand towards the tank.

"Horace?" He couldn't look her in the eyes. "Let's do a swap."

"What?"

"I'll swap your tank with mine, so you don't need to wait for yours to fill up." She started taking hers off again. "Deal?" He froze. Her hands rose to his grey face, and her nimble fingers, scabbed and calloused and copper-coloured, slipped delicately beneath the silicone on his face, relieving his skin momentarily before the panic crept in and he didn't dare exhale.

Within seconds the mask was over his head and the other was in its place. His eyes were watering from not blinking, but his chest rattled with a final release.

All he could hear was the fizz and hiss of the machine, then silence. Layla's trousers were dusted to the knee, her pockets bulky with wires, as she got back to work. "You good?" She asked nonchalantly, but he heard the genuine care in her voice, He nodded, and it was the truth. He was okay. "So..." She continued, changing the topic. "You a fan of Shelley?" She really was good. "I prefer Byron personally, but that's just me."

"Yeah. Byron's good," He answered weakly, "But the man had a hell of a reputation. Even Shelley had some strange stories."

"No way! They were mates?"

"Best mates, I would say. Though," He winced as he got up, "they couldn't stand each other."

She shook her head and smiled. "Only on earth."

He laughed along, moving closer to meet her after she moved on to the next station. "Only on earth."

They spoke through the night, passing the time under the Embassy, whose lights never dimmed. Every so often, they stopped, and listened to nothing in particular. If the city was anything like what it was desperately trying to be, there never would have been a dull moment. Layla didn't need to be a New York native to know that, but even in her hometown, an old mining village in England, the night was never quiet. Earth was never quiet, like this, and like her, it hardly slept.

Horace's breaths had become more regular, she noticed, less dragging, each inhale wearing out the wheeze, and struggling less with each exhale. It reminded her of her father's breathing, how he used to come home and cough clouds of soot into the air. He always told her to stay in school, so she could take her mother away from all this, but he never said anything about himself.

"We will have to leave one day." Horace said, at dawn, while Layla's tired hands fiddled with the final button. She slammed the door closed.

"Someday soon?"

"Unless the war ends very shortly, and if that was the case, we wouldn't be dealing with these things." He knocked on the first in the row of Oxygen stations, all whirring silently one beside the other. "From the look of it, we could be here for a while." Layla nodded with a blank expression. Part of her wanted to go home, but the other part of her was tied to this place. She had, to a great extent, made this possible. Horace, too, had become attached to the orchard in particular, mostly because of the way Layla's face filled with warmth when they stepped inside, and the way that the air wasn't as empty and dry as it was on the outside. "A long while."

"You should sleep."

Layla emptied her pockets into the pile that had grown all through the night. There were hundreds of wires, all waste, thrown into the machines by an amateur. "What can we use these for?" She picked at the plastic casing of one of the wires, pricking her finger on exposed copper. She did it again, but her calloused fingers didn't bleed. "We could use this copper for something, but I doubt the plastic is of any use-"

"Layla, did you hear me?"

She sighed, shoulders drooping. "Can we go see the orchard first?"

They almost sprinted through the streets, both consciously putting more and more air between them and the cement cuboids that cluttered the skyline. When the glass dome came into view, the sparkling of the sunrise almost blinded Layla, whose eyes had adjusted to the darkness inside the machines. She blinked. That couldn't be right.

Horace spoke up as they neared the dome. "Is that…"

Layla broke into a run, weighed down by the full tank. A single person was in sight, the botanist she had spoken to the day before. She was leant against the glass, oxygen tank between her knees, arms crossed and eyes open. She was like a statue, unmoving, yet with a dominating presence.

Layla skipped past her, making a beeline for the entrance to the orchard. The trees, shrivelled and clinging to life, could be seen through the spaces between the metal bars that blocked the door, keeping all outside.

Layla, without thinking, kicked at the metal, and the echoing clang made the woman stir. "I told you. I told everyone."

Horace caught up to them. "What's the meaning of this?"

The woman couldn't help but smile. "This," She began, "was too communal. We were too happy, and to be happy about something so communal is a sin." She laughed. "How ironic, on this red planet."

"But we made this. We have the right to be proud."

"Oh sure, we do, but that's not what the people back home like to see. They want to see America in all its urban glory. Imagine how it looks to them, that we value anything that doesn't radiate – that doesn't reek of – of-" She seemed at a loss for words. Giving up, she rested her head against the glass, her cheek catching a film of dust from it.

"Aren't you gonna do something?" Layla pleaded.

"While those doors are closed, what have I to do? If they let me die here, I'll die, and then it'll be their fault," She smiled, self-assured, "and the world will see all."

"You're just gonna sit and let the air run out of your tank."

"Exactly. It's simple, but effective. They either make the right choice – the easy choice, or I die. Either way, I win."

Horace held out his hand, and the woman shook it with satisfaction. "We leave tonight."

"God bless you on your journey." She closed her eyes

"And you. We hope to see you again on earth." He added in his mind, "If we get that far."

"I'd rather die right here." The two turned to leave, but she called them back. "I ask one thing. If I die, and you go home, make sure everyone knows my name." They looked at each other, then back at her.

"What even is your name?" She smiled.

"You'll know it when I'm dead." She tapped the metal plate of her oxygen tank, which bore the name of each owner. Horace remembered he still had Layla's. "One more thing. Did either of you happen to see where that rocket went?"

Truly, they didn't. Neither of them ever saw anyone moving the rocket away, and in its place was merely the shallow pit it had created by blowing away the soft sand upon landing. They shrugged, and that was the end of it.

Layla never saw her again.

She pondered over her pile of wires sifting through them, picking out the ones not too weak or damaged, and cut the stock down to a mere fistful of copper threads. This was the convenience to having no earthly possessions: packing to leave was too easy. Leaving was too easy.

Mars was no place for earthly things, so why confine everyone to the most Earth-like place, when there was a whole new planet to explore and make their own? It was only time until they all realised that this city was an infection of something pure, bound to rot sooner or later. A blemish on the surface of the planet that would soon disappear beyond the horizon.

"So," Layla broke the silence. They had been sitting with their backs to their baggage, watching the sun hide behind the city for the last time. "My dad was born in a mining village during the Depression."

"The Great one?" He was trying to joke.

"Yeah, that one," she continued, trading lightly, "He worked there all his life. He said that sometimes he used to come out and forget how it was to breathe clean air. When he coughed, it was… Do you remember how kids in winter like to watch their breath?" She hugged her knees. "It looked like that, but instead of a white cloud, it was a black one."

"That sounds horrid."

"It was, to see. I couldn't imagine what it felt to live it, every day, 'til death."

"He died?"

She dug her heels in the ground. "Yeah, just the month before we left. He knew I wanted to get far away from that place, but I never specified how far." She laughed against the pressure on her rib cage, remembering the way his blue eyes sparkled behind his coal-dusted face and white hair. "The way he used to cough, that's what I remember most clearly, and I thought I'd gotten away from that, like everything."

Gotten away… she thought leaving would bring her peace. Instead she got stuck with me.

Horace felt a tickle in his throat, but he resisted the urge to clear it.

"He used to tell me to stay in school, but I had… bigger plans, I suppose." She sighed. "Bigger than earth. In my mind, I was walking on Mars before I walked out of my graduation."

"Jeez, kid. It never occurred to me, but you are probably the youngest person here." She nodded.

"On my last day of school, all I could think of was that I would be so much more than everyone else. I looked around and I saw people who could be doctors, lawyers, soldiers, most of them. I just thought, 'I'm going to Mars. You are nothing in comparison.' Now I just wish I'd stayed, and been one of them."

"A soldier?"

She shook her head. "Soldiers aren't people. Not to the people who matter." Her eyes drooped; she hadn't slept since before the fire. "Maybe it's the same for us here." Her mouth stopped moving. She had fallen asleep, but Horace lay awake, taking in the sunset while her words ran through his mind. A mind so young, and yet so honest. Burdened with knowledge nobody should have at her age. Bereaved of the innocence of youth.

There and then, he determined to get her home. Away from this land of redness and boredom, she would fly.

Layla awoke in the middle of the night, in the cold, alone, still leaning against her baggage. Through half-lidded eyes, Horace was nowhere to be found, though the lights of the city were illuminating the ground they fell on, casting a long shadow when Layla stood up on shaky legs, almost awake. To pass the time, she looked at the stars. One major difference between Earth and Mars were the stars, which shone so much brighter. An ocean, overhead, of light.

Dust storms often plagued this part of Mars, so a clear night was valued by all insomniacs, including Layla. If she couldn't learn to love the silence, at least this could distract her. But the silence was short-lived tonight. The sound of rapid footfalls broke the momentary peace and she looked around, finding the dark figure of Horace against the night hobbling in her direction as fast as his weak legs would carry him. Behind him, the dome mirrored the starry sky.

When he came into focus Layla saw the sheer panic in his expression. The yellow light cast writhing shadows on his horrified face. He was carrying something. "Horace?" He kept running, not slowing down even as he got nearer. "Hey!"

As he passed her, he grabbed on to her hand, pulling her down and behind their baggage.

"What is wrong with you?" She demanded, wrenching her hand out of his. She massages her sore fingers with her free hand. The old man was stronger than he looked, though he was again gasping and choking for air beside her. "Hey, man, breathe for a minute."

"I don't think…" He gasped, "I don't think they saw it."

"Saw what?"

Horace opened his arms, letting the object fall limp at his feet and clang against the steel cap of Layla's boot. "Shhhh-" He scrambled to pick it back up.

"Is that..." Hollow and light, the woman's oxygen tank.

"Yes. Look at the name. Read it and remember it." She took it with shaking fingers, squinting at the plaque in the darkness.

"I can't see it."

He groaned, pulling something from his coat.

"I was going back to ask her to come with us, but when I got there..."

"What happened to her?"

"I was too late, kid. I was too late. They already got her." Layla's heart dropped. Got her? "Two men from the embassy, they took her mask off and just... watched her. I watched them do it." He covered his mouth and breathed deeply into the mask, the breath whistling in his throat.

"I don't believe you." Layla's knees buckled under herself, and she lowered herself to the ground, her right shoulder bumping the baggage as she went down. "You're lying. Are you sure?"

"I knew what I saw, kid. Now, read it quick." He shone a flashlight onto the metal, and she rubbed her eyes to clear them of sleep, and droplets of moisture that may have bloomed into tears had she given them the chance. "Matilda S. McCarthy, 1941, January $2^{nd}$, Female." He switched the light off. You'll know it when I'm dead.

"I'm sorry, kid." Matilda S. McCarthy. "They got her." Matilda S. McCarthy. "We need to leave, now."

"I need to see it first." Horace stopped moving, turning to look her in the eyes, which shone in the darkness even now. "I need to see where it happened."

"Kid, they took her away."

"Where?"

"I didn't see, I just grabbed the tank when they took her away and ran."

"Where did they take her away?"

Horace was silent for a moment. "They went into the city. But we can't go back, we have to leave."

Layla turned away and rose abruptly to her feet, but he grabbed her by the shoulder firmly and brought her back to his level.

"What makes you think we're any different to her? If they saw us, what makes you think we'll have a different fate?" He got up, lifting her by the shoulders, still eye to eye. "Layla. You're a genius, but trust me this one time. When I got there, she was within an inch of her life, and they just pushed her that one inch further. I saw her head fall limp and I saw the crack in the glass where it hit." Layla said nothing, but took a half step closer to him.

She turned her head as it fell to his chest. He felt her unruly hair brush against his chin and brought up a hand to rest over it as the other wrapped around her lean shoulders. "I don't want you to end up the same as her." His hand rested on her back, between her shoulder blades, and rose and fell with each silent sob, drowned in a sea of stars. "I want you to get home."

How did it get like this? Just days before they had all they needed. A garden to sit in, and peace and quiet. Now they had nothing but their arms around each-other. They had the night and a blanket of darkness to hide them as they ran away. Them. That would have to do for the time being. She felt his heartbeat near her head. No tears.

"Kid." With a deep breath, she left the embrace, and it was all over. "We have to leave." His voice was barely a whisper, but it was commanding and comforting all at once. Only Horace had that ability, to tame a beast and appease a child all in the same tone, and in this instance, Layla was both. She took up her tools, and the empty oxygen tank, and they set off side by familiar side, drifting further and further away from Odyssey's orbit.

Either way, I win.

## 1986

Odyssey reached its tenth year in the darkness.

It had always been a city of darkness. At least, the past eight years had been a funeral. With Layla and Horace's departure, everyone felt something had shifted in Odyssey's air. It felt heavier. Lonelier. Louder.

Every other week, the ground shook, but no rockets came to save them, or give them new orders. It was the rumble of a fallen soldier, a collapsing hollow tower crushing through the air and sending up a cloud of red dusk sky-high as the others held their positions, watching their brother descend to the red purgatorial ground. At night, the lights came on, because they had to. Because a certain young woman was instructed to make them turn on at sunset.

Still empty, the buildings lit up. They lit up the path for others to follow, Horace and Layla's path, away from the city under its watchful eyes.

For the first time in ten years, the lights did not turn on.

Those looking for the city on the horizon caught their breath, and held it. With almost empty tanks, they were used to waiting for night to wander into the city, fill their tanks and clear out before first light.

Most of them hadn't seen another person in near half a decade or longer, but forced by necessity to see each-other in the daytime, they could at least share in the panic.

The power had been cut through the entire city. That meant the oxygen stations, their only destination in this ghost town, were rendered useless. Words of fear were passed between them, half a decade's silence was broken. They spread out, looking for the girl.

For eight years, the old man and the girl, her streaked with grey hair and dead dreams, disappeared off the face of the planet, vanishing on the horizon and only returning to replenish their stores of oxygen in the hours of the night when everyone shirked away from everyone. They always carried a spare tank beside them, its name plate removed and worn around Layla's neck like a noose, her face darkening as the rubble came into view. She kept her eyes fixed on the orchard until the city became unmissable, then let out a sigh that carried with it the years' worth of hatred she had held onto, leaving it out in the open for all to see. When they approached they brought with them a wholly foreign feeling, not of earth but certainly not Martian, like they returned from their secret hide-away in the stars.

Nobody had found them. They came of their own accord.

"This is too familiar." Layla muttered; head hidden deep in the inner workings of the first machine. Her necklace dangled out of her shirt, clanging against the metal, a spark of life in the dead silence of the city. The last few buildings that stood overlooked her. She felt their dim eyes on the back of her head. Invisible to her, she was exposed. "I hate it." The Embassy was one of them.

"We'll be out of here soon enough, don't worry."

"At this rate, I don't expect to finish before sunrise." At least they wouldn't be disturbed. Nobody lived in the city now, even the embassy tower was flooded in darkness. She worked by the light of the stars and the torch that Horace held over her shoulder, but he wasn't watching her work as usual. His head was far away, in the sky. When the lights were on, they had drowned them out. The star themselves seemed to be begging for more time. What a privilege, for time to run out. "You know what I'll never get used to?"

Layla dug deeper into the machine, making a dip in the dirt with the tip of her shoe. "Hmm?"

"There's two moons, and I can't see either of them."

"You don't wanna see them, trust me." Layla's voice was close to a whisper, echoing around the innards of the metal cube. "They're all kinds of weird."

The top half of her body emerged from the darkness, and she straightened up with a crack that ran all the way up her back. A strand of hair had fallen loose from the knot at the back of her head, and snagged on the hinge. It fell from her scalp too easily and dangled in the half-darkness. "All done here." They moved on to the next one. "What I'm wondering is…" She propped her foot up on the side of the machine, the froze, letting it fall to the ground.

"Let's… try a different way." She opened the door by prying it open with the head of a screwdriver. "What I'm wondering is why they all shut off right now? These machines are connected in parallel to the lights, so the break must have come from the source, not the fuses, and that's-"

"Kid, I know nothing, you're talking to a wall right now."

"They aren't broken, someone turned off all the power to the city on purpose."

"Why would anyone do that?"

Darkness hid secrets. Now, the power had been off for at least four nights, and not a single ambassador had said anything. And neither did they.

As soon as Layla had fixed the first machine, the grateful citizens had filled up their tanks and fled. They were, once again, alone. She wished only to be alone somewhere else.

"So… you don't need to fix anything?"

"No, just switch them all back on."

"But that one you just did isn't on."

"It is, but we need to let the oxygen come in from the source. It won't dispense unless there's a constant stream. They're built that way to stop people stealing them from the city." To keep them coming back. Keep them dependent. "Otherwise it's a hassle to disconnect them individually and I am not doing it again."

She pointed to a small cubic box at the edge of the city, half buried in the sand. "All the oxygen from the orchard comes through there, the branches off and comes to each station. It must have jammed when the power was shut off." She wiped her brow. "Actually, can you go there and check it? If it's on, then you should hear a sort of fan noise, like a whirring, and see it turning." She took the torch from him, put the end of it between her teeth and ducked back into the machine.

"And if it's not on?"

She mumbled in the sides of her mouth. "It will be." She stuck one hand out and waved him away dismissively.

Horace tried to keep his eyes focused on the edge of the city, avoiding eye contact with the shattered windows and piles of rubble from collapsed walls that would never have lasted the decade. As it came into view, the box seemed very fitting for the city, almost as large as the stations themselves, cubic and grey, made of cement, and reminded Horace of a city he was commissioned to map one time.

Everything was squares and sharp corners. Where it wasn't red, it was grey and dead, the new Brutalism. Even brutalism meant "raw," but not here. On Mars it was just brutal.

A large translucent pipe ran from the orchard to the front of the box, and out the other end, where a dozen more pipes ran out a couple feet and then turned directly into the ground.

The only sound was the hissing on the wind running past the pipe and smacking it with a spray of red grains. Other than that, there was silence.

He could see the fan, obscured by the plastic, but definitely unmoving.

"What now..."

He dropped down to one knee and felt around the dust-caked side for an opening, then prised it open with his fingers. It came loose way too easily.

He'd left the flashlight with Layla. Soon realising his mistake, Horace sighed and squinted down at the mess of wires before him, beginning to decode the maze of colours within the little box.

Simply put, everything was in order. The matching colours of wires were plugged in the jacks with the right colours, as far as he could tell, that was right. So why wasn't it working? He closed the panel and stood up, dusting off his knee. "Well, when all else fails..." He drew back his foot in a wide arch behind him.

He turned his foot, so the uncapped heel hit the side of the box. The clang carried far, unsettling a layer of dust atop the flat box and shook his ankle to the bone. It still felt the buzz as he knelt back to peer in through the tube.

After a moment, nothing happened, but soon enough the sound of the sand hitting the pipe (and the faint echo of the clang) was joined by a soft whirring. The fan was spinning, slowly at first, then blurring into a single, seemingly unmoving solid plate. With a self-satisfied nod he started blindly walking back, shielding his eyes from the city's skyline and keeping his eyes on the footprints casting shallow shadows in the starlight, following them back like breadcrumbs.

"What did you do?" Layla's voice demanded.

He looked up, guiltily. "Hmm?"

"You fixed it. How did you do that?"

His shame was painted in a red flush on his cheeks, barely visible.

"I... Uh, I kicked it."

"You... You kicked it?"

"Mhm."

He couldn't tell exactly what her face meant to say. His talent of reading faces failed with the irregular shadows obscuring her dark features. She looked black and blue. A smiling bruise.

At least her nostrils weren't flared. That would mean she was actually angry. And he'd only seen her truly angry once, and he hoped never to see it again.

"Kicked it," she whispered, bewildered. "A bit unorthodox... But it worked?"

"Yeah, the-the fan turned on."

"It sure did, dude!" She gleamed, like her eyes were stars escaped from the black canopy above the city.

"I just thought I could save us some..." His feet refused to move further. "...time." The air turned to clay, hardened, brittle. He was refused movement.

"What's with the face?" Layla brushed aside the stray hairs from her face, but the wind picked up and kept blowing them back. Like the curtains of a haunted house. This was a scary movie. Horace's blood ran cold. "You've gone all pale." His eyes wandered to the black sky.

"Dude, you're scaring me. What are-" She pivoted on her toes and followed his line of sight. "Oh shi-"

The air shattered with an ear-splitting sound, like the sky and ground were crashing into each-other.

A flame had been lit behind the clouds, but there was no sun. No morning light. No warmth of sunrise to start a new day.

Behind the Embassy, fading in from the atmosphere, blurring through the clouds, a familiar sight sent the two of them back to a day eight years ago, the advent of their self-banishment.

A rocket was soaring above the city.

*****

Layla and Horace stood at the edge of the crumbling city, just staring. Occupying one half of their vision was the rocket, standing tall, upright. It had made a gentle landing, at least. The other half was flooded with smoke.

The Orchard was up in flames.

The shards of glass hung off the melting metal skeleton of the dome, drooping inwards, limply hanging down like vines among the trees.

Horace regretted standing dumb while the dozen old men, the government officials, pranced out of the embassy and strolled past them as if they were invisible. Even as the Colonel himself paused at the entrance, laid down his oxygen tank, and looked out on the horizon, Horace did nothing. He merely watched the old man door behind him and start walking.

Maybe they could have stopped them from leaving, or maybe they could have run on board themselves, saving themselves from the fate they were living out right now. Perhaps the least they could have done was stop the rocket from taking off.

Layla's mind snapped back in that moment, watching the pillar of flames rise into the sunburnt sky, now glowing with the sunrise, too.

She took off towards the distributor. Horace heard her struggle with the heavy tube, but stayed unmoving. It gave way just in time, just as the flames began crawling towards them through the translucent plastic They flooded with a roar, shaking the tube in her hands but she didn't drop it.

She didn't drop it.

Instead of spreading into the city through the oxygen sources, the flames spewed out of the detached end, and in an upward cascade, combed through Layla's hair. It licked at the brown flesh of her neck and jaw, searing it as the singed hair flew back. Her hands finally let go and flew to her face, but she couldn't touch it. Already salty tears were falling down her face into the wound.

She used to sleep on that side of her face, the cheek resting on the cold pillow. She wouldn't sleep again. In the hours she lay awake she would always be thinking of this. The selfishness of those men, who left her behind and flew home as she burned. She didn't wish fire on them, hellfire or other. She didn't even wish them to lie awake as she did, sleepless.

She only wished them nightmares, like the one she was living in, and the one they escaped.

## Chapter 4

# HORACE

1987

She only realised she was awake when Horace coughed. Through some miracle, she had blacked out long enough for the sun to cross halfway over her head. But she didn't feel a second rested.

"How much longer?" She asked, alarming Horace, close to dozing off himself. He cleared his throat again.

"We just entered the radius, but if we don't find anything by midday we have to turn around." She looked to the West, where the giant wall of dust was clearer, like the clouds from the sky were drooping and melting towards the earth, sand and sky and wind all blending into a blushing desert.

"Sleep well?"

This isn't normal. "Yeah, pretty well. No dreams, though, again."

"Really? That's surprising."

"How come? I rarely dream."

"Well, you were talking the whole time."

Layla lurched forward, dazing herself. What had she said, and, more importantly, how much?

"No need to fret, kid, it was just some old nursery rhymes. But it seemed like you were struggling with a few of them."

"Which ones?"

"Well, for starters, you forgot all the names of the churches in 'oranges and lemons.'"

Layla scoured her memories. She'd visited some of those churches, but their names escaped her. She looked to Horace for help.

"Saint Clement's is first, then Saint martins, Old Bailey, Shoreditch, and Stepney follow that, and then Bow. But that's just the first stanza."

"There's more than one?"

"There's more than six churches in London, kid. How do I know more about this than you?"

"What's that supposed to mean?"

"Firstly, tone down the sass. Second, You're younger and also British."

"Hey! Only half-British…" She crossed her legs and folded her arms self-importantly. "Fine, what's the rest Mister Nursery Rhyme expert?."

"I… only know the first verse."

"Okay. Maybe We'll find someone who knows the rest." She reclined again and closed her eyes, playing the tune in her head. Oranges and lemons, would she recognise the flavours if she ever got the chance, or will her mouth reject the sourness after eleven years of living on protein, fat, and hardly recognisable artificial flavours? Grapefruits were foreign to her taste buds already, but what she would give to taste it, just once. Even if she ended up hating it, the experience alone would be something to boast.

"Can you miss something you never liked?"

Horace didn't need to think long. "Sure. You can miss the feeling of hating something almost as much as you can miss something dear to your heart."

Layla scrunched up her nose. "That doesn't make sense. You're supposed to be happy when a bad thing is gone."

"That, too. Do you remember what happened when the orchard was first destroyed?" She nodded. How could she ever forget? "I guess I never explained…" He trailed off, then blinked, snapping back to reality. He brought his chest close to the steering wheel. Layla followed his line of sight, ending at a dark spot on the horizon. Far too small to be what they were looking for, but just the right size for what she always dreaded. "Give me the map."

Layla opened the glove box, where half a dozen rolled up maps were arranged, and pulled out a specific one. He unrolled it, marking the space they just saw with a cross. The rest of the map was littered with dozens of scattered crosses, most of them circled, showing they had been checked out. Beside the maps in the glove box was a small metal chest: an old toolbox, now heavy with the weight of all the metal plaques they had taken from the oxygen tanks of the dead they discovered on their adventures.

There were less plaques than crosses. Sometimes the outposts were just abandoned, and that meant another survivor. Another Nomad, like them.

But, more often than not, the small shacks, tents or even just lone vehicles, were inhabited by the deceased. More than a few times they had had to leave a perfectly good truck or recovered caravan out of respect. The planet claimed these, along with the lives it snatched.

Everyone had a different approach to their new situation. Some didn't cope with the boredom well, and resorted to the one escape off this planet. Others perished from loss of oxygen. Very few starved, not realising their own starvation. It seemed food was the one constant to most. That is, something they could use to feel alive, Earthlier. Though hunger was scarce, a good many people on the mission had never truly been hungry on Earth either.

The two accepted the task of keeping their memories alive, and their names in their minds as often as possible. One name didn't go into the chest, however. It was the name of Matilda McCarthy, whose plaque always hung from Layla's neck, the metal warming by the heat of her heart, resting above the pale scar that bloomed above her heart, snaked up her neck and jaw, and ended with a light streak over her eyebrow.

The flesh was much paler than Layla's tanned skin, but she never ignored the tenderness and softness that remained in the aftermath, while the rest of her untouched skin aged, that part remained youthful.

Another exception was the plaque of a lone soldier they found in the early days of the new life after the sacrifice. They entered the outpost of a man, who used his last moments to write a confession to whoever had the misfortune of living longer than him. He claimed the man whose name he bore never even received his letter, and that he'd intercepted it to come and sabotage the mission, ensure it would never succeed.

He also felt his mission of sabotage had taken effect without him lifting a finger. Beside the note were a sealed box of seeds he stole from the orchard before the fire. The note was signed with the man's real name, which Layla inscribed herself into a new piece of metal, which joined the names in the chest. He was a victim, too.

One day, she thought, those names will all be remembered and forced to be gazed upon by those who sealed their fates, even this one. Maybe they already erected a memorial for them, or erased them all from history.

*****

Layla rolled up the map and closed the glove box, tracing the name on her necklace with the thumb of her right hand. She caught her reflection in the rear-view mirror as they drove past the outpost, watched it disappear behind them, then let out a sigh of relief, licking her bottom lip to wet it, and touching the tip of her tongue to the pale scar that disappeared between her lips.

When Horace was teaching her to drive, they started an inside joke about looking in the rear view mirror, knowing there would never be anything worth seeing behind them, but as the cabin shrank in the distance, she never let her eyes wander from it until the speck on the horizon was gone.

"Will we have time to check that out?"

Horace sighed. "Probably not," He said, "Even if we find nothing, we'll need to hurry back if we want to miss that storm." He felt a rising tightness in his throat and coughed it into his shoulder. A spray of phlegm splattered the beige uniform. He had grown to hate it; the years of wear and grime had dirtied it enough to camouflage him to the planet. Layla's at least, was stained with a black scorch mark over the shoulder and collar. It stood out. He blended in.

Layla cleared her throat, feeling his mind start to wander. "So, how can you miss something you hated at the time?" His knuckles tightened on the steering wheel. She would ask to switch, but the so-called 'sleep' hadn't worn off yet. "Open up, man. You know everything about me."

"You miss the feelings you have at the time, and the people that stuck with you through it. My story is no fun, trust me."

"Lucky for you, I'm not looking to have fun." She leaned back in her seat. "Just fill time." When Horace hesitated, Layla urged him on, clicking her fingers impatiently.

"You talk enough for the both of us." His chest was still tight holding back the words he wanted to say. Memories of decades past, that he held, suspended, between forgetting and reminiscing. Yet to make a judgement, they stayed static on the borders of his mind. All his thoughts since then had been on one thing only. The urging clicks persisted. If only he could make the truth less painful, but then it would all be a lie.

"Only in my sleep, apparently." She clicked again, and the volume shocked her almost out of the daze. She flexed her hand, entranced by the swirls of her fingerprints. Still the same. The nails, though chipped, were nothing different than when she was just a girl at school. *I should take better care of myself.*

She imagined herself going to a hairdresser. *No, maman would do it.* She had kept the "We can do it!" attitude from her time as a nurse in the British army during the war, and nothing could shake it out of her. She swore nobody but she would touch Layla's hair on her wedding day.

"I suppose-" Horace's voice startled her, and she closed her palm. He didn't notice. "Well, I'll try to keep it short. Stick to the facts, you know?" Layla nodded but he wasn't looking at her. "You know I was raised in an orphan's school. I think that goes without saying, because, well… look at me."

"You can't really tell."

"Thanks, kid."

Layla muffled a yawn. "Keep talking."

"Well, I signed up for the army at sixteen, because I thought there was nothing worse to do than stay in the same place. I can't tell how exchanging the streets of Seattle for the French trenches was a good deal, but I was just excited to make my own mistakes for a change.

"When I returned, I had nothing but my name, and what was called "shell-shock" at the time. I also had a pack of cigarettes that belonged to a dead man. He became my dearest friend when we had each-other, for a short while, but we never even knew each-other's name. We just called each other "Tommy." Nobody used their own name. I even lied about my age.

"The cigarettes, among other things, helped me forget. The next few years were the most important of my life. I know this because I don't remember much of my time, but I remember the lessons. They became part of me.

"I somehow became apprenticed to a prolific artist that was living in Seattle at the time, and was sleeping on his couch most nights when I wasn't out drawing, or drinking the city dry with my friends. Of course, I wouldn't tell him where I went, but he had his own secret stashes, and if it kept my grubby hands out of them, he wouldn't think twice.

"One morning I came in to work and found only a note that said he left to find his family in Russia, and I was supposed to take over for him, even leaving all his money and clothes to me until he came back. From then, until he returned, I was to use his name and do his work for him, and I knew from the second I finished reading the letter, that he wouldn't show his face again. I couldn't remember my real name anyway, so I took his. "Horace Desmond" sounded much better than anything I could come up with."

"How did you know he wasn't coming back?"

"He instructed me to burn the letter and any traces of him. But first I learned to copy his signature. I was now him, and this opened a new chapter in my life before the last one ended."

"So you took his identity? What happened to the guy?"

"Disappeared." He shrugged. "Without a trace, just like he wanted. Nobody even noticed until I left the studio for good. But my time as one of the artistic elites of America was bitter. I regret even now leaving behind my life for a fake one, no matter how poor I was before."

"Why?"

"It was beautiful. Everything I stand for is what I picked up in those years as an apprentice wandering the streets, drinking, smoking, drawing. When you're a man like me, you define bliss using those words. At least I used to."

"It was still poverty. It was painful, wasn't it? I know it was." Her throat felt hot, and she pressed the back of her palm to it. Even when she didn't speak, it trembled with each breath.

"How would you know?"

"You know exactly what I meant."

"You and I are very different. We endured very different species of pain."

"Pain is pain, poverty is poverty. Stop romanticising your past just because it's over. Let it hurt. That's what makes it all real."

"And you, the poet? What's real are the lessons I learned in humility and patience; two things you wouldn't find wandering another street. If I ended up like everyone else, where would we be then?"

Layla didn't dare say out loud what she was thinking: Not here.

"I hated living in someone else's home, no matter how comfortable. I missed my friends, my self-proclaimed "tortured artists," who didn't ask about my name or job or where I'd been all this time. They just took me to their new find.

"It really sprung up right under my nose. I should have spotted it from the studio, but I was too drunk to even tie my own shoelaces.

"An entirely new town just appeared in Seattle, overnight! When I saw it, I knew it was the place to be. I left everything behind, but took the artist's name with me. Even if I said nothing, I did recognise among my friends the styles of artists I used to study. We all flocked to the Hooverville. I dedicated my days and nights to the study of the misshapen and misaligned streets that wound around the barren land like roots.

"Every day was a new adventure that took us deeper and deeper into the very heart and soul of this urban jungle. The roads I'd become familiar with morphed and twisted each and every way when I looked away for a moment, and every day I started again. "I could never get bored in a place like this," I used to say. The town itself was alive, amorphous, always changing and always challenging me. It was an ongoing battle until dawn. My maps then were the best work I'd ever done, and no sum could force me to part with them.

"This didn't sit well with my artists, who followed me with the promise that I could make us all a little bit less tortured. We all passed our time drawing, smoking, drinking whenever we found any, and washing down the drinks with stories, which I only listened to. It was our currency, and I was poor again in a new sense of the word.

"Suddenly I had nothing again. I'd drank and smoked away so many memories, and thrown away all the money. It was only time before they threw me out as well. At least, that was what I thought. One thing about artists is, they stick together, and they appreciate a quiet one. Most artists never shut up, and most writers are often lost for words." He tipped his head towards her as he said this.

"I suppose we're both exceptions."

"Indeed we are." Misfits among misfits, the two of them. "It was easy to pass time like this in the Hoovervilles, given you had enough booze and enough stories. But when they both ran out... Then it got hard. Time stopped passing. It bled, and you could feel it in your skin, how a second bled into hours. When you're bored – or sober – your skin crawls with it. Time," Horace said, "is the cruellest mistress. She always gives you more than you want and less than you need."

"It was that boredom that came between the safe and sober, between one smoke and the next, and between one sheet of paper and a drawing. That truly tortured my artists, and I couldn't stand to see them like that at my benefit. There's no glory in seeing your friends suffer for your joy, you can't romanticise that.

So we started preparing for war, but Hell would have had to swallow us all up before we joined the US army, so we pulled together all we could to get us each a one-way ticket to France. The last night we spent in America I felt very strange. Almost in pain, but not there yet. I assumed it was sobriety mixed with nerves, but when I woke up in a hospital bed it was clear that this wasn't alcohol's doing."

"Why was it clear?"

"Because It's hard to miss the fact that one of your lungs is outside of your body.

Layla inhaled sharply and held it, though the breath too deep, burned against her ribcage. It would be insensitive to sigh.

"That first pack of cigarettes was bound to catch up with me, and my friends had to sell my ticket to get me the hospital bed. There was a clock next to me, and I counted the seconds until their ship departed. I knew I wouldn't ever find them again to thank them, and instead thanked the nurse who fixed my oxygen mask when my sobbing moved it from my face.

"Her name was Darla, that's all I remember of my time at the hospital, and she had red hair that was short as a man's. I asked her why she kept it that short, and she told me it was her last week of work in this hospital before she transferred to Belgium. She told me her fiancé loved her long hair, but it took up too much time to keep it looking nice, time she didn't have to spare, and she wouldn't be caught dead with messy hair. The solution was to cut it all off. "Can't have bad hair if you have no hair.""

"And what about her fiancé?"

"He would be too busy getting shot at to worry about her hair."

"They were both going to war together?"

"Same place, too. She said it would be better, because if something happened to him, she didn't want any of the other nurses undressing him."

"Did they ever return?" She shifted her feet, and the steel toes of her boots tapped the metal box with a ding that was drowned out by the retching engine.

"I didn't stick around to see. As soon as I was out of that place I found the key to the studio, sold everything, and ran away to Europe."

"Where did you go?"

"Where didn't I go? I went around for a while before someone recognised me. It must have been one of the architect's old friends who used to come around the studio. He was eager to know what happened to him, but I had to break the news to him that I had assumed the guy's identity. If he didn't know, then Horace Desmond was dead.

"He agreed to help me find a place to stay until I got myself settled. That was in Amsterdam. Within months I was teaching architecture in a University. I had to learn Dutch pretty fast-"

Layla jumped. "I knew it." Horace jolted with the shock, his elbows drew back, and the truck swerved, knocking Layla into her broken door, which opened and she half-dangled off her seat. Her right hand hovered inches off the ground rushing below her when Horace caught hold of the fabric of her collar and drew her back. She pulled the door closed along with her.

They sat in silence together for a few seconds, both just breathing. Layla blinked awake. "So when you were a teacher-"

"Are we gonna ignore what happened, then?"

"Yes. Anyway-"

"How did you know I was a teacher? How would anyone know?" He asked. "I never told anyone, and I barely taught a handful of classes."

Layla scoffed at being interrupted. "You're just the type, you know?"

"What-what's that? What's a type?"

"It's something you can tell about a person without asking or being told. You just have to pay attention or spend long enough time together to pick it up. You're the teaching type."

"I don't believe you can actually do that."

"It's not for everyone. I'm a people watcher."

"There's not many people to watch around here."

"Except for you. You're people, too." Layla's sudden change in tone sent a cold spark up his spine and he almost swerved again. Why did it scare him so much to be a person, the way she meant it? "What type am I? Guess."

"Why don't you just tell me?"

"That's not how it works. I could say anything and it might not be true even if it feels true to me. Types are all about what other people think about you."

"You're not the type to care about such things, then."

She sighed. The joke was done. "Give me a real answer."

There was no real answer. Layla wasn't a type. She was so much potential, concentrated into a little person. She was the change in the colour of the sky as the sun passed overhead, and the ebb and flow of the wind's breath. She was the process of healing, and the heat of vengeance.

She was just Layla. Layla was.

And there was no conceivable world in which she wasn't.

"You're a know-it-all and a smarty pants."

"I can not believe you just said that." She pouted in faux offense. "And you who got offended when I called you a Geezer."

"I think I was more offended by your terrible American accent." He saw the start of a cheesy smirk and cut it off before she could begin to mock again. "Don't you dare, smarty pants."

She put a hand over her heart and closed her eyes. Chest puffed out.

"Ah pledge allegiance to the flag-"

"Please stop."

She wiped an invisible tear. "-of the United States-" She pretended to choke up and completed the phrase in a strained, staged whisper, "-Of 'Muricuh."

"That was worse than you calling me a Geezer, whatever that means."

"You don't wanna know." She stopped wiping fake tears. "Plus, you deserve it for the American words I've picked up. I feel like a traitor. 'Sidewalk,' ugh!" She mimicked a shiver. "See, you did teach me those, Mr Teacher-type." Horace received a playful; punch that hurt a little more than he thought necessary. "Really, though, I was a terrible student. Nobody can teach someone who already knows everything."

"Or thinks they know everything."

"That was mean. I thought I was a know-it-all, and a smarty pants. Go on, then. Teach me something I don't know already."

"All that comes to mind are more vile American words: faucet, garbage, ice pop-"

Layla clapped a hand over his mouth. "Noooooo. If you're not gonna finish your story then don't talk."

She eased her hand away and Horace kept looking directly forward. The twitch of a grin betrayed him.

"Don't..." Layla warned.

"Okay smarty-pants."

"Hey!"

"Anyway- I lived on campus, which meant no alcohol, but I had all the cigs I wanted. Not that I wanted any. My promise to myself kept up. I stayed off them for good. Those years teaching were the most peaceful of my life, even with the war going on all around me.

Layla nodded. "I stayed at the university until the end of the war, then started moving again, which is why it took years for news of my friends' deaths to reach me.

"The morning before the ship sailed out, we all got lawyers. I can't remember who paid for them, but they pulled a few strings. None of us had any living family, and one who did made sure they thought he was dead. So we all made each-other our next of kin. It was a short process. The guys we got were good. High up guys the government uses. They must have been the ones that found me as well. Both times.

"I awoke one day to a bundle of letters on my doorstep, plastered with postage stamps from different countries, and wrapped with a piece of twine that was holding on by threads.

"All of them were dead."

The wind picked up again, whistling past his sharp nose and jutting cheekbones. The wrinkled skin smoothed under a hard gust then slackened and he kept going.

"Tommy was the only one I mourned, but I never shed a tear for them. I guess I thought they wouldn't want me to cry for them. I wouldn't have. I always felt like I should. After all, they were my first friends by choice, not chance.

"One thing made the grief much easier to cope with, and this was something I only realised upon the second reading of the letters."

"What was that?"

"I tried to save the stamps when the letters turned to shreds. I carefully peeled the first one off and... I saw a-"

He cut himself short, as if questioning his own memory. Could it really be as he remembered? Layla put a hand on his arm. "What was it?"

"A swastika."

As soon as the word left his mouth he felt Layla's hand stiffen, and remembered how the paper seemed to burn between his fingers, tearing stamps from each envelope, one by one, but met with the same angular black gleam. "Then I started trying to forget, but it was too late. I'd already seared them into my brain. I burned the letters and the stamps instead." He felt the weight of Layla's hand leave him. There was space between them again, expanding. Distance.

"I've forgotten enough of my life to know to cherish memory, even when it stings. My artists joined the wrong side, but I was spared the choice. In that was I am grateful. We need to remember as much as we can because we are also being forgotten, and being forgotten is a second death."

"If you believe in that stuff." Layla yawned, "We've already been forgotten."

"Not yet. If we aren't dead, we keep moving. That philosophy hasn't changed, even since I was a boy. Until we stop running, we take our memory into our own hands-" he made a fist and shook it in the air, "-and the memories of those who need a little help."

All hopes Layla had of a big find blew away with the changing wind that beat on her other cheek. She dragged her jagged and bitten nail over the map, searching for the last marker. She thought about what Horace said.

Being forgotten is a second death.

It made sense, but what stung her was how forgiving Horace seemed. To Layla, there were people in the world who deserved to die twice. People who deserved to be forgotten.

She tried to sleep on the way back, but with the storm ever nearer, there was too much on her mind. She tried not to think about death a lot, especially not her own.

Layla had no plans to die today, but very few ever did.

*****

Layla stepped back from the door after knocking, as if waiting for a neighbour to answer about an errand from her father. The neighbours didn't like her much, but they hated her mother more, so if there ever was an errand to run, it was done in her father's name.

No sound from within, and no movement, as expected. Sometimes, silence was better. Not always. Horace reached for the handle. "I'll go in, see if there's anything we can take, and... You know." He blocked the entrance with his tall, square body so she couldn't see in.

Layla's grip tightened on the heavy chest, growing heavy in her arms. Why had she brought it?

She kept it between her body and the door as she leaned in, the cold edge jabbing her between the ribs as the scarred side of her face made contact with the metal door. Every sound from within sent a tremor through the door. She could feel it on her face.

She never really realised what she was doing at this point. It always came later. She would listen, imagining what the old man did in the time between footsteps. What did he see? What did he avoid when the directions changed? The unsteady shuffle of his long bowed legs sweeping clumsy feet through dust never failed to entertain her inquisitive mind. She mapped his movements in her brain. Choreographed his dance around the dead. He didn't call her in. That meant he found someone.

She always said "someone."

She guessed at the contents of the outpost. This didn't look like a lab, so maybe something new. New wasn't always good either, but it meant a new person, and that was always good.

Nobody really knew how many people were on the mission. Some said 150, others only counted a few dozen. It really depended on where you worked. Layla and Horace were single-skilled, unlike most of the others. One person with two special skills meant one less person to deal with, clothe, feed, transport. It was always a question of money.

Layla got unlucky. She was spotted too early to have found a second skill. All they focused on was her fluency in electricity. After that, everything else went out the school window. The French lessons, at least, she was glad to get rid of, but with the added price of her English lessons, her favourite. Not her best, by far, and in exchange for a chance to go to space... Nobody would think twice, surely?

When she got tired she would read poetry. When she got sleepy she would write it.

As for Horace, he always said his 'job' was just an excuse. Keeping to himself meant nobody asked questions. But it was mainly his age that puzzled.

The cold of the door was beginning to numb at her cheek, and the constant shifting against the door had moved her mask slightly askew. It dug into the sensitive scarred flesh. She blinked hard, her dry eyes wandering from side to side behind her eyelids, and when she opened them there were dark spots swimming in her vision. She closed her eyes again before they could make her any dizzier than she already was, but behind her eyelids flashes like electrical sparks teased at the edges of her vision. After a while, she stopped chasing them and let them dance just out of sight.

The cold was travelling up her face when Horace's footsteps returned, and she jumped from the door, unsticking her skin from the metal, and leaving a large red weld on her cheek, only broken by the grew silicone. The chest rattled with clinks as she tucked it under one armpit.

Horace tossed one look behind her as he exited, still blocking the door with his body. "That storm is getting pretty close. We should wrap this up and head back." He held out his fist, and between his knuckles the glint of a metal nameplate poked out. She opened the box and caught a glimpse of the numbers before he snapped the lid closed a little too rough.

"1960?" Horace nodded. "He was younger than me."

"That's neither of your faults." He held her elbows when they sagged under the weight of the box. He shouldn't have slammed it so hard.

"And what was he?"

"By the looks of it, a radio technician. There's a big radio console in there, looks broken, but – look." His look turned stern. He took her by the shoulders now. "That's not important right now. Whatever we've been looking for these past years," he took a heavy breath. "He found it."

"What?"

"Yes - but look. Kid, we need to make a choice – and fast."

"What do you mean? We could have saved all that time if we just stopped here first?"

"It doesn't matter now. It won't matter when we find it, too. The storm is coming, and we need shelter. If we want to play it safe, we have to stay here until it blows over. Until then, we can fix the radio-"

"It's broken?" There was electricity in her fingers now, and a spark of energy in her heart, like she was truly awake all of a sudden.

"By the looks of it, yes, but it's nothing you can't deal with. We can try to contact anyone around with a radio, and see if they're near enough to find us. Or if we guess well, we could even try calling home." Happy, hopeful tears were pricking his eyes, but he blinked them back. His hands were tightening around her shoulders, and she tried to wiggle out. "If we play our cards right, we can find a way to make this count."

Layla's eyes lit up. "Could we go home?"

Horace's hands fell to his side. That was always the end goal: leave this godforsaken planet, get Layla home safe. That was the promise he made to himself, and more importantly, to her. He nodded, but if he learned anything in the last eleven years, it was that promises meant nothing if they weren't kept. He hated it, but he couldn't get his hopes up just yet. She already had.

"We can't just sit here, then, we need to go and get a look." She turned and started toward the truck.

"Wait! We can't- he-" She stopped in her tracks. He couldn't see her face, but the wind was getting stronger, blowing her loose hair away. He could see the pale scar and the fingers that stretched all the way around the back of her neck.

"How... How do you know what he found?"

"Layla, forget it. Please." He shook his head, placing one hand on each of her shoulders, and though she never tried to force them off, he could feel her muscles tense, as if they couldn't decide whether to fight or stay. "It was just a note- I didn't even pick it up-"

"He left a note?"

Horace shook his head. "I didn't mean to say that."

"But did he?"

He paused, then sighed. There was no point trying to lie now. Bit by bit she was picking away at him, breaking through the things he did to protect her.

"He did." Layla answered for him. She flew past him without meeting his eyes, placed one hand on the door. "If you won't go, I will."

"You're not going in there."

"You said it yourself; we're already being forgotten. We can't afford to forget anymore." The chest was slipping from her other hand.

"Layla." How do you tell someone that every passing moment, you worry for their innocence? For their soul? She knew too much already – been overexposed for too long. What's one more mark on her conscience?

Horace felt an overwhelming need to pick up the girl like an infant and carry her away, far away – anywhere was better than here – but when he returned to his senses, to the sight of her eyes locked on the door, like they could pierce right through to the pale corpse on the other side, he knew she wasn't the child that he followed to this wretched red planet, but the friend he would die for, only to see her leave it.

"All right. You win." Was this surrender? He regretted phrasing it like that, stubborn and stiff, the very qualities he tried to eradicate in himself so many years ago. "But just... let me go in."

Before he knew it, he was once again avoiding the gaze of the dead creature beneath the layers of sheets, as if they were shielding the room from its coldness, not the other way around. Horace could only imagine the final moments in this young man's life. Curling up in his bed like any other night on earth, turning off the lights and knowing the tank of oxygen beside his bed was too empty to be worth waking up to. The shrill screams of the alarm warning him of critically low oxygen levels wouldn't wake him either. The tips of his fingers poked up out of the sheets, resting on his hollow cheek, staining his face with government-issue blue ink, the blue bruises blending well with the shadows under his eyes.

Why did they all look so young, yet so old all at once. It was as if everyone stopped ageing, but the corruptions of old age still tainted them. Wrinkles and greyness could be painted on, eyes hollowed like the craters of Earth's moon. Blushed faded, hair was streaked with white. But asleep they were all babes again. Smoothed skin lost the natural frown that everyone adopted or mirrored from others.

He noticed Layla stopped growing when they arrived. She was hardly shoulder-height before. That was at seventeen. He soon learned that the extras inches came from her own shoes. Now these standard-issue boots robbed her of those, too. Another thing to frown about. She rarely smiled and meant it.

Stop it. She's waiting for you, out there, all alone again. You left her alone again.

He tore his eyes away from the motionless child and skimmed the room again, locking his gaze on the desk, upon which was stapled a small stack of paper, the watermark of the US Government taunting Horace even from a distance.

Beside it, the screen illuminated with the warm glow of the desk lamp which somehow hadn't burn out yet, was the radio. The console looked like it had seen better days, but so did most things Horace saw. Its innards were spilled out like guts through an exoskeleton, and he could only wonder how Layla saw things like this as just a puzzle to be solved. Enticing, even. It looked like a dead animal to him. Or one playing dead, just waiting for him to make the wrong move. Fake carcass.

He snatched the sheets from the table, cursing silently when his elbow slammed past the lamp, knocking loose the hot bulb and drowning the room in darkness. Before the darkness could grow milder for his old eyes, a sliver of yellow light stretched across the wall. It widened as he watched, his back to the door, creaking open. The wall was papered with drawings. Child's nonsense, interrupted by the angular shapes of the real world: diagrams and numbers, letters. Sometimes whole words, otherwise symbols with secret libraries behind them. Beacons of knowledge on some other planet, but here they were a pastime. An escape.

He turned around, and there was Layla.

Windswept hair gathered in front of her shoulders, dusted with red. The same red that brushed her ankles in swathes as it followed her in. Her face was a shadow until the door flew open with a fresh assault of wind. She wasn't looking at Horace. All he could see were the whites of her eyes.

"Layla." Horace approached her, as slowly as his legs allowed, so he wouldn't scare her when he placed one hand on her cheek, turning her head to face him, but her eyes remained fixed. It was then that Horace saw the true effect of her insomnia. The white of her eyes were buffed pink with dryness, erasing the childish sparkle she once had. Beneath her eyes, the dark trenches resembled those of the dead boy. He traced the outline of it with his thumb, almost dipping into it. His palm hovered above the scar and her mask.

"Hey," he whispered softly, and saw her eyes start to tremble, them force themselves to break the gaze. "Are we good?" She pursed her lips, not realising her mouth was open until a cold breeze hit her throat. The room was telling them their time was up, they had seen enough and it time to go.

She nodded, following her feet because the rest of her was fixed. She vanished in the light of outside, but the storm that followed her in didn't leave with her.

He found her in her seat in the car, hands tucked under her knees, silent. "Layla, we can go back to the outpost if you want, we still have plenty of time." She shook her head. "Well... I see the wind's changed direction. We might avoid the storm after all."

"Have you read the notes?"

"I skimmed the top sheet, but" he said, "it might not be the best idea. Maybe another time when..." He couldn't find anything to end on. Was there ever a better time, or a less bad one? There was nothing but bad times, just convenience. "I'm not going to stop you." He held out the sheets, but to his surprise, she turned her head away.

"Let's go." She straightened her back and took a map from the pile. His hand remained, suspended in the air. When she looked back she looked straight past it, right into his eyes. Hers were blank. His hand fell before he broke the stare.

This was neither of their first times seeing a corpse. Horace alone saw enough for a hundred lifetimes. But that was what they found here, not a death but a life, suspended. Static. He was less dead than asleep, or so it seemed.

He started to drive.

In her drowsy sing-song whisper, Layla's first words after an hour almost went unheard. "What?"

"I said, do you believe in ghosts?"

He cursed under his breath, assaulted by another memory, forced into the background for so long. "I suppose…" he cleared his throat, then wondered why?

"What's that supposed to mean?"

"It's a long story," he hated saying that. "And I've talked enough about myself for one day."

"Time is our only infinite resource. You taught me that."

He cursed again. She was right, of course. "You know, just because I said something doesn't make it right."

"Are you saying it's wrong?" He knew her well enough to recognise when she was deliberately winding him up, and this was not it. She asked a genuine question. She wanted a genuine answer, no matter how long.

"I was told," he began, "when I was very young, that my parents were dead. So I started seeing them everywhere. Like guardian angels I thought they were watching over me. Of course, when I found out they were alive the whole time, the little divine acts of kindness stopped. I realised I was making them up to make me feel better. Less lonely. Somehow knowing they were alive made me lonelier. So I got over the loneliness, started drawing.

"I at first drew the only thing I could see: the school. This attracted an unexpected fan. The headmaster at the school was an old guy, very strict, but he took a liking to me. I drew him a few times and showed him, but there were many more drawings I didn't show him. I used to sit on a bench outside his window in winter, when the fireplace made the windows steam up.

"I would look up every so often to see a spot where the steam was wiped clean. Whenever I finished a drawing I would slide it under his office door, wait for his shadow to move from the seat by the fireplace, and then pack up and run back down to the dormitory. We never spoke but through the drawings under the door. I never went into the office while he lived.

"The old man died at his desk when I was 10, and his replacement came the day of his funeral, but she was a superstitious younger woman, the kind who thought the stars could tell the future, and she planted all sorts of ideas about ghosts in the other teachers' minds. So the office stayed empty, and the fireplace unlit. It was easier to see inside when the windows weren't steamed, but nobody ever dared. Not teacher or student.

"We buckled down then. Kept our heads down and hands clean.

"One particularly cold winter night, however, I snuck away. The office was kept unlocked because the old guy was buried with the key in his hand. Nobody knew why, but he asked for it. Perhaps he forgot to request it to be locked, but then I found out why he wanted it unlocked in the first place.

"I wasn't careful when I came in. I headed straight for the coals and built a nice fire, then I sat in his chair and drew with his paper and pencils. The fire stayed small enough not to send loads of smoke up through the chimney, but large enough to warm my stiff fingers. The armchair was so comfortable, and being so small I could just curl up on the seat. I must have fallen asleep.

"When I was woken up by the old cuckoo clock above the fireplace, I saw the fire had already gone out, and only a few glowing cinders were there to remind me of the best sleep of my childhood. I was lucky enough to wake up when I did. Another five minutes and the housekeeper would have walked past the window and seen they were steamed up. I got up, pulled my sleeve over my hand, and rubbed my eyes, climbing up on the chair to start wiping the steam off the windows. That was when I saw the drawings.

"Someone had drawn a rabbit, using the steamed up glass as a canvas and their fingers as brushed. I looked at the paper I had drawn on. It looked as if someone had been looking over my shoulder and copying my every stroke. That was when I first got scared. When I ran to the door, half expecting to pull it open and see the headmistress ready outside to pull me back to bed by the ear, I found that I had bolted it behind me.

"I was completely alone, and had been since I wandered in there, half asleep and half frozen. Maybe what the headmistress had been saying about the office was true. Either way, I never hid there again. The gardener left for the winter months, and there was a perfectly comfortable tool shed that became vacant."

Layla's mouth had fallen open at the mention of the rabbit drawing, and stayed agape until the end. "You're sure you were completely alone? And it was definitely drawn on the inside of the glass?"

"When I wiped my hand over it, it disappeared."

"Dude."

Chapter 5

# SMELLING OF BLOOD

"I am going to die. I've made peace with this so many times before, but I think this is time. I suppose I should first thank the people who took me so far, before I come clean. First time I was ready to die, that nice girl came and fixed our oxygen dispenser-

Layla read that last sentence again and again. She'd snuck the sheets out from between their two seats. If Horace had wanted to say anything with the glare he threw, she pretended not to see, and he didn't comment further.

He didn't expect to read about herself within the first paragraph. Maybe that was why Horace hesitated

-That was just about a week after we were abandoned, but I already lost all hope. She said she will find everyone who took one of the dispensers and fix it. The old man with her was probably too old to be her dad, but he acted like that. Well, it broke again, and she was somewhere far, so we left it and moved on. It was almost empty anyway. That wasn't too long ago.

I should say "danke" to Marta, even if she broke my radio, and didn't return before sunset, like she said she will. I might look for her if I have enough time after I finish writing my confession, but I have much to say.

I can't seem to stay on track. Maybe this confirms I am dying? Maybe it is the English...

I knew we will be left alone, before everyone knew, and my radio is too broken to prove it, and I lost the notes with the messages.

I shouldn't have signed up for that science camp last summer.

Not last summer, it feels just like it, though. I can't blame Marta. She only came because mama forced them to let her, so I did not go alone. We would be with her still.

It was in the year 10. I was using my personal radio to try and catch signals from earth. That wasn't allowed, but nothing stopped me, so I did it. I intercepted an error message, and in the next days, more were sent, printing on my screen and I wrote them down.

They were important, and it was obvious. The last time, the president's seal shined on the screen before a message. I can't remember the words, but he was saying something about the end of the mission. I didn't tell Marta. I should have told her, but I was scared. I told her after, but then it was too late. We all saw the rocket land, and we all saw it leave.

Marta says I shouldn't blame myself, but where is she to stop me? She told me not to follow her, maybe that meant she didn't want to come back, but I will look for her anyway. She never really liked me. I know she blamed me for her life. Not a life. She yelled at me when I read her comic. I guess she wanted to go home as well.

She thinks I am stupid; I didn't grow up. I did grow up, but I only had her around. She saw me growing up like her and didn't like it. I guess that is why I sleep so much, so she does not have to see me walking around, pretending to be like her. I don't know anything else. I will not know anything else but what I know now.

I am going to apologise again if I find her. Say sorry for me if I don't.

*****

Layla folded the first piece in half and slid it to the back of the stack.

"I knew I remembered him."

There had been a grace period. Everyone looking for her again. She assumed they all forgot her after she was done fixing up their dispensers. She sure did, well, most of them. That was the goal, then: get as far away as possible, not knowing why, just running. Distance was an infinite resource alongside time.

Now the goal was to reverse that mistake.

And these messages he wrote about, was there some way to contact earth even now? She remembered threading thick wires on high beams in Odyssey. Faux telephone lines. The hollow ropes swayed and snapped in the first winds. They were just there for show. Show what? That they still could call home if they wanted to. Not that anybody ever would...

"He doesn't sound that sad, knowing he was going to die." Layla said, tracing the softened edge of the second sheet with the pad of her finger. "He loves his sister, the way a little brother does. It's almost like they were never here at all." She looked around and wondered how someone could live a Martian existence, but still have Earthly troubles. Sibling quarrels.

"He's not the most poetic." Horace added.

"Maybe that's a good thing." Layla took up the next sheet. "Mars gave us many lessons, but poetry was Earth's creation. Not everything can be made to feel like home. No point fooling yourself with trying." She started reading again.

*****

I thought I was done with all this. I thought I would just die, why can't it all just end? I'm so tired-

"You don't have to read out loud."

"Do you want me to..."

"Just- Don't force yourself." He could hear the change in her voice, the hitch in her breath when she started the second letter. "Maybe you shouldn't read this one at all."

"I will," she said. "Sorry." Horace shrugged, defeated, and listened again. The engine quieted as they crossed smoother terrain.

I'm so tired but I have to keep awake and remember this.

I went to find Marta, and good luck to her, but I can't back. It's almost dawn, and I left the cabin around midnight, because I couldn't sleep. My footprints are still glowing outside from the stuff I stepped. If I look really closely, I can almost see the place glowing. Are they following me, or is that lightning? My footprints make a path.

I don't know, I'm so tired. If I sleep, I won't wake up, so I need to finish first.

I need to write this down, to make up for my last secret. Not too far from here, (north?) I walked for a long time. I hoped to find Marta, but I found what she was looking for instead. All those rockets we lost, yeah they're all there. Just standing up, lined up in rows like soldiers. Like graves? I could have been a soldier. They don't send soldiers to Mars. My mama thought I was too smart to die in a field, but look where I ended up. All the same at the end of the equation.

I went down into the place, and looked around. It was hard to see in the dark, but I noticed around the edges of the crater were some indents, like caves. I went in one. I saw a light, dim and blue at first, that started getting brighter and sort of beating as the thing came nearer. Then I heard it.

It sounded like marbles, sort of gurgling, and when I got out of the way, it came out.

It was pushing a rocket out with its head. It must have collected it from somewhere, and when the head emerged I saw it had no eyes, but gills that leaked the glowing stuff, that slid down its body and spilled on the ground. Its body was smooth like larva and thick as a train, and it pumped its accordion body noisily, sliding out of the cave and settling itself on its back to push the rocket up near to the others. I had to escape then, but I stepped in some of its slime. The stuff outside is still glowing, but my footprints in here faded when I turned on the light. Maybe that's how they cover their tracks. When the sun rises, all trace of them disappears after they've smelled their way home. Clever creatures.

I think it noticed me that way, because it turned its shiny round head, and I ran. When I turned around for one last look I noticed all the other caves around were glowing, and I didn't want to wait for its friends, so I ran until I got home. I didn't look to see if it followed me, but I worry now.

I'm so tired, and I ran out of oxygen. If those things followed me, at least I'll be dead before they get to me. How many of these things

are there? Where do those tunnels go? How far do they reach? They must be all over the place – even as far as Odyssey? Someone else will look. Not me. I'm done with all this. I'm not even scared anymore, I'm just so tired. Sorry again Marta.
Love, Markus."

On the back of this sheet was a hastily scrawled map, annotated with smudged blue fingerprints and a hatch of crossed out lines. Layla remembered his blue fingers, and his face, paler than the paper. She wondered how horrifying these creatures might really be, if he'd included a drawing of them, too?

When was the last time Layla had read something out loud? Her voice was already shaking. She blamed the reading, not the words. Words don't hurt. She coughed to awaken herself, and Horace jolted. "Were you sleeping?" she asked. Then he did something so unexpected. Something eleven years of friendship had never betrayed.

Horace ignored her. Craning his neck as they were passing over a dune, it was as if she didn't exist for a moment, to either of them. The engine strained against the steep incline, but Layla took the final sheet into her hands. They were shaking, but she didn't realise against the tremor of the vehicle that shook her whole body.

It was the letter of invitation that everyone had received months in advance of the mission. Layla still remembered burning hers. One of these was a rare and fearsome sight these days. It was a mystery why the boy would have kept it. Layla's questions were answered when she read the name at the top of the sheet, the only thing differing between everyone's letters: Marta K. Ludwig.

Where previously the job would be listed, for the first time, was a name. Who was this person? Person. That was a nice thing to be sometimes. Difficult most times, almost impossible now.

She tore off the top part of the letter, which cut off just after the name, and rolled it up, adding it to the names in her chest with a heavy heart. From what the boy said, there was no use going to look for her. While she still had the chest on her knees, she fished around, looking for the one belonging to the boy. She was sure he had told her his name when they met before, but it escaped her.

"Markus D. Ludwig." She returned the name to the chest, letting the lid fall, casting the plates in darkness, but relieving her of their sight.

Marta was his sister. They were sent here together, and they left with a Martian wasteland between their bodies. He died not knowing if his sister's leaving was to help or to condemn him.

Before she closed the latch her fingers pried the heavy lid back, eyes scanning for the plate she just added. Without really thinking, she fished it out along with the paper. It was still warm. With cold fingers she worked quickly, wrapping the plate in the thin paper scrap and dropped them both in at once. Back together, as they should be. Layla used to dream of siblings. Now she was grateful they stayed dreams.

Less mourning, less grief in the world.

The car slowed as it braved the incline. Falling sand skimmed past the tyres like water through fingers. Horace muttered under his breath, urging the heavy truck forward. Most of it was caught in the whistle and whisper around them, but between revs Layla could catch fragments.

"Come on, come on, come on–" She fell back as they lurched forward, now looking forward to the sky and clutching the door for stability. She hadn't used the seatbelt once since they found this, but now the sturdy band across her chest and stomach was a comfort.

As she clicked the buckle into place, she spotted something she missed on the letter, which fluttered around at her feet. Her boot pinned it into place, and she forced herself against the seatbelt to grab it. Her fingers captured the frayed top, and she drew back, slamming her back flat in the seat.

In the lower margin of the page, right above the government watermark, was an unfamiliar verse written in the same ink:

"Sing now while your throat is free.
While there are none around to hear,
There are also none to silence you.
Toss no coins, shoot no bullets."

These were not the verses of the boy, whose crude thoughts were painted on their pages with a scrawling script. Could these be the words of the sister? Funny how words can outlive and outrun you. Words are immortal, bodies are not. Persons, Layla - people. "This is it."

She watched the rays of light descend down his face, from the silver hair turned gold, down to the grey chin, as they reached the flat top of the hill. He slammed on the brake, and she shot forward, the seatbelt digging into her ribcage. "We made it."

Barely thirty feet of flat ground spread before them, before a sharp decline hid the crater's contents from view. Horace didn't let his gaze wander, unbuckling them both at once. As he exited the truck Layla's breaths became laboured and she screwed her eyes shut. She grabbed on to the top of the windshield and pulled herself up blindly. Beneath her eyelids the light of day was teasing her, but she held on, heart beating in her throat and wrists. The wandering scar began to tingle.

She opened her eyes.

The sun was almost blinding as it dipped behind the other side of the crater, but she didn't blink. She didn't even squint. The light burned into her weary eyes the shadows of the standing rockets' pointed noses. Dozens, she couldn't focus long enough to count.

Horace was to the side somewhere, equally silent, pacing the edge of the steep hill on the other side of the flat side.

They stood up like soldiers, standing to attention, chins jutted out, arms tight to their sides, all looking like one another. She ripped her gaze away and with teary stinging eyes stepped out of the car. The door slipped open, and she tripped, but Horace was too far away to hear. She waited until he made a full trip around the rim and was back by her side before meeting the landscape beneath them again.

However, the longer she looked, the more it started to resemble a graveyard, rather than an army. Each rocket signifying a lost soul, forever wandering, scouring the planet looking for home, but they will never find it here.

Horace's mind was elsewhere, rather the edges of the inside of the crater, which looked more carved than cut. These hills weren't dug by millennia of rivers and oceans, and they weren't forced into the planet's surface by any asteroids. Seconds and Millennia didn't create this place. It was creatures that dug it out. Creatures with claws or teeth as big as a digger's. The cross-hatching scars was evident that something scraped at these walls to mould them into this vast ravine – a hoard for its riches, or a dump for the invader's waste.

The caverns dotted around the edge mimicked drainage holes on the sides of a road. What intricate sewer systems hid beneath the surface of this lonely planet? What have they been walking on top of all these years, never thinking to look down? Catacombs drawn up in some mystic imagination never to be seen by man.

A cloud of dust stirred beside him, and he turned to find an empty space where Layla had been standing. He followed the sound of scuffling and rocks tumbling down hill to find her halfway down the steep crater wall, sliding on her heels as if surfing a red wave, spitting dust instead of sea foam in her wake. He took one last look on the horizon before following her. The storm really had changed direction, and was disappearing, withdrawing its crimson tendrils from sight and mind.

"Wait, kid!" Horace yelled after her, but she didn't look back until her feet were firmly on flat ground, then, her dark eyes were blurred behind a screen of dust. He finally met her at the bottom of the crater, no longer looking eye to eye with the rows of rockets, but overlooked by them. The looming monoliths, the giants who would carry them home - mechanical cocoons. It was so close to a reality, but he remembered the boy's letter. If what he said was true, they should be very wary of nightfall.

The solid boundary of the crater's edge was split between the red, ablaze where the sun still tread, and earthen brown below it. He counted less than an hour before they were cast in night's rich danger.

He noticed Layla eyeing the dark caverns with passive intrigue, but he knew where her mind already was: inside those rockets, deep in their mechanisms, untangling their wires like guts, reading their secrets like a prophecy. Then putting them all back together as if nothing had happened.

The contents of the metal shells beckoned Layla closer, but she resisted, sticking by Horace's side until the old man got his footing. His stride didn't follow him to Mars. He disguised his age with his wisdom for so long, but it was coming through now more than ever.

"Well, what now?"

"We've got to be careful, kid. You read what that boy wrote. There's something here that wants nothing to do with us, and we should respect that if we want to get home."

"They're nothing like what I expected aliens to be like, all... wormy."

"Layla, we're the only aliens here." He motioned with wide arms to the rows of rockets, "And here be our UFOs."

"Well, this alien is going home." She pointed her thumbs to herself with cocky disregard. The gleam was returning to her eyes, but the shadows under them were still dark and deep as bruises and cold as the unsunned terrain. She tossed a look over her shoulder at her oxygen tank. The level was just over two-thirds full, and so was his own.

"I go low, you go high?"

"I'll do that in a bit. These caves are really drawing me in." Horace added in mock British: "As you say, 'ta, love." He spun toward the cavern nearest to them, escaping the scowl she threw after.

Layla gave in to the rocket's magnetism. She submitted to its welcoming shade and what she would find in it. Invisible electricity reeled her in. She could almost hear it.

She wasted no time - prying the control panel door open, she unearthed a whole room of buttons and wires and bulbs that had seen no light, other than their own fluorescent blips, in a decade. But most overwhelming was the smell.

When they first arrived, the stench of blood was overwhelming, sickening, and Layla could barely get it into her head that it was iron, not real blood. Even then, she felt ill for months, but everyone was still getting used to everything. Little by little the smell faded, as did all of the effects of life on the new planet.

The air that escaped the room was rank and still, but above all, it felt like earth smell. There was the dampness she didn't know she would miss until it returned. Her dry skin softened just by stepping into the cold shade. Like stepping inside after a long, bright summer day. She let her eyes adjust the same way. In this way nostalgia flirted with her, and she let it happen.

Horace was in no rush, observing the handiwork of whatever creature dug this ravine. Much less like a ravine, it was quite small, and quite circular, like a deep pore. The steep walls he studied. Nothing was meant to get out without some difficulty. The ground felt solid beneath an ankle-deep layer of dust, but he didn't like the sound it made when he stepped in some places, like there was something underneath, just waiting to sift away the dust and swallow him up. He moved to the edge to ease his mind.

Impatiently he stepped into the cave's shade, looking back at Layla's oxygen tank anchoring her to the outside as she worked. The side of his face met the obstacle first, then his body fell flush to it. His right shoulder sank into the soft, fleshy substance that coated the sturdy wall that barricaded the entrance of the cave. He pulled himself away, unsticking his cheek, knee and shoulder.

As his eyes adjusted he noticed the glow. The whole cave was radiating a soft blue-green aura, even the residual slime on his clothes was aglow. The cold slime seeped through his clothes, which should have been waterproof, but now appeared penetrable. There wasn't much water to test it out on in the first place. The coolness on his cheek started to spread lowed, through his mask. He swiftly removed it and wiped the mouthpiece clean. The glow remained even when clean.

So, these creatures didn't like visitors. He could respect that. The recluse lifestyle appealed to him, too, but more recently it became something impossible, and frankly, unwished for. Loneliness didn't have the same comfort it used to have.

The wall was translucent beneath a liquid layer, and he peered through the gap his shoulder had cleared in it. On the other side, the light carried just a few feet, but he could tell the cave went far, deep, and sloped down.

Making a fist, he widened the gap and hovered his ear just above it, trying to hear through his whistling breath, heartbeat, and the natural ambiance the planet had. It sung to itself most times, but especially at sunrise and sunset. Apparently Earth did the same, but he never cared to notice. Only Layla noticed such things.

The distance was starting to creep down his spine, tugging at his sleeves. He should turn back. Layla wouldn't miss him for another minute or two, surely. He pressed his ear to the wall. Instantly the cold fluid coated his ear and hair, but he pressed it deeper, feeling the hard wall give in, not even half an inch, but it did give in. It was still fresh.

The voice of Mars behind it was clearer now than before, the clearest he'd heard it since he learned to listen for it. He pulled away, swatting the fluid out. The planet was waking up and they were wasting time. He would take what he could find and leave.

Horace turned on his heel and was dazed with the full power of the sunset's last desperate rays. While he keeled over, straining through the pangs of pain rushing from his eyes to the back of his head, he made sure his breathing was unaffected by this. He had come too close to allow his age to be a burden. Too close. He opened his teary eyes.

Layla was in the spinal cord of the rocket. The centre of control. Everything that happened, it all led back to this little dark room. She was sat, balanced on the edge of the entrance, just a foot or two above ground where her oxygen tank rolled around in the playful breeze, the tinny sound of fine grains powdering the metal danced in the wind. White noise. She yawned, her shoulders bobbing up and down, her hands tracing the route each wire took, where it came from and where it ended up.

She remembered how fun it was to rip out a whole fistful of wires, but nothing like that could happen this time. There was too much at risk. The lights around her were winking, twinkling at the sleep-deprived girl like stars, but she only saw them out of the corners of her eyes. She was busy.

No time for sleeping under the stars tonight. Maman used to say the stars would watch over her when she was gone, but she rarely saw the stars anymore. Maybe she didn't look for them anymore. Perhaps she should take a few moments, close the door, just let herself imagine these were the same stars her mother doted on to keep her company. Or did she mean they would protect her?

No. You are busy. Layla opened her eyes.

This place wasn't spared of the thin layer of dust plaguing everything on this planet, but this was different, this was dust all the way from Earth, and she felt an odd nostalgia brushing it away, wiping the greyness on her clothes the way she used to get scolded for as a child.

Dust on the mantelpiece. There was a clear spot where her mother's vase used to be, before Layla dropped it. She just wanted to hide it. It might have been a game, or it might have been revenge. She didn't know what for, but after her father died, she was so full of rage all the time. Hot rage, and nothing to aim it at. She felt bad it had to be her mother, even if only for a short while, that felt her full concentrated fury. Maman didn't mention the vase. The others looked uneven without it, so she sold them all to pay for her trips.

Maybe she really did miss home after all. But, then again, it was a million times easier to miss something when you were stuck here. It was a million times easier to forget all the bad things, and polish the memories of the little good. Maybe trying again with Earth wasn't impossible.

You won't get back at this rate. She opened her eyes again and focused them on her work. Wake up.

"Something's wrong here." Layla couldn't help announcing it out loud, maybe to keep herself from passing out, maybe to prove a point to herself. Pointing out the problem helps it come out sometimes. She used to wait for Horace to come back before trying to solve it. If he were there, working beside her, he would have dropped what he was doing, squinted and leaned into her work, waiting for her to start explaining her troubles. Not that he even tried to understand, but problems always want an audience. They live for the applause that comes with their own death. Layla would have to be her own audience.

The scuffling overhead made known Horace's presence, but it wouldn't do. She couldn't interrupt him. There was too little time. This would be a puzzle she solves alone. With a quick crack of her knuckles, she started from the top, closing her eyes and trying to forget everything she saw.

When she looked again, she found something new: a small grey panel hidden behind a tangled wall of wires. New was good this time.

"Got ya!" One of the wires stood out from of the rest, leading behind the panel. She followed it like a crumb trail, unscrewing the obstacles in her path with her fingernail, not bothering to fetch her tools from the car. Impatience is a Deadly Sin for a girl, she thought, looking at her shattered nails. Her mother's words echoed around the chamber. "I deserve to be a little impatient." Eleven years was a long wait, and with this little control room, stars twinkling all around her, it was coming to an end. Her eyes drooped, following the wire every way it split and strayed. The oxygen tank was rolling around more violently outside, tugging mercilessly at her face, constantly moving her gaze. She got lost in her own maze, the thread she followed wouldn't help.

Horace hardly paid any attention to the contents of the shuttle. There wasn't much of note anyway, aside from some old boxes and devices he couldn't begin to guess the purpose of. His feet were cemented to the ground, but his head was in the clouds. He did it. He would see this rocket leave this planet, with Layla and, ideally, himself, in it, headed for home. He took a deep breath through his mask. Not too long until it would come off for good. That would be a day to look forward to. He looked for something to wipe off the rest of the slime with.

Layla's fingers were tingling with anticipation. Behind the little metal panel was the key to going home. She prised the grey cover off, careful not to damage the wire as she dug out its source: a small red box with a symbol printed clearly on it. The stray wire was wrapped around it, branching off into a dozen directions, behind the line of view and into the very walls of the rocket. Whatever this little box was, it controlled everything. Now, the symbol-

Layla knew she recognised it, but where from?

She leaned backwards, taking in the whole view. What beauty. Everything coming into place like a jigsaw. Poetry, she could have said. The one missing piece was right in front of her, now, where did it fit?

Horace couldn't move. He wasn't quite sure if he could breathe either. The storm had changed direction, how was this possible? The red tendrils returned, twirling their fingers in his directions. The door was swinging on its hinge, shrinking and enlarging the dreadful image in front of him. How could this happen?

Layla?

His mouth formed the name but made no sound.

She tried re-focusing her eyes, but the edges of her vision were blurry, like they were only capable of reading one word at a time. Tunnel vision. This symbol meant something. Something bad. She cast her mind through eleven years' worth of fog, wading through the memories to catch the right one. A metal inscription. The symbol cast into the sheet of stained copper, painted white but looked pink in the light, like a drop of blood diluted in milk.

She scrolled down the list in her mind, finally landing on the right one. A circle, broken in half from east to west by two stars. The pale blue letters beside it spelling the word "Explosive." Ancient hieroglyphs. A secret language.

As Horace sped down the ladder, wind on his back, he remembered the images, black and white, of homes drowning in dust. This wasn't in black and white, but it would rip through them all the same. Or maybe it won't. Maybe it could be merciful. Mars wasn't always a planet of rage; red wasn't always a colour of death.

Its song ripped through his white hair as his feet touched the ground.

A dull thud, her head coming in contact with something big, heavy, swinging at top speed to the back of her. Her being thrown forward, catching herself with her palms. Now eye to eye with the symbol, the little wire dancing teasingly into the blur of her sight.

Even when the room was cast in darkness, the white seemed to glow in contrast, taunting her. "What now? What are you going to do this time?" It seemed to sing at her.

Her dry lips sputtered, words perhaps, but no sound come out of them, and other than the horrible ringing in her ears, nothing could be heard. Pushing herself up and further from the symbol, her tunnel vision didn't clear, but made the hundreds of twinkling lights spin around, winking, teasing. These stars will do, she thought. Here is a night sky I wouldn't mind getting lost in. Her eyelids were getting heavy, and something warm was trickling down her cheeks, but she wasn't crying. Her father told her not to cry, for her mother.

Maman would be proud, that's what it said on her grave, so it must be true. It must be forever. "Proud mother." If she were here, she would sing a song, but the ringing in her ears was enough. It was more than a ringing now. Melody was growing out of it – flourish – and she thought of little Lemon, her Canary. She tried to forget it, but that wasn't good. Father brought Lemon from the mines, that's why she only lived as long as she did. Her birthday present was gone after just weeks, but her song was finally coming back. Notes morphed in and out, in and out, loud and quiet. Poetry.

Horace clawed at the door's edge, Layla's oxygen tank swaying by his feet as the winds hurled at him, whacking wave after wave of grit at his skin, stinging his face and neck. "Layla!" He screamed, his fingers turning white with the effort. The end of the tube waved to and fro freely, but its middle was cinched by the door, jamming it closed, rendering it useless. Less than useless. He could hardly hear himself among the whirlwind.

She's in there. My girl is in there. She's dying in there. He grunted, pulling at the door with all his might, screaming from the pain. His fingers gave in, slipping off the metal edge, and a gust of wind pushed him onto his back. The breath was knocked out of him and stayed above him, out of reach. He fought to get back up. He had to get up. He had to get her out. He had to get her home. Breath or no breath.

In a way it was a beautiful song. It was nice to fill the silence with, when she's had silence for far too long. Something told her it was bedtime. Was it her father? Maybe he got home early tonight. That meant she would need to wake up early to see him off. She heard a thudding, far off.

He was coming upstairs to tell her goodnight.

Horace pounded on the door in frustration. Hot tears were streaming from his eyes, whisked away by the wind before they could reach his cheeks, or caked with dust on his wet lashes. "Layla!" He punched both his fists on the door. "Layla! Can you hear me?"

It couldn't be her father. He was dead. So was she. "I don't want to die." There was nobody to sing her to sleep, but Lemon was still here, or at least her voice. She always had such a beautiful voice. No chorus could out-perform Layla's perfect Prima donna.

"I don't want to die." She couldn't hear herself.

Where was that silly bird? Looking around, all she could see were stars, waltzing in and out of vision. The song was louder now, and she couldn't tell her own words apart. This was the perfect song: a song of chaos and drowning in your own noise until you can't even hear yourself. It was so poetic, so it was good, right? "I don't want to die!" Layla screamed until her throat was hoarse. She used to sing in the church choir. No. It was the school choir.

Horace never prayed. Not unless he had to, but in those Christmas church services, hymns recited half-hearted in a cold pew with another sleepy boy on either side, pleading for midnight to strike so they can finally return to their threadbare beds – no real prayer could cross his lips.

He never prayed when he was starving with a friend on either side, cowering by the fire in the streets in Seattle or in the trenches, warmed by the flames feeding off his latest failure. He didn't pray when his lung was lying beside him on a tray, and all that remained of his friends were his memories, and their shattered limbs lying somewhere in the French wastelands. He never prayed.

Horace was knelt outside the door, knees dug into the red dust as the whisper of the returning wind blew away the silent words from his lips as he begged – pleaded – for the life of his only friend.

Her screams pierced through the cold dead metal, twisting in the air until the wind seemed to whistle to match her pitch. "I'm sorry." He could only whisper. "I'm so sorry." He could only breathe.

"That's enough, girlie." Her father's voice silenced her. "It's time to sleep." Layla sighed, curling up in her warm arms. There was a storm outside. She loved the sound of night rain, if only that dreadful bird would quiet down enough for her to hear it. The stars outside her window were glittering, twinkling, but no moon tonight.

"Goodnight, dad."

"School tomorrow."

School tomorrow. School, where she would walk the halls alone, sit at her desk alone, eat lunch alone and still feel better than everyone. Her fingers clutched at the folded up letter under her pillow. This letter was proof of it. It would soon be over. Her father coughed as he closed the door behind him.

The warmth on her ears was dripping down her face now, and smelled like metal, but so did everything around her. She closed her eyes. One way or the other, she always managed to block out the bird. Maybe attention is what fuelled Lemon's song. If she ignored it for a little while, she would quiet down, and this chorus of chaos would be over. Layla hoped it wouldn't take long. She had a terrible headache.

Finally, as sleep washed over her, the song came to an end, smelling of blood.

"I don't want to die."

Chapter 6

# FORGET EVERYTHING

The broken record of Layla's muffled screams played over and over in his head, as Horace put distance between himself and the rocket. They cut through him. Their coldness, their distance so small but impossibly great, sliced at his bones and fixed themselves in his wrists as he gripped the steering wheel. Time had passed, he wasn't sure how much, since then. Now he was in the truck, driving, alone. He didn't remember walking away or walking up the steep hill.

His bleeding fingers pressed deep into the old leather, but the only trace of the blood was the smell, which even the receding winds and crisp nightfall couldn't mask. Why was it all so dark, so fast? His chest tightened, eyes snapping open and closed to stay awake. It was too quiet, even the engine, which sputtered and gasped worse than he did, was breathing the clear cold air. The air he couldn't breathe. It was all a taunt.

Straight lines no longer existed. He swam over the pecan surface of the planet, blind. All he saw ahead was the two broken beams of the white headlights, and the inches of light radiating from his own face and hands, illuminating the heavy mist – remnants of the dust storm that clouded his eyes and crystallised on the damp patches of slime on his cheek. He swerved again, and the sharp jolt knocked his mask to the side. He cursed aloud and pushed it back, his hand smearing the cold tears deeper under the tight silicone. He could smell them now.

The swerve sent the hollow metal canister spinning around at his feet, the rhythmic clangs shooting pangs of ice down his back as he hurtled through the night, the speed of the truck simulating the storm that had escaped his wrath, but hung around to watch his tears.

Frozen anger thawed in his stomach, climbing into his throat as he slammed on the gas. Without thinking he beat his fist on the horn, too long been silent. He punched at it, again and again with sore fingers, hands, and when the heat in his fingertips was too much to bear, he took them to his throat.

Deserter.

Behind the masking yells of the car horn, his mouth had cried into the night. Piercing, hollow groans that cluttered his throat and nose, stinging, itching to be let out. He choked on the air that invaded when he gasped, warm fingers dripping what could be blood again into the neck of his uniform. He buried his face in the crook of his elbow, blinking hard to squeeze the tears out, and when he opened his stinging eyes again, the dim blue that coated his shoulder and elbow twinkled in the reflection from the metal chest that sat in Layla's place. He stopped breathing for a moment, then broke free of its image.

The canister had lodged between his calf and the door, the dulled edge of the nameplate protruding slightly, digging through the thick fabric into the muscle. He realised is hurt, more than it should.

It hurt because he was hurting in ways he never knew humans could. He broke his promise.

The cabin came into view, perhaps a welcoming sight, but not what was inside. When he stopped the truck it was quiet again and he could hear his breathing. He wished it would stop, if only for a minute, so he could have peace.

But peace was the last thing he was ever allowed. Always chased, always followed, always running from something. He stopped short, hand on the door knob, the other holding the Layla's tank.

Horace's thin hair swung around his tear-stained face, sticking to the wet remains as he looked behind into the night.

Nothing followed. Nothing chased. What was he going to do now? After losing everything, there was nothing.

*****

"Aren't you angry?"

He spun around. The half-awake face of the girl stared back. It was her birthday today and she was choosing to ignore it.

Horace rolled up his map. "At what?"

"Everything," she said. "Everyone. Back there." If she meant Earth she would have pointed vaguely at the sky. If she meant Odyssey she would have pointed over her shoulder. So maybe she meant both when she did neither.

"Sometimes. I used to be so angry, all the time. Then I figured, in life you need something, because you are going to lose most things. The last thing I had was my temper, and I wasn't going to give it up. If I need one thing to keep me close to home, it's that."

He lied. He hated lying to Layla. Layla didn't deserve any more lies.

He was angry, still, and had been every moment since… Well… But at the same time as his wrath was born, so was his promise, and that kept him closer to Earth. Layla kept him closer to Earth, but he'd broken his promise and she was gone. He never told her, really, about the promise, because then there was the risk of it not coming true. Superstition, he called it, childishness. Something he crafted to protect himself, out of thoughts and words and fear. Things he couldn't afford.

But this was not a planet of fear. It was as empty as Earth was, as ignorant as it was to Horace. There was nothing for him in either place, but there was everything for Layla, and everything she thought she'd lost. Layla was never scared of anything, and now she was gone, it would not start for him. He never asked why she had no fear. He would have known it was because she already felt there was nothing to lose except him. And there was no way he would ever leave.

He cast his light into the small cabin and stirred the dust that had settled since they left. For a moment, he froze, because the figure swaddled in sheets like a child resembled the young girl, now sleeping miles away, in a sleep she would never wake from. If his blood could have run any colder, it would. The darkness deepened the colour of the boy's skin, until the paper white glimmered only in Horace's visible aura. The golden hue of Layla's face rested in his memory, along with her peppered black hair, that bounced in the wind and calm alike. This place could never take such a thing away from him.

Layla had made her own little planet for them, and kept it close, tangled it tight in those curls and took it everywhere she went. Maybe she realised what she did for him. Maybe he only realised it in hindsight.

The boy's skin was different. The coolness of the light that radiated from Horace was hardly strong enough to make out the details in his face. But the more he strained, the harder it was to tell it was actually a person. The darkness loved playing tricks as much as it loved to hug the beauty out of the beautiful, corrupt it, make it more dead than alive. Make a warm thing cold or a singing thing silent.

He owed it to Layla not to succumb to silence. To listen to the song of the planet that took everything from him, including fear, now, was his duty. He backed away from the boy, letting him rest.

Feeling around the void of the room, he placed his hands on the desk, raw fingers skimming painlessly over the flat surface until they met the staples still buried in the wood, no longer holding down a death-confession. From there he gripped blindly, through the memory in his arms he found the desk lamp, and the switch. Dead. Another memory burned in his elbow: a curse, a knock as he spun around, drowning in darkness. Familiar.

The bulb had cooled, and soothed his touch as he gently twisted it back into place, eyes closed without realising. The blue glow strained his eyes more than it helped him see.

Through the thin flesh of his eyelids he saw warmth again. The golden glow, a captured sun. The real sun wouldn't rise for a long time.

He sat at the desk and put the empty oxygen tank in front of him, using Layla's tools from the truck to remove the two screws from her name plate with trembling and dry blood-coated digits, making sure to keep the plate pure of both blood and the residue slime. He felt it drying on his skin and flaking off in the heat of the lamp.

He scoured the cabin for some thread to hang the metal from his neck, and remembered the times he did this for his artists both in the trenches and after them, until it seemed he was collecting names more than memories. Horace sucked the blood from his fingers before threading the string through the screw-hole beside Layla's name. He allowed himself to cry as it dangled above his heart before pulling himself together and pulling the heavy radio along the desk.

Strange that crying was something he needed his own permission for. It was coming either way, only this time it was justified. Like no other was loss was this. He realised Layla was nothing like his artists. He could not even bring himself to call them friends. They were tokens, people who were in the same situation at the same time. Mutual respect fuelled their connection, they did not like each-other, but their stories, and through a shared need, they kept coming back to each-other. Layla was different. The artists knew nothing about him, that was why they stayed. He and Layla knew almost everything, and stayed regardless. Neither needed the other, but they stuck together. There was hardly anything mutual. Nothing made sense. Nothing was perfect or constant. That was real friendship. Layla was a real friend, more than a token person.

Lucille. Why had she chosen Layla? The obvious choice would have been Lucy. It was questions like these she would never answer, and he should have taken advantage of the eleven years he had to ask them. They told each-other everything and yet there were still mysteries shrouding her like shadows. A long time ago he would have hugged those shadows on himself, kept them closer to his chest than any person. Now they taunted him and his tears.

It was time to get to work. The night was young, and the storm had caught up to him again, beating on the shell of the cabin with strength that rocked it like a ship at sea. He was safe in here, so he wiped his tears and put the broken console in front of him on the desk, covering up the ink stains from the final letters the boy wrote.

"Christ..." Any trace of optimism faded once he saw the mess of colours spilling out of the radio, its guts winding around each-other like snakes in a pit, writhing in his tired vision. Where did Layla even know to begin with these things?

Was he stumbling before he even began? It wouldn't be the first time.

Come on, eleven years, he must have learned something.

He closed his eyes and tried to forget everything he saw.

*****

Horace watched the night advance through the little port window beside the desk, avoiding glancing at the black reflective screen on the console, which displayed nothing but the pale reflection of the corpse's face, tilted on the pillow as if in slumber.

The static started an hour ago, blaring in the headset, the only sign he was doing something right. It was a harsh sound, that made his brain feel like it was frying, but it was a welcome break from the booms that pounded on his conscience with every gust of wind. The white noise also drowned out his thoughts, the images of the shapes he saw above his head when he looked around for help, scanning the diagrams on the walls for hints. The shapes morphed into a hundred blank eyes, watching him from above. Did that mean something? He was just glad to have an audience. Problems tend to solve themselves when someone is there, watching you untie the knots.

Layla hummed when she worked, but she didn't admit it. Perhaps she didn't realise it. Was it only this morning she was singing in her sleep? Murmured halves of broken nursery rhymes.

It felt like so long ago, her memory starting to fade even now. It wasn't possible. Him being there now, working his fingers raw into the nooks and crevasses of this godforsaken machine, this was keeping her alive, one way or another. This was keeping him alive. The grey of his fingers rubbed into fleshy pink as he worked, and he saw colour on himself for the first time in over a decade. Colour that wasn't blood.

London bridge... falling down... falling down...

The broken lullaby wasn't enough to break through the static, but his lips formed the words anyway, leaving the song hanging in the air. Perhaps the boy appreciated it. When was the last time he was sung to sleep? When was the last time Horace had sung?

He remembered the choir songs he used to mumble through at the orphanage, the Christmas carols in the trenches that took him through the cold winter and the deaths of his friends. The drinking songs he and his artists would grumble through as they roamed the streets, too drunk to remember the words, all singing different verses at the same time, in different languages. Then, the nursery rhymes he would mouth along to when the redhead nurse sang to the newborn or dying baby in the room beside him.

That was the last time.

Build it up with sticks and stones…

This song wasn't just about some bridge. It was a testament to People. It was an ode to humanity. When something breaks, you watch your work be washed away in the current, and still decide to make it again, learn from your faults and make something even better than before. That was what it meant to be human.

Horace straightened up and plugged a wire into a port, "Falling down… falling-" He stopped short.

The static had gone silent, and his own voice rang in his ears. His eyes drew to the glazed screen, the white outline of the face unmoved since the last time. The screen lit up.

"Yes!" Horace jumped up, hitting his elbow on the lamp and knocking the bulb again, drowning the room in near darkness. The only light came from the bright emblem displayed on the glossy screen, the electric blue flashing and flickering, casting icy light on Horace's face.

He knew the symbol at once. It was the same image painted on the door of the truck, the image sewn into the cuff of their clothes, and the image that is hidden behind black ink on their letters. It was the crest of Odyssey.

He tore his eyes away to screw in the bulb, but the heat burned his raw fingertips, and he drew back, hissing curses into his mask.

His headset buzzed to life.

"Markus?"

# PART 2

# OLIVER

## Chapter 1

# A SECRET EVERYONE KEEPS

Marta woke with the setting sun. She didn't open her eyes for a while, thinking that if she did, she would wake up from this dream. Maybe, she thought, it wasn't a dream, but the end. Did death feel so warm? Wait...

There was someone next to her. She couldn't tell exactly, but through her closed eyelids, a shadow moved across the orange sunlight that filtered through to her eyes. Her heart beat faster. Who was this? Where was she?

Her fluttering heart warmed when, through her half-closed eyelids, she made out what seemed to be an Earth hospital room. This reality could last just a short while longer if she didn't move. But her hand, sticking out over the edge of the bed, was too close to the figure for comfort. Her fingers twitched, and the warmth of the layers of heavy blankets on top of her beckoned it in.

The shadow stood up, looming over her, and a warm hand took hers by the wrist, tucking it nicely under the blanket again, before sitting back down. Her breathing ceased until the silhouette stopped moving again. Was it watching her?

Soon the sun would disappear, and it would be impossible to keep track of its movements. She would be totally blind, but it wasn't time to expose herself now. Breathing too fast, too deep, it would give her away, so she held her breath until she saw stars dancing behind her eyelids, then let go again. Silent. Slow. Dizzying. How long could she go like this? There was so little to be learned with closed eyes and a held breath.

Marta didn't doubt she could carry on long enough for her watcher to fall asleep, but she remembered Markus. He was still waiting for her when she lost consciousness. She had left in such a huff that he must be thinking she abandoned him. She still couldn't tell if that was true, but now was not the time. He couldn't have been left behind, not a second time.

She opened her eyes.

At first, it did seem like a hospital. Light blue paint on the walls filled with shelves with glass doors, obscuring dozens of bottles and boxes with red crosses printed on them. A papery curtain was drawn at the foot of her bed, and looking down, her blanket seemed to be made of dusty brown scraps of fabric. Government-issue uniform.

Her red hair was tied in a tight bun on the back of her head, pulling her skin taut as a canvas. Not a single loose hair. She couldn't have been sleeping for long, surely? Her eyes fell on the figure sitting in front of the window, only a vague dark silhouette since the bright sun shone behind him. The view through the short window moved with the room, but when she sat up, her focus wasn't on the shadow that had been by her bedside, but the dozen or so vehicles driving side by side, catching up and overtaking each-other, but always staying together. Always together on the canvas of the great red horizon. Both the usual trucks she remembered from the early days of Odyssey and some caravans that she had forgotten about that were probably looted from the city where they were held. She noted the cabinets on the walls also shook with every bump in the rough road they travelled. This must have been a caravan they refurbished into a makeshift hospital. Who were "they?"

It had all been a dream – a fantasy – she was a fool for believing they could have ever been saved or that anyone cared enough to try. Her heart sank into the blankets.

"You're awake." She took one hand out from under herself to shade her eyes from the sun. It was easier to make out the male figure's face like this. "You don't have to get up now. We're stopping soon anyway, and you can come and eat with everyone." He said this so casually, like a youth leader she remembered from over a decade ago.

Stopping? "Everyone?" Her voice came out weaker than she would have liked, and her accent more prominent than she remembered.

The man put up his hands. "Or not. You can stay here for the night if you feel like it." That was tempting. The sheets were so warm. The room so quiet, save for the gentle whirring of an engine, somewhere in these walls. "What do you say? Marta?"

She opened her mouth to answer, but the vehicle stopped abruptly, throwing her forward on the bed and almost knocking her on to the ground. The man jumped to her aid, but she held her hand outstretched between him and her. She caught sight of her fingers. Clean nails buffed and clipped. Pale fingers, palms pink from the warmth.

The man backed away slowly, putting his hands behind his back, which was comforting in a sense. She could tell he wanted to talk, but the door to his right clattered open. She threw her outstretched hand over her mouth, and her fingers touched her dry lips for the first time. Her mask was gone – and so was his.

"Don't worry, darlin', this room is filled with oxygen." The intruder laughed, closing the door behind him. "And there's two air-tight doors between us and outside. Breathe as much as you like." His own mask was dangling around his neck as he moved his attention to the surveyor, who was sitting again.

"Dante, we're waiting for you." When had the vehicle stopped? This sleepy state she hated, unaware of the little changes in the senses as they happened. She shook her head to wake herself more and the tight bun loosened.

'Dante' stood up, nodding to Marta before grabbing his own oxygen tank from beside his chair and following the other man out. She was alone again.

Alone again, ha! Eleven years, and then another nineteen before that, spent by her little brother's side, and always somehow in his shadow. Was she ever not alone then? No, this solitude was a blessing, she convinced herself. It couldn't be selfish, this peace felt at last.

The blue walls of this room, the warm blanket, the good air in here. It was less lonely than in that cabin. The cabin where her brother was all alone and probably scared. The moment of triumph had ended prematurely as she remembered her responsibility.

She owed it to their mother to take care of him, and having betrayed her a thousand times already, it was time to put an end to that streak. Markus never deserved to bear the full force of her vengeance. They had never been friends, but he was not the cause of her personal suffering. He suffered as much as anyone.

Marta slid out of the warmth of the blanket and peeked through the two glass doors. Something was happening outside. All the vehicles, identical exteriors to each other, huddled in groups of three, shielding each-other from the wind as the inhabitants snuck out and met like old friends.

The atmosphere being created was a throwback to the building of the Odyssey Orchard. Familiar faces with smiles under their masks, greetings and hands beating on shoulders in friendly nostalgia, as if nothing was out of the ordinary. A year ago those faces would have stung like curses when they met Marta's gaze. Out of fear, or a silent grudge, they would have both looked away at once.

Something tugged at her heart. It couldn't be envy. She hadn't yet figured out these people's motives. There must be around fifteen by then, with more arriving from other camps nearby. They all huddled around in their own cliques, but every person who arrived first went to Dante before someone else waved them over. Dante, sitting cross-legged on the ground, facing the nearest group and joining in their banter every so often, was leaning against the caravan opposite to Marta. If she went out now, he would be the first to notice her.

There was something kind about his face, even from afar, something fun. How she could see the rosiness of his cheeks still, when everyone else was grey and hollow-cheeked? Some had made attempts to maintain beards or haircuts, but eventually let them grow wild and long. Dante looked like he shaved fresh this morning, and his was the only head of hair that lacked the characteristic grey streaks. He stood out, and she could tell everyone knew it, and knew why.

He was the one living among a troupe of corpses.

His skin, hair and eyes all glowed with life, with the familiarity of something they would all likely never find again. He was reminiscent of the home they all left behind, where they were someone else's first priority, someone's reason to be. Where the reason to live wasn't spite or fear.

It was miserable seeing just how alive he was, but they flocked to him. They didn't see that his existence was a mockery of their decay, and he loved the adoration they unconsciously gave him. She could see he loved it, every face that met his, searching deep in his eyes for fragments of the past.

Yes, he adored that they adored him.

That feeling was back. Something pulling at her chest, moving up her throat. She hadn't been hungry in so long, it must be the oxygen in this room doing this to her, or seeing how everyone else practically inhaled their own nutrition bars. An appetite she had never associated with the food (though it would hardly qualify as that) unearthed itself.

Dante picked at his own meagre meal, dropping chunks under his mask and letting the crumbs fall on to his uniform. Why did she detest that?

One by one, the visitors finished their food and left, but not without stopping once more by their mutual friend's side and saying goodbye. Not even their dinner-mates got that kind of treatment. The group thinned, the last few diners retreating to their own caravans, lights turning off, but Dante's bright eyes cut through the dark like two stars. Who knew when they would stop again? It was now, or never. Marta picked up her oxygen tank from behind the first door, seeing it was now full, and reluctantly put the mask over her face, passing her hands over her nose and pinching her cheeks for old time's sake.

"I saved you one." Dante held a white wrapped nutrition bar, his elbows resting on his knees. "I hope you're not too picky." He must not have realised how patronising that sounded. They all knew there was only one flavour.

Marta took the food, masking her hunger and pretending to fumble with the wrapper for a moment, but couldn't resist breaking off a large chunk and dropping it behind her mask. She had lost count of how many of these she'd eaten, but none had had such richness of flavour, almost melting on her tongue. The sweet taste of honey spreading warmth through to her skin and sending shivers down her spine. This was nice. Hunger at last felt nice, different from the indifferent emptiness she'd survived with, but filling the hunger felt better.

He was just watching her, knees up to his chest, and though she stood over him, she couldn't help but feel so small in his presence. Marta hoped he would just look somewhere else, or drop that taunting smile even when the face was obscured by the grey mask.

"Is it good?"

"Mhm." She could only grunt. Suddenly she was very self-conscious of her voice. She was trying so hard not to like him, but the melodious way his voice sounded in the Martian night made it almost impossible. In another world he might have been romantic. In this world he was an anomaly.

She cleared her throat.

"I was asleep... how long?" Whatever English she had learnt all those years ago was coming back to her. Markus insisted they speak English to each other at first, to fit in with everyone else, but that lasted only until the end of the first year. Nobody spoke to anyone outside their own group, and for her, that was just her brother.

"We picked you up three days ago, around this time. We fixed you up in there, and we've been on the road since, so we never got you settled in..."

They were driving for three days, who knew how far they were from Markus?

"We must... turn around." She made a circular motion in the air with her finger while chewing. "Where I was... My brother is there."

"Your brother?" He asked, and widened his eyes. "What is his name?" Even the idea that he knew her name made her uneasy, but what was there to lose?

"Markus. My brother."

He looked into the night as if reading the shapes of the clouds on the horizon. Midnight was upon them. His eyes suddenly focused again – on her – and Dante pushed himself up off the ground. "Markus." She stepped back but was caught off guard by his firm hands gripping her shoulders. He looked at her like a teacher, and though he was nearer to her height, she still somehow looked up to meet his eyes.

"Can I be honest with you?" he asked, tightening his fingers on her shoulders. She hoped he would let go, but he only kept talking. She didn't have a choice now. "I need to be someone that everyone can trust, and if that means bending the truth to make everyone happy, so be it." Even while incriminating himself, his sombre voice evoked sympathy.

"The truth is, I've been following someone else's lead this whole time. They all think I chart these paths, find all these amazing things through some deep calculated moves in my head, or psychic miracle – but none of this would be here without… him."

"Him?"

"Yes. They follow in my footsteps, but I have to track him down first. Whatever he leaves behind, we claim. It's how we survive. It's how we can grow and thrive, even in this… predicament we find ourselves in." Marta didn't like it one bit how he described the situation.

"Why do tell me?"

He looked down. "You need a real reason. I can't lie to you. We can't leave this place until I find him again." He answered. "I lost his tracks when we stopped to pick you up and that was the last place I tracked Desmond to. It's like he disappeared into thin air…"

Desmond. If she found him, they could go back after. "You lost your guide?" He let his hands fall to his sides and turned away from her, avoiding her eyes. "You haven't told anyone else?" Dante retreated, and the weight off her shoulders with him.

"We will speak in the morning. Let me show you where you'll sleep."

He led Marta to the caravan he'd been leaning against, opening the back door to reveal it was much smaller than it seemed on the outside. There was nobody else inside, which she silently thanked him for, but the free space inside was greatly shrunken due to the walls being lined with thick drawers, cupboards and stacked crates, leaving room only for a mattress only big enough for a child. It had been cut in half and sewn on one end, and someone else was probably sleeping on the other half.

"Sorry about the squeeze. But, hey! While we're moving tomorrow, you can find something in one of these drawers to occupy yourself with. What's your profession?"

"Chemistry." That was the one question she didn't need to think twice about.

He scoured the walls, finding one cupboard and opening it to reveal twenty small boxes of various powders. "I'm sure you'll find something to do with these. We all have to make ourselves useful here." He disappeared into the moonless night, waving a quick good night before closing the door on her.

One door. There was no escapism here. The lines on her face had just healed when she was forced to put the mask on again, and the grey silicone cut deeper than before..

Three days, driving across the red watercolour landscape, putting fields of crimson dust between them. How much oxygen did her brother say was left in his tank?

Maybe if she hadn't told him to stay put, he would have followed, and they would have been found together. She'll convince Dante to turn around. Markus would survive, somehow. He wasn't the sixteen-year-old boy she was sent to babysit. Eleven years away from home should have made him into a man, but he was still the child that she followed into space. Aside from the grey hair, not even his features changed, not his voice. It was like time stopped for him while Marta had to face her own deterioration. That was another reason to be jealous of her brother.

Three days, leading all these dozens with no real aim, the illusion of a destination giving them all hope. She couldn't help but admire it. Keeping the façade up, even to one person, must be exhausting. Maybe she judged him too soon. Whatever force it was that kept him alive gave everyone a bit of comfort, and in turn kept them from the ill-fated end they were all facing. Better to face a more forgiving view.

But maybe he wasn't living a façade. Maybe what he told her was known to everyone. Each made to feel special keeping his secret from the rest. Keeping a secret everyone kept. Loving him because he made them feel loved. Caring because they felt cared for. It was all too rehearsed to feel real. The hands on her shoulders were too familiar, lines that he must have rattled off how many dozens of times? She knew too well not to let a nice face and kind voice get the best of her. Words meant nothing anymore. Too many times they had promised truth and delivered something else. Too many times they had betrayed their own purpose.

The powders in her hands she recognised as testing samples of fertilisers from the Orchard. None really took too well to the new soil, but the trees had seemed to grow well enough without them. Then and now, they were just as useless. She began searching the drawers beside her bed. There were instruments she couldn't begin to name, and tools she had forgotten the names of, never thinking she would see them again. Beakers and Sextants, pencil sharpeners and a cracked magnifying glass lens. The final drawer wouldn't budge, blocked by the edge of the folding bed. She could have just tried to go to sleep, left it until morning, but three days was enough sleep to last a lifetime, or to lose one.

Marta stood up and folded up the mattress, tucking it between the drawer and the door, like a makeshift barricade, barely half-stuffed with synthetic cotton and who knew what else? It started off feeling like a treasure hunt, finding all these bits and bobs that could have been someone's whole purpose here one day, but now, surrounded by devices, half of which she couldn't master in a dozen lifetimes, was truly depressing. How many life stories were in this room? How many of these tools would never see their masters again?

The drawer was jammed. She could swear it was slightly ajar before, but nevertheless she sat down, placing one foot on the drawer beside it and pulling at the knob with both hands. Something gave way, slamming her backwards into the wall, jabbing other doorknobs into her spine and she erupted into a string of curses her mother would be crossing herself over. When she opened her eyes, Marta was holding the broken doorknob, and the shut drawer hadn't budged. The hole where the knob had been looked at her like a single black eye.

Okay, time to improvise.

Almost an hour later and the pile of wood chips at her feet boasted what her blistered fingers couldn't. With a blunted and broken scalpel, and another three on the floor beside her, she stared with pride at the radio console she dug out of the stiff drawer. It took a bit of dusting and some searching her memories before she managed to get the thing to even turn on. Batteries survived. The headset was deeper in the drawer, but she fished it out in perfect condition as well.

"Talk to me." The heavy console rested on her knees, lifeless. Not for long. She whispered to it in German. Either to urge it to life, or to keep herself company in the silence of the night.

Every moment she spent fidgeting with buttons and wires she was thinking of her brother, three days away and so alone. Had he gotten the radio fixed yet? The radio she dropped too hard on the desk out of rage, or frustration, or whatever she had been feeling right then. Emotions were never her strong suit, but Markus always found ways to get through to her.

Even as a child, when her mood swings confused everyone around her, even herself, he would suddenly toddle in and as if by some magic intuition, getting rid of the very thing that was stressing her out. More recently he couldn't even stay awake long enough to notice her rages. He almost slept through her breaking his radio. Then slept immediately after.

She wished he were here now, guiding her on what every dial did, explaining to her why the static in her ears kept cutting in and out, and just being there with her, an assurance that she was doing the right thing. She took breaks by reading anything she could find.

In one drawer there were stacks of pamphlets, instructional manuals mostly, and one of the acceptance letters, the original ones from when the mission was still hiring from a pool of professors and specialists. Her hands went cold when she read the name at the top.

"Matilda McCarthy." Her name became famous with her death, and Marta remembered a cold night, it must have been three or four years ago, waking up in sweats as the memory of her discovery played over and over in her head. Her cold, lifeless eyes and limp body sprawled on the road beside one of the skyscrapers. Nobody believed it was a suicide.

One brief conversation she and Marta had once repeated itself as the image of her silhouette flashed behind her eyelids. She had forgotten it now, but copying it down on the nearest piece of paper she could find, it started to look a lot like a fragment of a poem. It was only when she woke up that morning that she realised she'd defaced her own letter. Markus had lost his own years ago, but he liked to read the English out loud to pass the time when he got tired of speaking to her. She didn't let him look at the letter anymore after that.

Maybe if she managed to get it working, she could at least tell Markus to take care of himself until she found a way back. Or, even better, he could find a way to her. Surely Dante wouldn't mind keeping still for a few days. Everyone would appreciate a good rest and she could get to know all these people who should have been her friends by now, if the official plan had ever had a chance of working out.

The taste of honey from the nutrition bar lingered in her mouth, and she sucked at her teeth, waiting for something to happen, to change. She desperately gave the radio a last bump with the base of her palm.

The static cut out and didn't start again. She sighed, thinking the headset might have finally given up, but when the screen lit up, her breath was cut short. She looked to the blue square, then to the patch sewn on to the lapel of her uniform. It was the same emblem.

A red flag, rippling in different hues of crimson behind a blue and green sphere, the portrait of home.

It was the flag of Odyssey, which disappeared after a moment, leaving her in silence. Another second passed, then another, and she began to doubt there was anyone on the other end. It was after midnight, and Markus liked to sleep early. His philosophy was that sleep made time go faster, so it was almost like time skipping until someone found a way home. It became a way to avoid his half of the work.

The screen printed some English words she only half recognised, and the rest were glitched and cut off, then the lights died. Then it was quiet.

A loud thud boomed in her ears, and she fiddled with the wire on the headset, but her hand fell when she heard the distant hiss of a curse.

"Markus?"

Silence from the other end. She must have heard wrong. The static left a residual hum in her ears, and it must have filled the silence with imaginary sounds. It was funny how quickly the imagination takes over in moments of sensory deprivation. Perhaps in the morning she will have better luck. She took the headset off.

A muffled sound came through the earpiece. Too quiet to have a voice, but the sounds were there, forming words in the empty space: "I'm sorry."

She put the headset on.

"Hello?" She said in English. It wasn't Markus. "You are sorry?"

It was nice to hear another voice, but the person on the other end was not her brother, though his German was almost convincing.

"I am sorry for you."

"Why?" She changed to German again, more comfortable in her native language, but still wary of the stranger on the other side. "I could say I am sorry for you just the same. Should I?"

"I already do that enough."

"Why?" She asked. The voice on the other side seemed to hesitate.

"Am I not allowed?"

"I'll be the judge of that." What did the man know? Clearly he knew something about her, otherwise why would he have begun in German? Marta was getting tired of people knowing more about her than she knew about them. She looked at her oxygen tank and spied her name. So that was how Dante knew her. Dante didn't seem like a real name. So she knew even less than she thought. The man started talking again, she hoped he forgot to be sorry for her.

That was her job, and she had avoided it for a long time.

"I had one goal, and I blew it. Now I have nothing to do but wait to die here. It doesn't look like a long wait either." Self-pity was so butter. Almost selfish. But Marta couldn't say that, so she tried something else. Something that occasionally worked on Markus.

"Do you remember when the Orchard was destroyed for the first time?"

This was supposed to make him feel better? "I may be old, but my memory isn't quite gone." Horace added "unfortunately," in his mind.

"Everyone was so devastated. We had all worked so hard, putting in a little bit of ourself in that little bubble of life. We created a space where Earth could live on, outside our memories, but in the real world. And when that shuttle came, and half the trees perished, it felt like a piece of everyone was shattered like the glass."

"But we rebuilt it."

"Of course, we rebuilt." He could hear her smile when she talked. "But we never forgot the first time. We just moved on, keeping the first in our hearts when the second came along."

Layla's name dangled on a string around his neck, and she was asking him to move on. Had it even been five hours? The truth was he would never forget, but how long until his age would betray him? How long until the memory would cease to exist, just like him, and all the names in the chest turning to dust as the centuries passed? He figured it would be better to humour the girl than ignore her. Humour her now because what was coming after would need something more. Already his initial plan was ruined, he needed time to improvise a new one. How to break it to her than her brother was dead beside him>

"What's the next step? After I move on, I mean."

"The next step is just the next step you take. Who knows where it will take you?" It could take you my way, for example, she thought. "But you need to take that first step for the rest of the road to make itself clear."

"What you've said is very eloquent. Have you rehearsed this?"

"My brother used to get... discouraged, often." Her brother.

An icy pang went through to his heart, and he was reminded of the breathless figure behind him. "He has his own ways of getting through it, but it feels a lot better to hear it from someone else."

It sure did feel better to talk to someone again. These few hours felt like decades when he was alone for the first time..

"Your German is very good, where did you learn?"

They were getting further and further from his original point.

"Germany." He excluded small details from his story. "During the war I moved around a lot, so I know enough of most European languages. Enough to get by, anyway."

"The war? Ah, you were a soldier." She smiled. An old picture of her father unearthed itself. His soldier uniform, his handsome and proud face, furrowed brow. The red armband, the swastika. Her smile faded, along with the picture. Up in flames, at the mercy of her mother's lighter. The red-hot weld on her face from her slap, her punishment for snooping. He was never meant to come back, and she made it clear that way. Would her talents have been used in the same way as his, had she been given the same opportunity? The same command?

"Not exactly. My efforts in the first war made it impossible to join the second. As well as... what happened between..." His cracking voice must have given him away already, but he could pass it off as emotion.

"Have you been to London?" Magazines, postcards, movies and novels had painted such a romantic image of London in her Head. It was a shame, she thought, she never got to see it before she left.

"I did, briefly, but that city wasn't good for my lungs... lung." She sensed they had wandered into a personal topic and changed the subject.

"Under different circumstances we would have once been enemies." She laughed. It did feel like a joke, to lighted the mood. She didn't want him finding out too much about her before she knew his intentions.

"Are we enemies?"

"N-no, I never said that-"

"That's enough for me. I should probably ask some pretty obvious questions, but I'm afraid it might seem out of character for someone in our situation." Here it was. Questions. She hated those, especially ones about her.

It was hard to avoid, but there was little else to talk about to anyone, and eleven years of the same conversation was exhausting, more so than boring, with her brother. She sighed into the headset.

"Then, let's ignore the situation. Pretend we are making each-other's acquaintance on earth. Perhaps in a school. I'll go first: What's your name?"

"Desmond, Horace. Oh, wait, force of habit." Marta's mouth fell open, and she gaped around the room, looking for something and nothing at the same time. "A school, then... How did you know I was a teacher?" She was deaf to the laughter on the other end. She had to find someone, to find him. "What's your name, Fräulein?"

"Uh, Marta Ludwig. And it was a lucky guess." So, thought Horace, he really was the type. He didn't sense the urgency in her silence.

"Would your luck go as far as to guess what I taught?"

"I'm no magician, Herr Desmond." Keep talking. Don't freak out. Dante will probably come in the morning. He will figure everything out. "What other obvious questions do you have?" Keep him talking. He'll lead you to Markus.

"You're right. My mistake. I suppose I could ask why you're here, in the first place."

"Here, as in...?"

"Mars. Forget the school. What made you decide to come here in the first place?"

She sighed. Again the conversation turned to her brother. Just after she'd accepted the challenge of talking about herself. There was no use getting angry at him. How could he have known?

"I made a promise to my mother, to protect Markus. He was invited, and he couldn't say no. I had to come along. Eventually it was decided my skills could be useful, and we were both brought here. If it was my choice I would have just stayed home." She added, "But, in hindsight, I think we all feel that way."

"We all?" Horace fiddled with the earpiece. "Who else is there?"

She'd given herself away. Not that she was hiding anything, but it all was moving a bit too fast for her to manage. "I'm not sure exactly. Dante didn't tell me exactly how many people are here, but there couldn't be more than half than we were at Odyssey."

"Dante is the leader around there?"

It wasn't Marta's secret to tell, but it wasn't hers to keep either. "Seems like it. But I only just got here-"

"Marta, I am going to be very honest, and I think you might not like what I'm going to say." He took a moment to let her answer, but she was silent. "You'll need to come back." Nobody said anything for a long time, but Marta was the first to break.

"Are you using my brother's radio?"

"I'm so sorry."

"Where is Markus?"

"I'm sorry. I'm so sorry. If we were a bit earlier, we might have saved him, but we were too late. I was too late." He began choking on his words. He'd taken them off to sound clearer through the microphone but regretted it now.

"I don't believe you." Her throat felt hot, and there was a clump of pressure building up in her neck. She wanted to tell him to be quiet, but she listened to his sobs on the other end, because it was clear he was sobbing for someone else.

"I should have been there. I should have been with her."

The tides came in and washed out again. Over and over and over, a cycle of emotions on repeat for the rest of the night. They cried together, miles apart. They found safety in strangers, and in their voices. Safety that hadn't existed before. A friendship forged in grief.

Marta's eyes were beginning to close, as her mind was just wrapping around the fact that he was gone. He was free, and with nobody to follow anymore, so was she.

The sun was rising, and engines were coming back to life, when Dante took the headset from a half-asleep Marta and introduced himself to Horace Desmond.

Chapter 2

# MENTOR, FRIEND, MEMORY

Horace wouldn't open the door, not to Dante, at least. When Marta walked him to the hospital, he stood tall in Dante's presence, but Marta felt his quivering muscles, his arm hooked around her own threatened to slip all the while he towered above the crowd that had gathered to greet him. They cheered for him, and for Dante, drowning out the shrill beeping of the empty oxygen tank that trailed behind as they made their way to the hospital caravan.

"So, who is really in charge?" Horace asked. He swung his knees off the bed and rested on the edge, breathing in slowly, hesitantly, the lightness of his face still unusual, and always keeping the newly filled canister in view. He didn't let himself relax yet. "It couldn't be that Dante, he's just a kid."

They spoke to each-other in German, partly so they couldn't be overheard, also because there were nuances in the language that neither could express in English. There was a secret language within the regular one. The two had taken to each-other immediately because of this. Without even saying a word, they had singled out Dante before they even set eyes on each-other.

"Technically, you are." She sipped cautiously at the lukewarm tea someone had served them at the door. Horace hadn't touched his. She took notice of it. Dante made his first appearance since Horace had shooed him from the door of the desolate cabin. No offense appeared on his face, but Marta noticed that no real emotion ever did. Past the glassy perfection of his smile, bright eyes and clean complexion, no thoughts could be spied. All defence, she thought.

"We've sent an advance party to the directions you've given us, and from the boy's letter. I hope you know how much I appreciate all your help. What seemed impossible last year may just be achievable, thanks to you." Dante had a way of smiling, but only with his mouth. His eyes, no matter how full of life they were, stayed stony and sincere, which somehow made his genuine smiles petrifying.

"I'm sure you appreciate it." Marta was shocked by the sudden change to English. Horace, who had by now been as gentle in his tone as in his language, was suddenly cold, somewhat aggressive. He was scary, and his height added to his overbearing presence in the room that outweighed his thin frame. "Let me ask you one thing. What was your job? Back in Odyssey?"

Dante cleared his throat, but his face stayed stubbornly pleasant. "I was registered as a multi-skilled individual. I think that was what it said on paper... Gee, I haven't been asked that in a while. I mainly worked in Odyssey the first year-"

"In the city, or on the city?" Horace turned his head to the side, and gave a skewed smile that sent chills up Marta's spine.

"I-Is there a difference?" Dante looked defensively to Marta, but Horace demanded his attention with the snap of his long fingers.

"Is there?"

There was a knock at the door, and Dante let out a silent breath of thanks as he disappeared without a word to them. Marta let her shoulders fall, not realising she had brought up her own defences. Now that Dante was gone, and Horace more laid back again, it felt almost embarrassing to have been intimidated by the old man. This was a person who could never be fully understood through a voice in a headset. The voice and the person were like two different entities, and Marta saw them converge into one before her very eyes.

"What was that?" Marta picked up her teacup again.

He picked up the cup of tea, then set it down again with a clatter, his hands starting to shake but he waved the tremor away. It could be disguised no longer. So, he did feel fear.

"I noticed it the moment he walked in the room. Didn't you?" Marta shook her head. "The way he talks, the way he carries himself. He feels weightless, I bet. He's a type." He caught his breath. "He's the type of person I've met one too many times in America. They find it fashionable to be among the suffering, but the subconscious doesn't let them truly relate to them. In a way those who are really suffering don't realise they're just entertainment. Classic wolf in sheep's clothing." He nodded to her. "If you were more fluent you would pick it up in his words. They can change their appearance, or their attitude, but they're stuck with the same tongue."

Listening to him, Marta couldn't help but feel inexplicably privileged. Until now she had thought everyone was in the same boat as her: that everyone who had come here was a professional of some sort – an elite, like herself, reduced somewhat with the abandonment. Now she saw the man before her had lived a life a hundred times fuller than her own, seen a hundred times more than her. Now she saw someone who could see through her blindness. Things she had only a juvenile awareness of, brought to full view at his side.

She emptied her cup and lifted his to his lips. He didn't back away, but he didn't accept it either. A puzzled look met her determined one. "Drink."

"No thanks, sweetheart." He smiled weakly. "I don't much like this fake tea, the water–"

She didn't repeat herself, but tipped the lip of the cup to his dry lips, silencing him. "While the mask is still off. Drink." With a sigh he brought his hand to her pale ones, grateful for their stability. Before his lips touched the tea he became painfully aware of the thirst that had accumulated his throat for the last decade, and found himself taking mad gulps of the cold, sweet liquid.

When he had drained the last drop, he sat back with his hands between his knees, passing his gaze over the loaded shelves on the walls, wondering if there was something in them that could reverse whatever was happening to him. Nothing could turn back time. Rust can't be made to shine again without scraping it off.

A hospital room. He'd spent his whole life trying to escape familiarity, and here he was now. At least there were no tears this time. The past few nights had drained him of tears, but grief still boiled deep in his old bones..

The advance party returned near midnight. So, Markus was making himself useful even after life. Horace received the news with no change in his expression.

Marta heard him turning in the night. She though perhaps one of them should be crying.

When her brother was buried at sunrise, she tried, but found her eyes dry. Almost all her life she was only following him around, picking up after him, wiping his own tears… Now, he was as rested as she wished she could have been. As the red earth hit his cold body, and the sun warmed the fresh gravestone, she was finally free.

She had read Markus' letters before handing them off to Dante earlier. They had moved her, but only closer to what she already knew: her brother was ready for his death long before it came. He was more ready for it than home. They forgave each-other, and both slept well. She didn't dream of her brother after that.

*****

The cold aura of death had lingered even after the body was removed, as if the ghostly aurora of the dead boy refused to leave when he could. Desmond had kept the company of a corpse for three nights. How could he have been talking through the days, knowing that thing was just watching over his shoulder? Dante closed the cabin door behind him, lighting the makeshift torch, an old helmet with a headlamp from the Orchard days. The afternoon light seeping through the window only illuminated the empty space where the boy was laid, not the rest of the cabin.

The wide circle of light that trailed over the rest of the interior exposed drawers upon drawers, another small bed on the opposite side of the room, and every inch of walls and ceiling covered in layers and layers of paper. Childish drawings of memories or dreams or things not experienced by either of the siblings, things imagined from another's life documented in grey lines. Above the desk it was as if a different person had occupied that wall. Numbers and letters, diagrams of complex systems and wavelengths littered the patchwork of sheets as much as they did the young genius' brain.

Dante's feet swept up the newly formed layer of dust that settled since last night, shallower than the layer covering the rest of the decrepit cabin, and he was reminded of his grandfather's tales of the Dust Bowl. The similarities he could draw between here and there... He only wished some of them were good.

Even Dante needed some reminding of home sometimes. Looking in the mirror that hung above the sister's bed, he spied what others overlooked in himself. Beneath the black richness of his hair lingered a memory of the gold flecks through chocolatey curls. The passage of time, the silver taints, at least, were disguised. Shoe polish or soot did the trick, though they stained grey the soft cotton neck of his father's old jacket, the only thing he thought to bring from home. The still pools of glassy water in his eyes struck ice into his expression, the afterglow of sunsets over two glimmering lakes now frozen over, shaded by heavy eyelids that gave him a sultry, welcoming air, and atmosphere of mystery.

Even the rosiness of his cheeks, signs of life, were just a lingering stain from the enduring fever that returned every night, that woke him drenched in sweat, though a comfort from the dreams he escaped then. It was these symptoms of his deterioration that followed him, made him distinct, attractive in his difference. Variety was, indeed, the spice of life, and everyone looked to him like their next meal, with eyes hungrier than stomachs that would be emptier still without him.

But in the plague that time had suffered each and every one of the settlers, he hadn't been spared the common scar. Even while appearing to age at a significant rate, boasting grey hair and greyer expression, the younger half of the colony had missed out on a decade of maturing that was expected of them. It was, in part, their responsibility, to create a society by growing into it. That was why they started looking for promising minds in schools, not only residing in the heads of lecturers, but in those of students. It was this scar that was the same across every face of youth, that begged to be washed away to reveal, beneath it, a mind more packed with experience than one hidden behind the wrinkles and blemishes of age.

Dante himself was well into his mid-30's but the lines under his eyes hadn't suffered a new addition to the ones already creasing below his them when he first stepped foot on this planet of suspended time. If, when he got home, he took off the mask, there would be the deep red lines, but they wouldn't be there forever. Soon the redness would ease, cease burning into his grey skin, and it would be as if the mask was never there. It would be as if none of this ever happened. Like he had nothing to show for the past decade, or even since his late admission into adulthood.

He was always taken at face value by all except him, and now someone new came along that saw through all he had worked hard to establish in the last year. He wouldn't be broken. All he had to do was break him first. Now he had the directions, what need was there to follow Desmond?

They didn't search the cabin until the morning after the funeral, and it took until afternoon to put everything back into place, all without protest from the sister, who didn't know it was happening. Dante was well aware of the unspoken alliance that was forming under his nose. They had a language in common, but nothing else. He didn't worry about their friendship. He didn't really consider Marta herself a threat, he could win her over as easily as he did the rest of them. Desmond, on the other hand, was a problem.

He made Dante feel small. Desmond knew something. No problem, Dante knew just as much, if not more. He just needed the right ammunition.

That was not why he was sitting among the dust in the empty cabin.

He emptied all the desk drawers by his feet, and put one drawer between his knees. Out of habit he licked the tip of his finger, but the dryness left a warm scratch on the surface of his tongue which faded slowly as he turned his attention to the tall pile of loose paper, notepads and envelopes. He picked up a ring notepad first.

Among the pages and pages of doodles and drawings were sheets full of writing, titled "Dream tonight," and a date. Most of the pages were separated into two or even three sections for every night. If he had known German, Dante would have read them all, perhaps his own dreams only lacked variety... He laid the notepad down into the drawer and started the first stack. There were perhaps a dozen notepads similarly filled.

He remembered the long lists he had to check and double check, special items requested by each traveller, months in advance. Almost everyone requested notepads, diaries, plenty of ink and pencils. Looking at the giant pile of paper beside him, clearly none went to waste.

After notepads and loose sheets with more of the same drawings and notes, what was left behind were letters. Ink faded and smudged, there was no chance anyone would read these again, but he stacked them up anyway. They were all letters from home, all over a decade old, and almost all addressed to Marta. The softening and yellowing of the paper showed they had been re-opened and re-read countless times. Clearly someone else was still hung up on the past. The letters slotted nicely into the edge of the second full drawer, the first having been filled by notebooks and half the loose sheets.

Only one item was left on the floor. It caught his eye even without shining the light on it.

His finger felt up the flaking spine, thumbing the dog-eared corners and dusting off the vibrant front cover. In his hands he held the most valued possession a boy could worship: a comic book. The German words on the front were highlighted, with holographic text that caught the light, spelling out the title and trailing behind the superhero, standing victorious on a skyscraper overlooking a beautiful city. The moon and stars glowed in patchy silver ink, and the scuff marks on the page gave the inky blue sky more constellations.

"Egon." Did it hurt to read those words again, or were the hot tears trailing down his cheeks born from the memories those words unearthed? Dante didn't need to know the language to recognise the story. The English translation almost jumped from the faded pages, but more memorably, it was a story he had read and heard dozens of times before. It was a story he was living through now. He wiped away the tears, vaguely aware of the crowd anxiously awaiting his instructions just outside.

It was the tale of a hero abandoned, left on his last legs by people he thought were friends. The tale was not one of revenge, but desperation – survival. Doing all that he was able to, to save the world. Lies were only ornaments to his genius plan, but when a new hero came along, Egon looked at himself and saw his lies had outnumbered his truths. He had turned villain, and realised too late.

Distraught, Egon begged the hero for a second chance, his deep purple armour cracking at the edges and falling from his body, plate by plate as he kneeled, clutching the hero's cape to his chest-

The last page was missing. Ripped out in vengeance or by accident, Dante's eyes scanned the room, but he didn't need the final page. He never needed it. Dante already knew the end of that story.

He wiped his cold tears from the penultimate page and closed the comic book, but as he slid it into his jacket something fell out of the dust cover. He gingerly picked up the half-burnt picture, studying the name and face for several minutes. In that time, suspended in time and space, Dante let the tears dry trails into his red cheeks. The rest of him had turned cold and pale and his fingers were trembling as he put the picture back.

Could time be so unforgiving, he wondered, as to carry the worst of the past forward? The best was always yet to come but pain made itself be remembered, always. Hate prevailed. Dante stood up.

The name was foreign to him, but he would recognise that face any day, no matter how many years he tried to run from it. The best and worst chapter of his life had been punctuated by that face. His hand on Dante's shoulder left a weight that would never lift, and the story-telling voice echoed in his ears even now.

A mentor, a best friend, a memory buried and hidden now clawing its way back up. The picture itself ripped holes in his heart, being a copy of the same picture he found that day he was forced to part ways with him. The only difference being, in this one, he wasn't wearing his armband, or it was on the burnt side.

If only he could see where Dante was now, and all because of him.

To the innocent and ignorant, he was just a government researcher working on getting the American people one step closer to victory against the Russians, Koreans, and anyone else added to the list. A genius that appeared out of nowhere. To Oliver Keen, this was a fact. Dante knew better – the truth.

The truth was here, framed in flames, with the black eyes of a killer mimicking his own glossy reflection. The same genius brain that got a man into orbit had composed the atrocities of the most awesome act of human evil that history had ever been burdened with.

Father, killer, friend. Who was he really? The legacy of Rudolf Ludwig and that of Frank Horn were worlds apart, and half of it died right where Dante stood.

In the eyes of the world, success meant sometimes turning a blind eye. That was why Dante knew his own legacy would die here as well unless he and Horace Desmond managed to come to an agreement, or one would need to be disposed of. Whatever it was that Horace was holding back would have to come out, sooner or later, but Dante had his own weapons. What his poor old mind probably didn't remember was their first time meeting each-other.

The crowd outside was growing restless, looking for him, and Dante sprung to the mirror again, checking his pallid face and pinching at his lips to sting the greyness out. He brushed away the salty flakes of crystallised tears from his inner eyes. Then, he straightened up and picked up a stack of letters from the drawer. With a fresh smile, he headed out, just in time to be met with a serenade of car horns and cheers. Times like these his smile was less fake. He waved to them with his free hand and kept walking.

One of the scouts from last night still sat in the truck she arrived in. She leaned out and said something to the nearest person, who then came running right to him. Dante didn't hear what he was saying.

Horace was outside the infirmary car, standing straight with his full oxygen tank in hand. Dante gulped down the shock at seeing him so tall after reducing him to an invalid, clutching at his bedsheets in a hospital bed. The gentleman was a giant, no less. His presence commanded attention, even when it was Dante at the focus of the crowd. Applause and cheers all aimed at Dante. He relished in it, but couldn't keep his focus on the praise. Horace's knowing smile was all that registered in the man's conscience. All else faded as he pushed through the adoring crowd, still singing his praise as he waved them away, with promises of a swift departure, but instructed them to start dinner without him. When he looked back, Horace had already disappeared back inside. He noticed Marta wasn't by his side.

He grabbed a nutrition pack for himself and one for Horace and stacked it together with the letters, painting on a fresh smile before stepping through the double doors.

Horace's mask was off, and he was already eating. That was fine, Dante could just say he had grabbed one for Marta. She was, after all, the one he was pretending to look for. Easy lies came to him like second nature. Big lies had to be worked after.

"Dante, my friend, you are an enigma."

"How so?" He spied the room for Marta, but she was nowhere to be found, so he tucked the stack of letters into his jacket, bending a corner of the comic book as he slid them in, and it felt like he just stubbed his own toe. "I'm an open book." He wished the man would only sit down so his heart could stop racing. Even on opposite sides of the room, they were too close for comfort.

The giant scoffed. Was it the height, or did the room actually shake with the force of the sound? "You still gotta read open books. Most people forget. I think I figured you out, either way. My only question is… what could an actor contribute to a Martian society?" He was clearly musing, poking at him to find the sensitivities, of which, Dante recognised, he had too many.

"Pardon?"

Horace motioned to the crowd outside, and his long swinging arm almost made Dante flinch, but he stood his ground. "You're certainly trained to handle applause. You adore being at the centre of a crowd. Tell me I'm wrong." Dante found himself unable to speak. He wished he had kept his mask on. Now there was a door between him and it, and two between him and escape. This old, sick, weak giant, but a giant, nonetheless, had him trapped. Horace took a step forward and it took everything in Dante not to step away, knowing his back would be against the door. Improvise. Lie.

"They're applauding you, not me." He refreshed his smile and tried to sound flippant, but it came across as defensive. He regretted opening his mouth.

Now almost face to face, the Horace's matching grin mocked him. "Are they? Really?" He guided Dante towards the chair he had occupied when Horace awoke the first morning. The chair he occupied to greet every new arrival as soon as they opened their eyes. He thought the first thing they needed in that moment, after who knows how long spent in isolation, was a friendly face.

"There's one difference between them and me: I see through you." Horace's nostrils were flared, and Dante half expected steam to shoot out of them, like some cartoon villain. "You see, I don't need to force myself to ignore the obvious... not like them."

Reluctantly taking the chair, he was lowered even further.

"Marta won't admit it, but she already fell for your little charade before I got here."

"There's no charade," He felt compelled to call him "sir," but resisted. "My intentions are there for all to see."

"Then tell me. What are your intentions? What is your plan?"

His neck was getting hot. "My plan is to go home."

"That's not a plan. That's the end result." He sat down on the bed and Dante wondered if it was out of fatigue. Maybe he wished it. Horace's voice softened, making him somehow scarier. "Look, son. You've surrounded yourself with people who will follow you, help you, let you take all the credit with no second though but... You knew you were leading them to dead ends this whole time." He shook his head. "The truth is... You were lucky to find Marta. She was lucky to find me. We're all running on luck right now and sooner or later it will dry up. That's what luck does."

Dante sniffed back the tremble in his voice. The student being scolded by the teacher, close to tears, would never admit defeat. "What do you suppose we do?" He cocked his head in faux confidence.

"What you need to do is be honest for once. You've spent so long pretending to be a hero that you forgot to actually be a leader." He looked out through the doors at the crowd dispersing into different cars, awaiting their guide. "I'm old. You can see it. I can feel it. I'm no leader and I know you know it too. That is why you need to sort yourself out-"

"Or what?"

He regretted the words as soon as he said them. Horace's icy eyes remained fixed on the door. The corner of his mouth twitched, and he thought for a second it was smile, then it curled into a sneer. "Or we're all doomed to dust..." He broke contact with the door and Dante froze when his icy eyes met his. "And it'll all be your fault."

The blood in his veins turned chill, and he was sure his heart had stopped minutes ago. Here was this man. This dying titan who would have blown away at the slightest gust of wind, fixing him to his seat with a mere gaze. The door opened and he breathed a prayer of thanks.

"Marta, dear." Horace stepped toward them, and Dante's feet snapped away from him. Get a grip. "What do you have for us?"

The sound of rustling paper caught his attention. Oh no. Not this.

"You should have burned this." Her broken English taunted him, waving her ugly truth before his eyes. "Oliver Keen. Ambassador to Odyssey, Mars."

"I knew I knew you from somewhere. Don't suppose you remember me?" Clenched fingers dug his nails into his palms. Dante tossed his head back.

"No. I do, of course."

"You thought I would be the one getting tricked." It wasn't a question.

"So you're going to expose me then. Now? To all of them?"

Marta passed the letter to Horace. "Not yet." The key to his past was folded up and tucked away. "You get a second chance."

Horace cut in. "A benefit of the doubt." He tapped his chest where the sheet was hidden. "Now you know what's at stake for you, you might consider the consequences of betraying their trust." There was a long silence when Dante felt like he should get up, walk out, lash out, anything... But he didn't move.

"Don't think I don't understand-"

"Oh, do you?" The growl in Dante's voice shocked even him. There was real pain in it. The realest thing he had shown yet. "As soon as that rocket left the planet I was the prey. I had one choice, and you know it. Adapt, or be killed. Join the hunt, or be the hunted."

He wiped a tear and passed it off as pushing hair out of his eyes. "That's funny, actually. Everything you told me... I told them. One year ago. "You're all pretending to be heroes. Don't you see we're the villains here?" I remember it like yesterday because those were the words that sealed my fate." He stopped wiping his face. "For Chrissakes. If I just shut up none of us would be here."

There was a heavy hand on his shoulder. Marta knelt by his side. "You're right. We would all be somewhere else. All alone. Most likely dead. You have done good things among bad."

"Yeah? And who's going to believe you? They'll kill me now just like they would have then." The heat was rising, rattling in his chest, heaving and gasping, "They won't care. They won't see. What I had to do." As his vision started to darken, a cold palm landed softly on his chest, right above his beating heart. Right above the comic book. He slid his own hand into the jacket and pulled it out for all to see.

"Where did you get this?"

"I need to get up." Horace jabbed his finger into the shorter man's chest, pinning him to the backrest.

"Answer her."

"Help me up."

"Not until you talk-"

"Help him up. He can explain later." They each took him by a shoulder, Horace digging a bit harder than necessary, and lifted him on bucking knees. He pointed to a metal shelf on the wall and guided them through the array of bottles until his limp hand touched on a black glass vial, hardly the width of a finger. His limbs suddenly reanimated and started moving as if by primal instinct, uncapping the medication before tossing his head back and letting the full contents run down his throat. The chill liquid stung going down, but it gave him the strength to shake free from the two crutches, who watched this process with quizzical looks.

When Dante opened his eyes again, blinking through the fog, he almost felt the medicine coming back up, but held his nose until he was sure it was down. Then breathed a sigh of relief, as if the heat, the shaking and rattling had just disappeared with the breath.

"I'm sorry about that."

"Take your time, son." That was meant to be patronising, he was sure, but it only brought back memories. Being called "son" when he ought to have been punished. He was never punished, only taught. "This been going on for long?"

He wanted to say it had, because it felt like he'd been living with this for decades. "When I was a little boy, I was very frail, weak. But I grew out of it. Seems I grew back into it when I came here." Marta saw him staring at the comic still in her hand. Instinctively, she flipped to the back cover, but before she could unfold it, she saw Dante's eyes grow wide.

"Wrong vial?"

"No. It's not that." He cleared his throat, and it stung his nose. "I hope you won't think it evil of me, well, more than you already do. I didn't mean to pry. I knew the cabin would be searched for valuables, anything we might use for the journey, and I didn't want any personal effects falling into the wrong hands."

"You mean anyone else's hands?" Horace sneered. Marta smacked his arm lightly.

"Let him talk."

He gave her a look of thanks, but Marta's glare remained stone cold.

"I never snoop. Heh, I couldn't if I wanted to." His joke flew past both of them. "But I couldn't help taking a look at that comic. Every little boy's dream is to be a super hero, and I was no exception. If I couldn't run and play with all the other little boys, that really limited my opportunities for making friends. I found the bookworms. The movie geeks. The boys who spent their lunch money on comics. We all wanted to be big. We all wanted something more. And if it wasn't fighting aliens from outer space, it was fighting crime on our streets. I hadn't seen one of these in so long, and it just brought it into perspective… how wrong it all went."

Nobody said anything as Dante traced the gold highlights. Then his eyes re-focused and he sat straighter than before.

"Then, I found this in the back cover."

The half-burnt photo appeared in his hand and Marta froze.

Horace scoffed. "If you weren't snooping you would have left it there." Dante ignored him.

"It was a little different than I remembered, and the name on the back was different. Of course, I should have known better than to pretend I knew everything. A son and daughter, too, that he never mentioned, but still. For a time he was my best friend."

"What time?" Horace and Dante alike were taken aback at her tone. She didn't stumble. She didn't stutter. "If you answer wrong, any chance of the benefit of my doubt will disappear. You say he was your best friend. Were you one of the fiends he worked with? Were you a heathen too?" Dante's fingers were hot as she snatched the comic and the photo, as if the cinders were lately extinguished.

"Please, don't misunderstand. My heart was as broken as yours when I learned who he really was. Truly, I had no idea that the man who taught me everything I knew was a killer. If I did, I would never have let him convince me to apply."

"That is all I need to know. If all you know comes from him then all you know is hellish." Within seconds the picture was torn to shreds. The hand that had comforted him just minutes before were now blackened with ash and pale from gripping the old comic as if out of fear it would vanish before her eyes. "I hid that photo in the one place I knew Markus would never look. This comic was mine. I wanted to be a hero, too. And I might have had my chance stolen from me, but your hands are redder than mine, and it will be my blood on them."

"Stop this!" Dante's new-found strength took him halfway to the door. "He betrayed me, too. Now, I have to live with the knowledge that everything I might have one day achieved was because of the favour of a monster. Does that make me a monster as well? I tried to stop everything before it began. There were twelve of us and eleven in favour of leaving you all here to die." People were starting to knock on the outer door, peeking in and calling out his name, at which he paled. "Is that not enough for you?"

Marta spat at his feet, and he recoiled. Loose threads of red hair accentuated the angry blush climbing up her cheeks and temples. Her furrowed brows pointed unspoken curses his way, arrows in the form of darkened glances between each eye, yet unfocused and swimming with unescaped tears.

Horace held her back by her arm, but he felt her muscles fighting against him and knew he wouldn't hold out against all she felt, manifested in flesh and bones that ached for movement, unstoppable forces. Through gritted teeth he hissed, "You have one chance to redeem yourself. Perhaps knowing the stakes will make you think twice about your actions."

Neither of them had listened.

"I see." He put one door between them and equipped his oxygen tank. "Good luck to all of us."

The cheers of his name fell on deaf ears as he walked away from the caravan, towards his own truck, where the scout had already vacated the driver's seat. He heaved a sigh before gripping the steering wheel with trembling fingers. His knees hadn't recovered yet, but as he shook his head, feeling the comforting warmth of wool on his neck, a plan was already forming in his mind.

Good luck to all of us.

Luck hadn't gotten him this far for him to give in to some newcomer's threats. Home was close – closer than he needed luck to take him, and in the end it will be him, that brought everyone home, not some old man or mumbling redhead.

This wasn't a bargain anymore.

It was just another story with the last page ripped out.

Chapter 3

# LOSING

Somehow this all boiled down to what happened on that one birthday. Was it the thirteenth or fourteenth? Irrelevant now that she was dead.

It all came down to Lemon, and her song, and her black throat that gave it such an edge - a deadly edge that took her from Layla too soon. The sharp edge of the song that sang her to death as well, but her father died similarly, in the dark, throat dry and black and stuffed with soot. Like Layla, like Lemon, like him - trapped in the sheer permanence of it all, of the big "what's next?"

"What's next?"

That was always the big question. Never could just live in the present, always had to think ten steps ahead, ten lives ahead. Sure, Layla could have something now, but when – not if – she lost it… what then? Permanence was a reward to come after death, until then change was inevitable. Embrace it, the temporary of life, make no attempt at friends or such idiotic luxuries that will not last.

There is no such thing as permanence of self, so change everything.

Lucille, Lucy, Lily. Layla was Maman's favourite. Speak English, French, English again. Adopt a fragmented identity, live each parallel life as if it is the truth. Her life was an anthology of different characters all played by herself, back to back with no breaks between the lines, an endless enjambment-riddled poem that never ended, never conformed to one form or rhyme scheme. It may have been called "free verse" but really, she was shackling herself in the cycle of discontinued, half-finished livelihoods.

Summer begins but an end comes with it always, so embrace the fact that ends will always follow beginnings. Father in the spring, Mother next summer, Lemon every night in my dreams.

Horace was an exception.

Since the beginning, he was the first one she didn't want to throw away, the one she wanted to hold on to, but letting go came too easy by then. Layla had to fight even herself to keep him. To a girl who could only ever justify apathy, training and mastering it over the years, the fall that taunted every attachment came laughing back, sneering. Something like friendship festered between it and her. A man of smoke from the fires of a war long ago extinguished, the flames of a different war than the one raging around, lifetimes away on a different planet. He made it easy to forget, but in the same way, too easy to remember.

He was the first person that, when she looked at him, Layla didn't see impending death. Maybe that was the mistake that killed her.

It was too easy to look down the fall when it was staring right at her through those warm grey eyes, tucked away behind grey skin and smiling lips, sympathetic murmurs that didn't provoke, but welcomed the way she never could, the way she feared someone would – one day. So selfish, was I really that selfish? How did he even put up with me?

He was just another temporary to that girl he picked from the rest all those years ago, who was still mourning the fact she was mourning in the first place, but he would never know. That would be an invitation. He was just a phase and then the war would end, and Layla would get back to the next phase and the next and the next until the temporary would expire. Paralysed in her search for permanence. What was more permanent than death?

Maybe he knew, maybe that was why he chose her in the first place, the mentee he would shape and mould into something new. Maybe he was like her, but not quite. While she picked up and tossed around a mound of clay, trembling at the thought of making a dent, he dug his digits into the cold wet mass, splitting and exposing it to the outside, plucking a fraction of the world and planting it inside, then letting time do the rest. In the end they both put the clay back on the workbench and moved on to the next.

He wasn't scared of his hands, or the damage they might make in his pursuit of art, his permanence.

All that for eleven years, she watched him exist that way : a parallel to herself. He had hope, she liked that he had something. She played along to his hope, watched him play into her whims: the flavours, colour coded and diligently noted in the little notebook behind her lapel, when they both knew there was only one flavour, and honey repulsed her. That was just the kind of person he was. In time, maybe Layla fooled herself as well as her tongue. It kept them both busy.

He stopped being the exception when they drove over the rim of that crater, when Layla allowed herself a flicker of the hope he'd carried for eleven years, a hope that she left behind on Earth, thinking herself the intellectual, the nihilist - and somehow proud of it. Always high and mighty.

With every blinking bulb the light of opportunity blinded her to the illusion she'd been living on this red planet. This wasn't meant to be. It was never meant to be, and she should have seen the truth so long ago. She wasn't meant to go home. She was meant to stay here, to let herself be happy, let herself have a friend she wouldn't have to lose. Layla was meant to be lost first, maybe that was what jinxed her, or cursed, maybe, the door to close on her, or the wind to change direction, or the ambassadors to leave them behind. The truth was she was happier here. Not here. But, here with Horace, with a friend and a purpose and more time she could ever ask for. That was what poetry was, in human life: more time than you know what to do with, with death only impending, but never coming. Always in sight, but never close enough to touch – hold – study, poetise!

When she looked at Horace, Layla did see death, but it wasn't his.

The bitter purgatory in the dark of the shuttle was anything but silent, but neither was Hell, and neither was Heaven. Echoes of the storm outside long subsided, it had stopped swaying hours ago, or had it been days? Horace must have been lonely. She heard the prayer he whispered long after it was too late, pulling at threads long ago unravelled, clasping ribbons of wind in his hands and pleading them to stay, braided around his fingers, slipping away with her life.

That was the kind of person Horace was: the kind to try and catch the wind in his grasp, to catch the final rays of sun behind his eyelids and dream of sunrise. The kind of person to be tailed by hope around a desolate planet and pretend he was the follower. The path home hid behind the horizon, and only he could see it. That was why he was the exception. That was why she had to let him go, before he reached his goal, and she lost again.

For now Layla drifts in between life and death, taunted by permanence with nothing to see but the fatal imprint of the white symbol painted onto the wall, wires snaking out from behind it and into the inner shell of the rocket's body. A bloody warning was scrawled, almost readable, beside it, and above, and below, on every surface she could grasp while her eyesight still held strong. Whether or not her warning would be heeded, Layla might never know. Nothing was certain to the dead. Even death – true death – was out of reach for now. An eternity might come and go, and she might still be there, dreaming of honey and blood and the poetic selfishness of her life, haunted by the cold corpse below her, curled up like a child gone to bed.

It's – Layla couldn't say her - eyes shut as if sleeping, but the eyelashes were caked in the blood that dried in pools below them, pouring from its ears in steady trickles like red tears spilling down its hollow grey cheeks. A spider web of blood-black threads shattered its marbled flesh, leaving a horror to behold even afterwards, the look of dying carrying on long after the death was complete.

After a while it became sort of... beautiful. A testament to the final unselfish moments of its life, where blushed, stained fingertips scrawled messages of warning for those who may never come, might never find it.

If Layla could but forget it, forget the fact that its blood was her blood once, she might have seen it by its beauty alone, might even have had it in her heart to poetise the sight, like she tried now with the rest of her life.

Being forgotten is dying twice.

But one look at the cold little curled up child and she can feel only pity, because that was how she will be remembered. I refuse to die twice in here, out here, far from home… What even is home anymore? There is no home for the half-dead, so where does she go to die?

She believes Horace was on his way, as much as a dead thing can believe in life. But then again, nothing is ever certain, especially for the dead. She begins counting the minutes before she lost all hope in death as she did in life.

Chapter 4

# THERE ARE NO BAD GUYS

1970

Oliver knew he would be big when he was older. A hero. Why wouldn't he be, when he saw himself in every book, every comic and movie. In mirrors, he saw his heroes, and what was coming for him. Every page and every year that passed he glowed with anticipation, breathed deep and clear the words that promised him glory, and a fated otherness from his peers he was yet to find, but recognised as his destiny.

His father thought the same when he enlisted and left for Korea. He could hardly find it on a map, but when he returned he did so with a new sight, a sort of vision, of the path he had followed, the path of his kind of man, and the path he would steer his son far away from. He was just a toddler then, but already the glimmer of heroism shone from his eyes like a flare. It was the same glimmer that he'd seen fade from his own eyes in the mirror, and in the eyes of his fellow soldiers. He promised himself he wouldn't live to see that glimmer snuffed out, and he knew exactly how. He knew the type of man to never be called to arms, and though he had once been that kind of man, and resented it, the path towards his son's safely was paved among those whose hands had never found themselves on a trigger.

He excused, therefore, the comics, the costumes and the toys, all to be expected for any young boy. He encouraged them, actually, in the spirit of make-believe, of the impossible. The impossible was stressed. The medicines weren't in the plan, but anything that kept him safe from the draft wouldn't catch a complaint from him.

He knew his son was not like the other boys. Of course, Oliver was never meant to know that. What kind of father kills his child's dream? Oliver also didn't know that the brighter that glimmer shone in his eyes the deeper his father worried. He was getting better, or the medicines getting stronger, it was hard to keep up with him, and by his teenage years, the boy that stood before him appeared almost…normal.

His biggest fear had been realised.

He called in his favour, with an old friend, from Korea. They hadn't spoken in years. He made sure Denver would take care of him.

Oliver Sr. crept past his son's room, catching silent sobs that made his ears prick. He was 19, and while all his school-time friends had received the fated slip of paper begrudgingly calling them to their destiny, he would linger behind. His chance had been ripped from him, and he wept for the first time. Outside his door, his father smiled. At least he would be saved, his job was done.

A week went by, accompanied by more tears. Oliver's mother was making lunch, his father wasn't home, and nobody heard the man walk in through the back door. They watched him drag his spotless black shoes over the unwashed tile floor of the kitchen, his mother still half-dazed from the teacup that now lay smashed by her feet, white chips of porcelain littering her fluffy slippers like snowfall. Noiselessly the man drew a letter from behind his lapel, nudging the steel cylinder beside it with a wedding band. Maybe it was a threat, maybe it was meant to excite him. Either way, Oliver's interest pas piqued at the sight of the gun. His father never allowed weapons in the house.

"This," the stranger tapped the letter, "to your college. And this," He drew another, smaller envelope, "For you." His mother shuffled; painted toes curled in her slippers, as the suited man who had floated into the house retreated with a nod to the doorstep. "Save your tears, men like us don't die like this."

He came and went in less than a minute, never leaving a footprint on the tiles or disturbing the lawn, but Oliver would never forget him. As he crossed the threshold into their freshly trimmed yard, Mrs Keen urged her perfect roses to glare back. Oliver saw nothing. His fingers gripped the two letters like they were made of gold, and retreated to his room, leaving his still trembling mother to sweep the teacup's remains from her feet.

They waited for his father to come home before they opened the letters, the one for College first. Oliver's fingers shook as he fetched a spare envelope to reseal and address it, but something made him halt at the top of the stairs. Once the heavy beating in his heart and the whispers that tickled his throat subsided, the hushed pleading from his mother carried far.

"You can't fool me, Oliver. You knew about this..." He made a single step down. "What did you tell them? That he's some sort of boy genius? Whether he's holding a gun or a pen this war will get him. It gets us all." She was crying now.

"I swiped his name off that list. You know he was weeping when he didn't get called up? You think I would make him weep like that out of spite?" Oliver's bare feet touched the cold tile of the kitchen. From then on, his mother passed off the tears as marks of pride. She started spending lots of time in her garden, knelt among the roses, tending to them so tenderly, as if they, too, might be ripped away from her.

He used to watch her from his window, looking so peaceful among the green, but like an army general, she meticulously ordered everything in its place, tormented by every leaf and thorn inching out of order. The turbulent mind planting bulbs into earth like landmines. No further visits were made.

He first met Horace Desmond at the end of that year.

He listened, mostly. He wasn't yet permitted to speak, not while his trial period was ongoing (it never really felt like it ended.) They had disguised it as an apprenticeship, and well enough that his college let him graduate early.

He was still the only one, aside from the Colonel, that was working on the programme, though he wasn't allowed to know exactly what the programme was. He assumed it was to do with housing, having snuck a few glances at the maps currently being torn to shreds by the man whose hands had traced each line. Oliver felt he should have brought out another of the dozens of copies, but held firm, mirroring the Colonel's stiff, but commanding body language from a few steps behind him.

He coughed a single time and stifled it, puffing out his cheeks. Seizing the moment of interruption, the Colonel cut in.

"You lost the rights to this project years ago, archiving it under an alias in Yugoslavia, need I remind you? You're only lucky we got to it before the opposition did."

"I should have destroyed it then. I shouldn't have even created it in the first place. Mine was at least a work of art. This -" He planted his hand on the table, crinkling the paper, "- is a satire. It won't work."

"Whether you choose to sign your name on it, or not, it will go forward…"

"Are you hearing yourself? It's suicide!"

This back and forth lasted hours, punctuated by coughing fits from the old man, after which he refused help or even a drink of water. Something told Oliver he was afraid to even grip the glass. Horace had a cane, but never used it other than to gesture at a map, or to the Colonel, and on rare occasions, at Oliver himself. It didn't register, then, that Horace's was more than a stubborn or rebellious kind of defiance. He should have taken it as a warning.

Oliver used to stare at the ceiling of his old bedroom. There wasn't much to look at, but it saved him from catching a glimpse of the walls, or the backs of his eyelids. He used to watch until his vision twirled images into his brain, white on top of white. He wouldn't think. In fact, he tried to think as little as possible, especially when his ticking watch did all the thinking for him. If he did think, it was to recite the times, dates and codewords he would need to remember the next time he was picked up. The meeting were getting more frequent by the summer of '71, and he'd stopped trying to figure out what the programme was about now that more people had been signed on beside him. It was becoming increasingly obvious what the next play in the was going to be.

He forgot what wallpaper used to hide behind the layers of posters he bandaged it up with. A patchwork of heroism that stared him down as he tried to sleep, or study, or just stand motionless in the doorway, almost trying to encourage himself to walk in, afraid to meet the eyes of his heroes, afraid to be unworthy of their gaze.

Most were bought, some gifts, very few stolen. Ripped from lamp posts or theatre walls or bookshops. From a thumb tack above his pillow hung his father's dog tag, except they had omitted the "sr." from it, so it might as well have belonged to him. It might as well have been him. He resented that it wasn't for him.

There were footsteps outside his door. Bare feet in slippers, shuffling past. A glance at the clock told him it was midnight.

He fell back into his pillow, into the bed that was too small for him, in the room that was too small for him. The world itself, he felt, was too small for him.

He bolted up again, squinting in the dark.

As his mother shuffled back past his door she stopped to listen, but he didn't notice the slippers fall silent over the sound of ripping paper.

By dawn he had built a mound from the posters and comic book pages, and set it ablaze in his back yard. His parents awoke to the smell of smoke, but by then all that was left was a pool of soggy ashes. The rain had come too late to save them.

They watched from the back door, afraid to move. Lightning shattered the sunrise.

It took him too long to figure out why he didn't like watching the posters at night. At night there was no light to bring out the gold and silver, to distinguish the bright letters from the busy backgrounds. In the dark, all he saw was red, and white, and blue. Red and white stripes and the blue night sky, white stars stamped on it like a tapestry.

Every page, every book, every poster.

His fingers were cut and stinging, but he crawled back to his room to see his finished work in the light of the sun, curtains torn open. He made sure no tacks remained in the walls. The room already felt bigger without them in it, and as the light drifted in, the canvas of his childhood was bare once more.

The night sky was painted on his walls. Real stars dotted the walls, and rockets and planets swirled around his medicated conscience. He'd left the dog tag drowned in the grey mulch outside.

He would get something better. Something with his own name on it.

## 1971

Jobs and ages were all they got at first. That was all they were. Not names, not even states. Just what they did and how long they'd been alive. All the necessary information. "Chemical engineer, 20, Geologist, 39, 40, 44, there's three of 'em. Uh… Cart-oh-graph-er? 74."

"Maps." His companion lit a cigar. "Drawing them." The sour smoke drifted upwards, pooling around the ceiling of the small office. Oliver tried not to breathe too hard.

"Ah, I see how that might be useful…" Oliver didn't see anything; he was just grateful for the company. "They're still on the lookout for talent, though. I hear they're combing the private schools now."

Frank was the only one that talked to him. None of the other ambassadors even considered him a part of the group, and, if he were honest, he didn't feel he would have related in the slightest with men who were deep into their careers before he was even born. Frank wasn't like that. He was nice. He was different. He had a funny accent.

"When are you thinking of going?" Frank inquired, as if about a holiday.

"Not for a while… '76? Might be sooner."

Frank puffed out his cheeks. "That's plenty of time." He took a hearty puff of the cigarette, and Oliver's eyes started to sting. "Still, you can never be too ready." Frank reached into his own pocket. "Do me a favour. I always wanted to go to space." He held out a small picture, a portrait photo, the kind someone would cut up and put in a locket. "Take me along for the ride?"

Oliver smiled at the soldier in the photo, younger then than the man before him, but recognisable. Aside from the uniform and soldier's cap, stern, straight look that could crack stones, the man in the picture was every inch his friend. "Will do, sir." Frank waved his hands dismissively through the smoke, batting a cloud into Oliver's face.

"Stop that. Not me." He held out a fresh cigar. "You smoke, kid?" Oliver found it funny that Frank called him "kid." Maybe it just sounded funny in his accent. It felt like such an American thing to say to a 23 year old man.

"No s- no."

Frank shrugged. "We can't all be perfect." A clock on Frank's desk rang noon. He muttered something under his breath and swung his feet off the table. "Better go. I've got a meeting in here." He spun in his chair and opened the windows in his small office stationed above an Italian grocery. Discreet centre of operations. The Italian family downstairs were none the wiser. They thought Oliver was visiting his tutor. It helped that he still wore his school tie every day. He wasn't sure why, but he felt he had to look smart for Frank. Frank was the type of man to look your best for.

"Men in uniform make America. Ladies in uniform make Americans." Frank laughed at this, and Oliver laughed along, though he spent hours trying to decode it afterwards.

He heard the other ambassadors tutting about Frank sometimes, but he was important. He wasn't coming along for the ride, or else Oliver might have actually had a friend for the long-term.

He'd moved out of his parents' house by then. At least, that was what his parents told their friends and neighbours, leaving out the part where he was relocated by a confidential government programme, and they currently had not the vaguest idea of their son's whereabouts, or the next time they would see him. That was the deal, and that was what he agreed to, what they agreed to, and it would be final. It was put in ink.

"Once you put something in ink," Frank said, "not even an earthquake can shake it." Oliver got this one straight away.

## 1972

"Frank... Frank!" Oliver hissed in the dark. He glanced at his watch before knocking again. In his head he prayed Frank was still in his office. Maybe he fell asleep at his desk again. Please. Please. "Frank?"

The door swung open, cutting short his final knock. The man that opened the door rubbed his eyes, cigar ash falling from his collar. "Oliver? What are you doing-"

The boy brushed past him, slamming the door shut behind him. "You gotta help me. Please! They're gonna kick me off the project." Frank lit the lamp on his desk, illuminating the boy's tear-stained face. "I messed up. What am I meant to do? I can't go home like this..." The streaks down his cheeks shone like gold in the lamplight.

"Hey, calm down. Did you... run here?" He took him by the shoulders. "Look at yourself, boy. That's not how you enter an office."

"Sorry, sorry. I'm sorry, sir - Oh, I keep messing up." He slapped his hands over his eyes so hard that sparks swam behind his eyelids.

Something tapped the back of his hand, and he removed them, taking a second to see through the rippling vision. He saw stars, then a cigar pointing toward him.

He took it.

"Tell me. We have all night."

They had ganged up on him. Eleven grown men, all of them his seniors in both age and rank. He was trembling by the time the meeting ended. "I overstepped my authority." He held his hands out in front of himself. "That's what they said."

"Sure did."

"But doesn't it seem... wrong... to you? That they're starting to look in schools?"

"Sure does."

"So I was in the right?"

"Not in the slightest."

Oliver was more confused as the sun began to rise, perhaps marking his last day on the programme. And now, the man he looked to for sense – for advice - was not helping like he thought he would when he ran over here in the dead of night.

"Look at it this way. You wanted to be a hero. Everyone does, in this day and age. It's everyone's dream to die for the country they love. When did you think you were ready?"

Oliver couldn't think of an answer. Truth is, he never really imagined death would be involved.

"I'm guessing twelve... thirteen maybe?" Frank answered for him. "Well, if they're ready to go to Mars, they're ready to die for it. It's a commitment." The cigar was only a stump now, but he held it like a prize between his fingers. "Honour has no age limit. They're getting a head start this way."

"I'm not ready to die."

Frank's eyes glittered in the lamplight. The sun was rising behind him, and the room was filled with smoke, which looked like it was floating straight out of the fire in his eyes. "This is something to die for. If you don't like that... Then you're not ready for the mission, and they were right."

"They weren't right."

"Make up your mind, Oliver." His feet were both suddenly flat on the floor – anchored, planted, like a tree.

"If it was you-"

"I already made that commitment. I did my time. I'm not making the decision for you."

Oliver's hands were shaking, and he wished he had his medication on hand. Since the start of the programme, he seemingly felt healthier than ever. Maybe he was just distracted.

He realised her never asked Frank how he got this position.

When would he ever get a chance like this?

The tip of his tongue still was slick with the taste of the cigarette. He put it on his tongue for just a second, and shoved it into his pocket when Frank turned around. He never even lit it, but the second he parted his lips his head felt like it was screaming at him to stop. Funny. He didn't even need to light it, to know he was a coward. And in front of Frank, too. What if he'd turned at the wrong time?

He won't mess up again.

"I want to go on with it. I'm ready for it."

"Good. I'll put in a good word." He winked.

Oliver sprung from his chair, almost bounding across Frank's desk, but the wooden edge cut into the top of his thighs. "You will?" Frank nodded.

"Honestly, they're just bullies. You have to put up with them one way or another. But, you want to know something about bullies?"

Oliver nodded.

"It's a hierarchy." He motioned layers in the air with his downturned hand, starting below the desk and ending above his head. "There's always someone on top." He pointed to himself and laughed, and the sun had fully risen. "Come on. You'll miss roll call, or whatever they do over there-"

The older man's speech was cut short. He'd stood up to open the door for the boy, but with his hand still on the doorknob, he met an obstacle.

Oliver was hugging him.

It was the hug of a child, weak and short, and though he wasn't particularly tall, Oliver practically towered over him. But it was the hug of a friend above all. That was how it felt to Oliver.

"All right, boy. You'll be just fine." He wrapped one arm around his shoulder, nudging him toward the door, but when they split the boy's face beamed, and the dried paths of his long forgotten tears curved with his smile. "Run along, now."

"Thanks again. Thank you, Frank."

"You're welcome, kid. No, you outrank me now." He straightened up. "Sir." He saluted as he closed the door, leaving the boy to sneak past the waking family downstairs with a hidden smile behind his icy eyes. Everything would be fine.

## 1976

Dr Frank Horn stopped in his tracks; his feet barely crossed the threshold of his office on the third floor. The smell of fresh fruit drifted in through the open window, intermingled with the stench of years of cigar smoke, that he was now numbed to. He saw the flame first, then what Oliver was burning.

"Morning, Frank." It was barely 5 am. His feet were on the desk, ankles crossed, but his eyes were on him, icy, blue, pools of water frozen over. He could lose himself in the turbulent streams behind that ice, crash into the sharp rocks that hid beneath. "But I know that's not really your name. Or have you managed to fool yourself, too?"

"Oliver. What are you doing, boy?"

"Boy..." Oliver whispered. "Haven't we exhausted that already?" He tossed the remains of a cigar into the flame, and Frank wondered if he had smoked the whole thing. His voice was so clear, so deep, like the fire. It burned when he spoke.

"What are you doing, Oliver?"

"I'm doing the only thing I'm good at. You know, six years ago..." He swung his legs off the table, letting them fall to the floor with a thud that felt louder than it sounded. "I took all the posters off my walls. They made me dizzy. Too many stars and stripes, they messed with my head, and I didn't even realise it until they were gone, and I saw what was behind them. And I liked it better."

"Oliver, you have to go," Frank almost pleaded, the fixed himself up. "The Agrestas will be suspicious." The old family had started asking too many questions, but it was easier to evict them than relocate an entire neighbourhood of secret service agents. The new family had only been here for a month, and were already tossing dirty looks when Oliver walked up. Frank noticed Oliver wasn't wearing his school tie anymore. When had he stopped?

"I burned those posters. Now, I look behind your disguise and I don't like you better. You lied to me, and I hated the truth." Frank's mouth was glued shut. "You made me dizzy. Why?" He knew Oliver expected no answer. Didn't want an answer. He already knew. "A boy would ask for your real name. I'm not a boy. You made sure of that." Oliver held the thumbnail picture between his middle and index fingers. "Remember this?" He spun it once, as if refreshing his own memory. Suspended in the air between two fingers, the flames barely licking at its corner. "This here is your legacy. This name..." He spun it around, so the glistening letters faced Frank, "is your chance to start your story again, through me." His fingers threatened to release, the heat of the flame barely singeing the paper, darkening the corner. Oliver never broke the stare, though the hairs on his wrists were also singed.

"I'd rather die than give you the satisfaction." He dropped the picture into the fire, watching as the black speckles grew, consuming the paper until there was nothing left of it, but the face burned into his memory. "You just had to be one of the bad guys, didn't you?"

"There are no bad guys, Oliver." Frank spoke after a long silence, but his dry voice intermingled with the crackling flame. "There are only the right, and the wrong."

"You were very wrong, then." He flexed his burned hand under the desk. "Are you at least going to try and convince me you've changed?"

"I'm not stupid, Oliver. I won't pretend it will make any difference. I did what I did. I only ask that you think of the past few years, all the time we spent together, and ask yourself if the image you have just burned is who you see now." The old doctor traced the edge of the desk with the back of his hands, as if asking permission to exist in his own room. He remembered a time when their roles were reversed, when it was the man before him, still a boy then, pacing awkwardly in his office, unsure of the space he was taking up, frigid in his own shoes.

The fire in the ashtray was almost burning out, dimming the red glow on Oliver's face. He flicked a lighter out of his pocket and lit it, the spark stirring the water beneath his lidded eyes. The office was very flammable, Frank thought. All those books, papers in the desk, the curtains. "Look at me, at least." Oliver's eyes never wandered above the edge of the desk, his hands.

"You got one thing right: You aren't stupid. Never were." He pushed the chair out from under the desk. "That makes it all so much worse."

"Listen, boy-"

Oliver shot up, pushing down on the desk with his palms turning white from the effort. "I am not a boy." His heart was starting to skip a little, and he subconsciously reached for the pills in his pocket. There was nothing there. He extinguished the lighter, and the focus of the light dispersed, the room feeling brighter, bigger, with the natural light coming through the closed shades. Only rows of parallel lines shaded Frank's face like prison bars. "I won't burn you. You should be grateful for that."

"Oliver. Listen."

"Not anymore. Leave me alone. Just let me go and forget. Forget me too." He stood up from the desk, and floated to the door, guided by the breeze that entered through the open window.

"What if I can't?" Frank grabbed the younger man's arm.

"Then try."

"What if I don't want to?" His hand held tight to Oliver's shoulder as he tried to brush past through the open door, but Oliver swung back, letting his free hand fly in a fist to the man's face. He couldn't have hit hard if he wanted, but the confusion alone was enough to set him free from his mentor's clutches. He sped past, down the stairs, knocking over a fruit basket as he fell.

Frank didn't follow. Oliver appreciated that; it made him easier to forget if he didn't fight it.

He didn't come knocking later, or the next day, or even the night before the scheduled departure. Oliver had already forced six years of memories back, burned them as well as he could. He was leaving him behind, a lost memory, as all eventually end up. This was a different kind of fire: one that no amount of rain could put out, and the thunder only stirred behind his turbulent eyes.

## 1986

They called it a "new start" when addressing them all. To everyone else, it was a manifestation of something. Fame, Power, Superiority, The Dream? To Oliver it was the chance he'd been cheated out of, though he never realised his first loss was a salvation, still caught up in the stars and stripes he tried to cast off.

A decade later, nobody believed in the dream anymore. So, when all twelve Ambassadors huddled around the static, craning our necks to read the urgent messages that flashed on the screen one by one, Oliver was the last person who could have seen the end coming.

"We had our orders. Are you not one of us?"

Suddenly Oliver belonged. Suddenly they wanted to save him too, how curious. The better half of his life had been spent wishing he could have joined them, the other resenting their coolness. But it was the empty seat that would deepen their guilt. Another fabricated death to mourn back at home.

Thirteen seats. Twelve ambassadors, and Colonel Denver Thirteen lives to be saved.

"Do you think you are a bad person?" The question hit Oliver like a mallet to the chest. Blunt, not sharp, only stealing the air from his lungs. He'd run out of pills, using three years' supply in the first few months, but found something else, a row of brown vials, that worked almost as well. Thinking too hard made him breathe heavily then, and now he had a headache.

After all this time, he really didn't know. Of course, he had the intention to be a good person – a hero – was that not why everyone was here in the first place? That was the Dream. Survive, thrive, win the war, save countless lives in the process, return and be hailed as a hero. It had happened countless times in history, at this point it was all routine.

Colonel Denver sat across from him, hands folding around themselves, urging some warmth from each-other. The telling veins that peeked out behind his thin skin almost glowed blue. This place aged everyone.

"What does that mean?" Oliver fixated on the veins, following them beneath his superior's sleeves, wondering how far up they went before fading behind the grey flesh that mocked everyone's youth. "I have never wished to hurt anyone, not even now." He didn't mean to come across as so aggressive with the last word, given the consequences. The colonel was truly old, and Oliver heard it in his voice, too, in addition to his face. Aged by countless wars, his ears were made sensitive by decades of artillery fire.

"That's not what I asked." His hands stopped moving. "I asked if you think you are a bad person. I'll help you. I believe I am a good person, never doubted it and never will." His voice was so soft, he might have been confused for a grandfather telling a story.

"With all due respect, sir, how can you say that?"

Colonel Denver unfolded his feet under the desk, planting his feet firmly in the ground. "In our… humble existence, every action is directed by someone else. Whether we realise it or not, our every move has been calculated, drafted and re-drafted by another, higher power." The hard-boiled apathy in his voice had survived the years that degraded the rest of him. "It's a chain of blame as well as a chain of command. We all have superiors: Commanders, Colonels, Kings, Gods, et cetera…"

"You are that to me."

"And I have one as well, and so does he, and so on and so forth. Nobody makes decisions for themselves, so there is never anyone to blame. This world runs on that philosophy – that promise. That nobody is ever truly guilty," he took in a shaky breath, and Oliver felt the rattle in his own throat, "except the enemy."

"Then there are no real bad guys?"

"You are not a bad guy, Oliver."

He shook his head. "I could never live with the knowledge I let someone die while I saved myself," Oliver said. "And nobody is willing to listen to me. Have all my years… all my loyalty to you and the others… won't you even consider what I have to say?"

"All these years, and you failed to see the biggest, most blatant truth. Oliver, loyalty doesn't exist in this job. There are those who follow orders, and those who mutiny." The Colonel smiled. "Go home son."

There are only the right, and the wrong.

"There's no honourable choice."

He held up one finger, like Oliver had just realised what he was trying to say. "As long as you understand that you'll save yourself a lifetime of guilt." He got up, ending the conversation. "Go home, Oliver. You weren't meant to die like this."

"Not men like me." The words formed on his lips as the Colonel vacated the room, leaving him with the flashing message on the radio console screen, the one warning them of their salvation.

"What kind of man am I?"

He looked out the office window to the horizon, broken by cement monoliths, some collapsed, some still standing by some miracle. Beside them, the rocket, the first in near a decade, a vessel of fire and hope, but also a condemnation.

Looking out the window was like peering through a misty filter. Here and there a white freckle would appear, a scar of sharp pebbles flung to the glass by strong winds. If he didn't know better he would have pretended they were stars, appearing in the late afternoon.

The sky was different here, even the sunrise and sunset were lacking in heat, and no real moon dangled on the edge of the city skyline, showing some glimmer of a world outside of reach, inviting but terrifying at the same time.

He was living it now, so there was no use for a moon anymore.

He watched from that same window as the rocket left the atmosphere, knowing well his seat was still empty.

He had to get away before the bloodbath began. If blood would be shed, his would hit the ground first.

He left the Embassy for the first time as the sole authority on this planet, though he knew that meant nothing to anyone but his teenage self. Young, innocent, ignorant Oliver letting himself be hypnotised by his very walls. He hid in the city, waiting for the perfect chance to blend in once the chaos died down. It was easy to do so among a crowd that barely knew each-others' faces, never mind their names.

The next steps had to be very carefully calculated, he had to make each one count, or die knowing he tried, at least, to be different – be better – than what he was scripted to be.

He put on his father's jacket.

Chapter 5
---

# JUST DRIVE

She wasn't talking. That was understandable. He knew it wasn't her, but the blurring wind and the flickering peripheral taunts made him doubt himself, even if just for one moment every thousand. If only he could tear his eyes away from the horizon, then the nagging feeling that it was the same sleeping figure he was used to just inches from his elbow, would disappear. But then, so would the comfort of ignorance. If he fooled himself long enough, anything could be real on this blank planet.

He didn't want to look, because then he might have seen the wild mane of hair was peppered white in red, not black, that the flesh was a grey hue of white, not brown, the hands curled into fists were wide and short, not long and slender, like hands you'd see bewitching a piano into melody, hands often wreathed in electric sparks, stung too many times but tamed them every time. Every time.

"Everyone deserves a second chance," is what he wanted to say to her, but he didn't think that was what she wanted to hear, maybe ever. He wasn't sure she was even awake, and doubted he would get an answer if he asked. He wasn't even sure if he believed the words he wanted to say. He wasn't sure of anything anymore. Was it a symptom of something?

Just drive, while you still can.

So he drove, following the pull of recent nostalgia and old responsibility, because hope was waiting for him, keeping her company, if it couldn't keep her alive. If it couldn't take her home. Like he was meant to. Horace coughed into his shoulder, forgetting the mask, which slid off, exposing his nostrils to the harassing winds that swept past the dwindling whiskers.

Can't be forgetting things like this.

He pushed the mask back into place. The air that filtered through the old truck hinted at smoke, and there was a noticeable cluttering noise coming from within the engine. You too? He took a deep breath and checked the rear-view mirror, an old habit.

When he was teaching Layla to drive, it became sort of an inside joke. Why even use mirrors? All you saw through them was yourself, and sometimes a different shade of red sky, but they did it anyway, exaggerated at first to make each-other giggle, then smile, then just mutter a silent grunt and half nod. It became routine, to peek over to the mirror, and be disappointed every time, or was it really comforting, knowing nobody was following? That all that existed in the space between horizons was them, and the map in either of their hands.

He remembered once Layla pointed out how peaceful everything seemed from her perspective, the flat fields of red dust tumbling over one another in the wind. Even the storms could be playful in a way Earth's storms couldn't be because they had nothing to destroy, no buildings to topple or bridges to split in half, no waves to crash onto the shores. They were dancing over a blank canvas with no paint. "Mars is the Roman god of War. This is a perfect planet to have as its namesake. I could imagine him raging in an empty field, and infinity of anger and nothing to take it out on." A red limbo.

Was the crimson sunset the angry god finally setting down his sword and letting the darkness wash over him? Was he giving up or finding another fight to endure... perhaps another way to face it.

Of course, nothing was ever really red, but Layla made it look that way, because there were more romantic words for red than orange, so he amused her, and her distaste for honey, and fooled himself until he saw red wherever he looked.

Now the red-tinted glasses were gone, the brown of it all was clearer, uglier. This was the world without her to distract from it. No Roman gods or imaginary battles, just dust and wind that dried his lips and eyes, and sunsets that didn't glow red, just extinguished between perpetual grey, ghostly clouds. And behind him, crossing the brown plains in close pursuit were a herd of vehicles, as foreign to him as he was to this new planet.

Horace's eyes darted to the mirror, then back again in shock, heart suddenly beating fast, and he lost control of his arms. The sputtering engine complained as he swerved away from nothing, and the sleeping girl's hands flew to the dashboard to stabilise herself, eyes flung open out of sleep or some attempt at it.

Horace's back was straight against the seat, and he clamped his mouth shut once he realised it was open, gasping for air that wasn't there. He had lost himself in a dream, one where nobody was following behind them, where Layla would mutter stories in half-sleep beside him and slowly fall silent as a corpse. A world that was comfortably red, with her to paint it thus.

The figures in the mirror awoke him from this illusion.

Just drive. While you're still awake.

Marta didn't ask if he was all right.

Would Layla have? Would she have called him an old fool and offered to trade places?

Stop it.

He had woken her. As he willed his pulse to stop drumming in his ears her gaze pierced his peripheral vision. Mars was stirring behind her eyes as well as between him and the horizon. Somehow he found the energy to break the silence. Marta had already resettled in her chair, propped her oxygen tank firmly between her knees and was staring at her feet.

"Sorry for waking you up." He spoke to her in German, hoping it might make her more comfortable. She didn't acknowledge his attempt, but bent against the seatbelt to reach to the floor. Horace heard the tell-tale jingle of metal stirring as she grunted, heaving the heavy box on to her knees. His breath was caught. "Don't touch that." Like a child being told off, she sighed, letting the box down with a thud. After a moment he felt the silence too unbearable. "How did you sleep?"

"I did not sleep." She answered in her broken English accent, refusing to make eye contact, refusing a connection, and though their elbows were mere inches from each other, she was a continent away. "How much time until we arrive?"

"Not long. It's walkable, if I remember from Ma-" His eyelids flared open, and he banked on the chance she didn't hear him begin to mention her brother. "And the scouts returned quite fast, so we should be there before night." An unfamiliar sound had joined the harmony of noises the truck emitted: a shoe, steel-toed, tapping. "Can you stop?"

"Why can't I open it?"

The breath he took trembled in his throat, and he coughed away the tremor. "You're already upset," Or am I just scared? Scared of what? "I don't want you any more stressed."

"Speak English – please!" she said, firmly. Her foot was still.

Suddenly his mouth was dry of words, all it could spew forth was a dry-throated laugh that sent aches and spasms through his chest, tears to his eyes and a chorus of pops between the glassy bones in his back. When the outburst died out he looked at her again through foggy vision and found a horrified face looking back at him.

"Why are you laughing?" She asked, redness spilling out in a blush of confusion or rage from behind the grey silicone of her mask.

"Do you know, out of all the languages I learned in my life, French was the one I never quite got the hang of?"

"Pfft, French is easy."

"You should have heard it; the words were right but never sounded right. I was hopeless. My mouth just isn't the right shape to make all those little sounds that change the meanings, so when I first befriended Layla, I tried mimicking the accent that slipped through her English."

Marta saw a sudden rise on the horizon as she listened to him, hoping the end of their journey wouldn't arrive before the end of his story. She was still mad, but she loved a good story, and the horizon was still so far off.

"I thought I was making progress, but she never spoke French to me though I knew she was fluent. She mentioned before that her mother never really learned English enough to speak it in the house, and her father did his best to learn but they made it work without having to speak to each other much, which I thought was odd, but sweet. Anyway, it must have been three years into the mission. Nobody knew where we were, and that was how we liked it. No news, no contact."

During his extended pause Marta thought his story had ended, but when she leaned back disappointed into her chair he spoke again, quieter now, the laughter having faded entirely from his voice.

"She wasn't sleeping. I knew she wasn't. Whenever she dozed off she would jolt back awake, like she was trying to keep herself from sleep, like she was scared of it, so she occupied every second with some work. I made a mistake then, admittedly. Sleep must have changed my voice, or maybe I'd finally fixed my pronunciation. I don't know what it was, but it was convincing enough that when I told her off, she dropped what she was doing and, still facing away from me, started to sob."

"She thought you were her mother." Marta knew the feeling. There were few things she actually remembered about her father, from the very short time she was allowed to know him, but while she forced herself to forget his face, his voice fought to stay with her. She heard, on the radio once, an old speech of his, and she was so shaken that her hands were restless the rest of the day, and she couldn't get any work done. It was the single most terrifying day because she knew there was no reason to be scared, and that made her more scared. Could he really ruin her life, even after leaving it?

"I'd never seen her cry before, not like that. She said she thought she was having a nightmare while awake. Apparently her mother would frequently appear in them, speaking French to her. She died just before the mission began. Layla never felt she did enough to keep her alive, so when, sleep deprived and tortured with stress, she heard me telling her off, she thought her mother's ghost had followed her, all the way here, to tell her off."

What was he doing, talking about her as if she was only a memory from a time past? As the space between them grew shorter and shorter she still felt further away. Would she still feel far when he held her again?

"I don't believe in ghosts."

"She never was really sure either."

"Do you?"

I said, do you believe in ghosts?

What's that supposed to mean?

"I don't know." It's a long story. "I never spoke French to her again. She started sleeping better after that. Turns out it wasn't her mother's voice she was hearing, but mine, just distorted, blending in with her old memories until she couldn't tell them apart. She got better - well, as far as 'better' goes for us here."

The tapping had started again, not half-minded, but active, as if she was giving herself a rhythm by which she could listen to the story. "You can open it if you think you can stomach it." Marta didn't hesitate to strain against the frayed seatbelt and Horace winced again at the sound she created, all those names sliding past each other as the truck began its slow ascent up the skirt of the dune.

The sun had vanished behind the dune, but as the heaving machine struggled against the dust that slid through its blunted tyres Horace saw straight ahead the final strings of light threading through the cracks in the stone rim up above, fading with every second. The rush of adrenaline this gave him pressed his foot into the pedal subconsciously. Heart raced as tyres screeched, engine sputtered and choked. This would be her last trip. His, too.

The other vehicles overtook them.

Head getting hot, he silently urged the machine to hold itself together one last time, but the steady rhythm was disturbed, unsure about the destination. It was actively repelled while the followers crossed his line of sight, appearing from behind him and disappearing over the top of the dune. While you still can. Come on. The cold metal dug into his sternum; the name carved in it printing red welds in his soft flesh.

Marta had once again fallen silent beside him, and the sound of the lid falling on the chest only joined the chaos of the dying engine that spat at him like curses. The magnetism that repelled the truck only drew Horace close to the epicentre of something running away from him. The light at the top was gone, snatched away by the shade the other trucks were casting. They must be all rushing out, huddling around the rim of the ravine, perhaps Dante was already leading a few of them into the nearest cavern.

The front tyres caught on to the edge of the top and lurched the entire system forward, thrusting its mass over the edge before its silence marked its time of death. They rolled mutely into place as the sun disappeared behind the noses of the rockets that struck the sky like the tops of Christmas trees, only stayed still as statues in the wind.

Marta came out of the truck first, throwing open her door and then the steaming hood, unleashing a wave of heat in her face as she clamped a hand over her eyes. "Careful!" Horace steadied himself on the door and pushed himself up, but found he nearly buckled under his own weight. The adrenaline, having faded, left his knees weak as his heart still beat in his throat.

They were the first ones out of their seats after all, apart from Dante, who only stood up, neck straight, eyes fixed on the nearest rocket, with a steel crow bar in his right hand. The black dust that coloured his hair had stained the back of his neck, but nobody would ever tell him that.

As Horace watched him, standing stock-still, facing away from him, he found in himself a chill reserve of comfort or – God forbid – faith.

Faith, how ironic. How unaffordable now.

Chapter 6

# NAME AND A FACE

She didn't get to see his face before she died, but he saw her, and he saw her again, but she missed him.

She knew he saw her, because as soon as he did, she was allowed to leave. Forced, more accurately. No matter how hard she tried to hold on, feeling the push, the air pulsing around her, gouging itself into her pores, forcing whatever was left of her out before the door even came open. It was the detachment which she dreaded, and longed for – separation from the creature she hovered around. The empty vessel of what she used to be, baptised in darkness to its new existence, anchor loosened.

The connection had been severed and she was free.

She was taken first to her gravestone, the first one she ever received. In a little churchyard in the north of England, among mismatched rows of headstones and statues, granite and marble and others so riddled with moss and lichen that neither name, nor date could be read. Hers was already joining the multitudes: the "Gone too soons" and "Beloved mother-sister-daughter, etcetera…" that told nothing of her life, her special-ness. That was what she had on Earth. That was all she had here. This dead stone said nothing of that.

She looked around, unsure exactly what force was keeping her there, and thought about the world. It wasn't something she liked doing often, but now she was dead, and with plenty of time to think and plenty more to think about, this might as well be the first. In this graveyard she was situated in the southwest corner, where she could catch plenty of light.

Sandwiched between two others of equal size, standing firm, the year-old headstone bore her name. It was a safe place to be, between her mother and father, though it would not be her place of rest. It never would, but she liked to imagine there was something under there, something they put in to make the ceremony seem more real.

Someone had left her flowers, not too long ago. Whoever it could be, she didn't hazard a guess, but the wrinkled petals that littered the top soil of the empty grave were much appreciated, nonetheless. How would they have known the date was all wrong? The grave had for a year bore the name of a being that was still – debatably – alive.

She thought about the age-old question: if you fall in a forest when there is nobody around to see, did you ever really fall? She applied it to herself. If you live a year on a foreign planet, did you ever really live? Did she ever really die?

Yes, she did die, and "too soon," of course, as she was always destined to. The fated "before" that caught her now, existing in the dreaded "after." Because, after all, what did she really live for that could have been remembered. She was living in the world during the technological revolution, something she wanted to take full advantage of, she wanted to be there early. She heard a computer singing with its own voice, and a man planting his footprints on the moon. She saw, not even a decade later, an entire city built on the surface of Mars, and survive over a decade.

But where did she fit into this living puzzle? Why was there only a set of numbers beside her name right now?

If she couldn't have put knowledge into the world, the least she could have done was a couplet or two, some pretty words to outlive her name, because her name was nothing to her.

"Lucille." This was a fragment, so old and over-translated that its original meaning was as lost to the wind as she was. The church door opened, and she was gone before she could glance at her parents' graves for the last time.

"Lucy Smith." Another one of her aliases, was spelled out in corrugated cardboard, orange and red on a painted yellow cork board in a small classroom. Top of the pyramid of Notable Alumni, with a little hand-written paragraph detailing her life and time at St

Bartholomew's primary school. At least she was someone's reason to do their homework.

The picture they used was a cut-out from her class photo. The little girl in that photo, wearing blue cardigan over checkered dress, hair in pigtails and exaggerated smile - did she ever dream she would die alone on a different planet, her only friend praying for the first time in his life for hers? The morning bell rang, saturating her, or whatever made her up now, and she realised she'd been in silence for so long.

The classroom door swung open, and she disappeared. The young teacher that walked in blinked. Even if she saw the figure that vanished as soon as her eyes fell on her, she wouldn't recognise it for the little girl she saw in assemblies and presentations, face plastered all over the walls at school, giving the building its own face, its own identity.

It took her a minute to find herself, and her name, in the memorial gardens. Her name was carved in small, delicate print, on the side of a large marble block, crowded on all sides by other names. Two numbers accompanied each name, the first being their age when the mission began, and the second being their age at the time of their assumed death. She gazed in wonder at the shallow-carved "19" beside her name. Blatant lie, but who would know? The sound of car horns awoke her to the surroundings. The garden was not a garden at all, merely a small patch of grass encased in knee-high wrought-iron fencing.

A plastic wreath leaned against the monolith. This was New York, she recognised, outside the building where she had worn a suit for the first time, only to sign her name on a document ensuring her silence for the foreseeable future. She never wore the suit again. Above all their names, at the top of the stone, on every side was inscribed in large print "Fallen Stars." A car honked again, and she was gone.

Layla's garden (she had claimed the compound garden, long ago, without realising,) had grown. It spread, roots curling into every crack and crevice they could find until every inch of the compound was protected by a shield of flowers, most of which she couldn't name, but could write a mile of poetry for each petal, and the way they looked in the light of the moon, and sunrise and sunset, and how they seemed to belong to totally different flowers in each light.

Her name was written everywhere on these walls. In every thorn that pierced a curtain or thin plastic mattress, and in every bud that flowered under the rays of sun that flooded through a smashed window. Her face was painted on the carpet of leaves and shrivelled petals that gathered over the brief period of abandonment. The compound had all become her garden.

She walked (because she could walk again) through her garden, and cleared a path in the roses before collapsing the roof. She shrugged away from the brambles as the remaining glass shrunk out of any frame that was left, falling invisibly to the floor and exploding into shards of ice that slid across the concrete, the colour of which she could remember, but not place in this new garden.

She wandered down a hallway she remembered. Phantom tears, fake even then, warmed her cheeks, and the door didn't need a key anymore. An apple tree grey in front of the wall, but the painted symbols were still there, faded slightly but readable.

So, she had been correct.

She had a lot of work to do. Her garden had missed her, grew in every direction, searching the earth for her hand, the hand that gripped the wet grass and dug its fingers into the moving soil. It searched for her for eleven years. Now it was complicit, and so was she. They clung to each other, like old friends.

"Layla." They sang, poetised her name, and she recognised the voice, but from where, she couldn't place. It was the voice of an old friend, whose name she had spoken many a time, and would continue to follow her even in death. She was fine not knowing. The flowers would tell her one day, after learning their verdant names one by one.

Opening her eyes would no longer reveal a red sky veiled by clouds of longing – for a home she didn't know the name of. The sky was once more the familiar blue, the blush of sunrise indicating the return of life to the great blanket she had been trapped under.

She was free. She was home.

## Chapter 7

# CALLING HOME

Oliver hadn't moved from his spot overlooking the crater, though the sun had set hours ago, and tents and caravans were being hoisted up around him. His feet were firmly planted in the ground and the crowbar hung loosely by his thigh. The night breeze sent grains of sand skirting past his heels and cascading down the edge of the crater. Horace watched him intently.

"He's planning something," he said to Marta as they cleared her 'room' of the clutter she had left on her first night. They wouldn't find a use for most of these items aside from nostalgia, and everyone was told to pack lightly. She was shovelling wood chips out of a corner with her hands, but nodded in acknowledgement. "When we go down, I want you to keep an eye on him."

"Will we wait for everyone to sleep?"

"No," Horace answered, a grim look befalling him as Oliver began pacing the edge of the crater. "Nobody's sleeping tonight." Parties of explorers had already formed, and made a beeline for the nearest cavern. Torches in hand and whatever tools of destruction they could find in the other, their only thought was of casting their eyes on an alien before they went home. "We won't stand out."

Oliver's arms, back and legs held straight, as if measuring himself up to someone who wasn't there. As if he wasn't, just hours ago, collapsed and gasping in a chair. His knees almost gave out when he saw a herd of people making their way toward him.

"Do you think you are a good person?" Every pair of eyes flashed the question as they smiled and walked past.

He wanted to snap back at their silent faces. "You'd all be dead if I was." He wanted to cry, to beg for forgiveness, but words failed him. What was he really repenting? If he told them all the truth, would they even bat an eye, or tear him apart, cut his bones to splinters where he stood?

They wanted Dante, the man who didn't lie, unless it was to everyone else. The man whose hair was naturally coal-black, whose blush was a sign of life, nothing otherwise. He would have to be Dante for a few more days. Dante from the city and nowhere else.

He watched the lights disappear into the caves, every so often one would peek out and seek out his silhouette on the rim, watching for wordless approval, motionless contentment. What would they do without him? He wondered the same, kicking a pebble into the ravine and watching it roll noiselessly through the dusty hillside, tracing his long shadow cast by the cold headlights of a truck still running, the warm beams reaching into the dark like talons.

Another shadow joined his, and his eyes snapped open, heart jumping into the ravine.

Arms' length away, Horace was standing, wordless and breathless, staring into the dark void below, torch and toolbox in hand. Beside him, the redheaded woman stood frigid, casting him cold sideways glances. He wasn't ready for another confrontation, not yet, with his mind so occupied with the first.

"Nice evening for a walk. Wouldn't you say, Oliver?" He cringed at the mention of his real name, clearly resisting a glance around. If he didn't see them, they weren't really there, right?

Horace would have laughed if he wasn't dreading the next few minutes and what would become of him when he saw her face again. He knew it would never be the same as the last time he saw it. But even worse, it would never again have the light of life she left behind eleven years ago, that she was meant to get back along with everyone else.

The makeshift necklace around his throat reminded him of the unfairness of it all. But with more names in the box than Horace could count still walking at the campsite, maybe this was true fairness: death, indiscriminately. One could say, random. "Why her?" turned to "why not her?" and he shook the thought from his head, because he couldn't come up with an unbiased reason. He missed her. That was all that was on his mind.

With a sigh they both straightened up and Marta led the way down, skidding in places where the moonless night swallowed up the ground between streaky remnants of man-made light. It was like treading in a midnight ocean, where pitch black water engulfs your feet and threatens to pull you under.

Looking forward, the peaks of the rockets were barely visible against the backdrop of the sky that faded out in deep ocean hues of blue and black. Not far behind them, the white and yellow aura misted the top of the ravine's edge, drifting in and out with the sound of shifting wheels and engines. Horace didn't look back. His eyes didn't wander from the same spot, though drowned in darkness, until his feet were firm on flat ground.

Marta was scared.

To an untrained eye the scene could have been a momentary reminder of the skyline of a once-great city. Where the outline of the skyscrapers traced the darkened clouds that shifted behind their shadows, and endless emptiness rose up from the ground. But it could never be that way, there would have been too many lights, they would have drowned out the stars. Here, at least, there were still a freckled few behind the veil of clouds that seemed to linger permanently.

Putting more and more space between themselves and Dante, Marta could imagine herself walking through the streets of New York, where she didn't have to look up to feel the towering figures crowding around each other. She only saw the real thing once, but seeing this, she scolded herself for passing up the sight when she had it. Soon, she thought, I'll see the real thing again. And I'll just stand and watch.

Stand and watch. Easy to say, hard to commit to.

"Is he still watching?"

Marta glanced back up the lip of the crater, where an unstable silhouette was shrinking away into the hazy mist of light.

"He's walking away."

"Where?"

Squinting past the steady halo of light that glowed from her headlamp, she tracked the black silhouette as it shrank from the edge. "To his caravan."

"He has his own caravan?"

"I think it is shared with two others. I do not remember their names, but they helped me move out of the hospital car." She pictured the two, down in one of these caves, waiting to go home in the morning, looking for an alien in the meantime.

"What have they got in there?" Horace's oxygen tank fell to the ground with a thud. When she didn't answer, he glanced up at the top of the crater, following her line of sight. The top of the nearest one must have been Dante's because it was the one with the makeshift antenna on the roof. Horace answered his own question, while Marta struggled to find her breath. "He's using the radio."

"But... Everyone is already here."

"No, Marta, that's not it," Horace said, "He's finally alone with the radio. He's calling home."

*****

The door was closed, and so were the windows, but he had rolled up his thin blanket and patched up the cracks between the door and floor so nobody could even try to listen in. He also turned off his lights.

He wasn't hiding or anything, but privacy was hard to come by these days. At least, while everyone was out looking around, he could be alone. Just for a little while. Alone. Surely they couldn't hear his thoughts?

"Ambassador... Are you still there?" the tinny voice called out after a long silence.

"I just- I don't know where we went wrong. Where did we go wrong, sir? Did they tell you anything. Surely they must have told... where did we go wrong? Did they tell you anything? If anyone, they must have told you something-"

"Ambassador, please slow down-"

"Well, I suppose it might have been kept a secret. What isn't a secret nowadays, you know?" Oliver sighed, mask free, leaned against the cold backboard of the makeshift bunk bed in his caravan. "I suppose I was just calling ahead." The silence he was met with on the other end didn't urged him on. "Does anyone have any news about Frank?"

A murmur followed behind the headset. The new President was older, but Oliver didn't blame him. When they both spoke it was like they were trying to keep their voices from running away from them. He knew the President had questions, but Oliver had less time, and just a few, more pressing ones.

It was just his luck that a diplomatic tour was passing through, otherwise the shrill hiss of the unused radio would have gone unnoticed. The President was called in immediately, and with him a herd of staff, that now whispered among themselves the name of the very man Oliver hoped would answer.

"Anyone know Frank?"

"Is there, uh... a last name we can get, Ambassador?"

"It's Oliver. There's no need for that now. Not anymore, sir."

"Frank Oliver?"

Oliver sighed. He was growing impatient.

"Dr Frank Horn. My name is Oliver. Get me Dr Horn. He knows me." More silence followed. He was sick of silence. "Hello?" Radio silence.

"Be right with you Am- Oliver." Between silences there were coughs. It was well into the night, but every so often a headlamp would flash across the sky, and out of the corner of his eye, Oliver could pretend it was a lightning bolt that illuminated that cloud.

He wasn't allowed to use the telephone during storms, but who would he have called back then? Now he had the President on the other end, but given the circumstances, it was nothing to call home about just yet.

"Alright, sir, we might have who you want."

"Is he there?" It would be a miracle to find Frank still working after all those years. Nevertheless, wherever he could be found, Oliver had hope.

Just ask what to do. Frank always knows what to do. He always knew. I'll vouch for you, boy. Just find me. Why did it always come back to him, the only person he truly hated in the world, the only person that could save him, shield him?

More silence. Behind it, they were telling him what to say, feeding him lines. This one used to be an actor. How fitting.

"Ehh, no, but we know where he is." He cleared his throat. "But first, we want to ask you some questions first, if you don't mind."

Oliver sighed, glancing at the stationary oxygen level on his tank. His was the only caravan that was air-tight, so not even that could be an excuse for impatience.

"Sure."

A gleeful silence followed, then pens clicking. He could almost see them leaning forward, each with an earpiece, holding their breath. There must have been a camera in the room by now. He was becoming a specimen, a thing from the past, a faraway relic spouting documentable nonsense. At least someone was listening to what he had to say now, when it didn't matter anymore.

"Could you tell us where you are, for the record?"

He ran a hand over his eyes. "I already told you. I am in my caravan, on Mars, where I've been for eleven years. Where the last guy left us all to die. Now, did Denver say anything about me?"

"Can you state your full name, for the record?" Were they even listening to a word they were jotting down?

This interrogation was a waste of time, but if it meant Frank would be brought to him, he would comply. "My name is Oliver James Keen," he said, "Junior. My father is Oliver Senior, and my mother is Rachel Sheila Solomon." His mother's name on his lips was the first truly sweet thing he'd felt in over a decade. "You'll find them easily if they're still alive. But maybe you took care of that already."

Nobody interjected on his last comment. It would be edited out in before being broadcast anyway. They also avoided his question about Denver, which meant he made it back. Even worse, he made it back alive. They would have said something otherwise.

"Are you gonna tell me where Frank is, now?"

"After this last question. We are aware of this mission you are part of. It is also common knowledge that it terminated over a year ago. Hell, we pass the memorial with your name at the top, every morning and afternoon."

"Memorial? Seriously?"

"Of course, there ain't a person with a radio or television that doesn't know your name…" He heard more murmurs behind the President's words, "You're a hero."

Oliver's heart dropped. Sitting cross-legged listening to the static silence he heard the words he dreamed of earning his whole sorry life.

So…Denver held up his end. Maybe even sparing a few words to applaud Oliver's dedication, or whatever he could scrounge up between pitiful prose about honour or pride. His name was written in stone.

"Which brings us to our last question:" Someone shuffled the microphone closer to the President's mouth. "How… are you alive?"

He saw the pale beam of light cross the sky, following it through the narrow window as it trailed over a cloud. "You should know." He was met with more silence.

Of course they destroyed all the records: half a decade of training, body modifications, diets and medications to withstand the temperature, fatigue, gravity or whatnot. He wondered just how long they waited before doing so. Nobody wants to stare into the flames of their own failure, much less watch it spread.

"I've been wondering that for a while." He straightened up. "I'm not answering any more questions. Where's Frank?"

"Can you first answer-"

"No I can't."

The President stumbled over his words. "Of – of course. Give me that- no the… that one." The shuffling of paper sent static through Oliver's headset. "Misburg, Hanover." He heard the tell-tale bump of fingers snatching a microphone and another voice interjected. "Germany." The words were bit out of the air before the mic was set back down, forcefully.

"Well, send someone for him. I don't have all day." Oliver's cockiness escaped him. Perhaps it was the suspicion of being recorded that made his shaking leg cease. There were ears again listening to him, and urgency had to be dressed up again. He peered at the rockets outside. It would take weeks to repair all of them. Even if they could make enough space inside for half a dozen each, they would still need fuel-

"I think you misunderstood, Oliver. That is the location of the graveyard. Now, you said you are calling "in advance," can you elaborate-" Graveyard.

"Shut up."

"Excuse me?"

Shut up shut up shut up-

"Oliver? Are you there?" Suddenly the silence that replaced his name felt much sweeter, much kinder. Oliver. How unfitting it was now. He sensed the President gearing up for a new barrage of questions.

"Be quiet, damn you!" Oliver snapped, and they obeyed.

The graveyard? His lips formed the words noiselessly. Mumbles on the other end filled his ears with cotton that shuffled into his brain, blotting out the words he couldn't come to say out loud. He's dead?

"How did... How did he..?"

A tentative voice read aloud: "Dr Horn was dispatched after the mission was terminated. He... went looking for his two children."

"His children..."

"A girl and a boy. Well, when he found them, he... couldn't take the guilt."

Where are you Oliver? Why don't you cry anymore?

"He was buried near to his wife, if it brings you any comfort."

It's over.

Dante gripped the sides of the radio on his lap. He spoke with fire in his voice. "We're coming back. All of us. We're all coming home. We found the rockets and we're going to fix them." He was burning himself more than the others, manifesting the smoke in his chest into the air, and yet a wide smile was stretched across his cheeks. He felt the fever blush spread to his temples. "I'm not a hero yet, so scrub my name off that damn memorial." His fingers were pressed white into the sides of the box.

"I'll prove us all right, and be the hero. But I'll live. Ha! - I'll live to tell it myself." He grinned at the uncomfortable silence on the other end. For the first time, he had the upper hand, and Dante was the louder voice. He was being heard, and he could have bet his life that the cameras and microphones were hurriedly shut off, but now after his promise, his life was something to preserve.

Against his will, Dante started to laugh. "You made me want to die for heroism. Now you force it on me, watch me earn it. I'm bringing everyone home." Watch me.

It was the sort of uncontrollable laugh that overcame him, one that hurt but didn't forfeit to empty lungs, only urging more air out, more noise. The kind that stretches the skin taut over ribs, heaving chest, that rattles with every fresh bout that booms in the ears. Hot tears glued his eyelids together.

He laughed because he remembered that last page.

The laugh had bloomed in his throat and spread like wildfire. In mere moments it reached its natural end, but each spasm of the chest or deep inhale sent electric tremors down to his fingertips, that still clutched at his chest, shirt balled up under a curled fist though the pain had come and gone.

"Oliver?" His smile dropped.

A darkness fell over his eyes, a numbness over his bones. Complete silence flooded the air and he lost control. His hands flew to his ears as he recognised the voice that uttered his old name through cigar smoke and nightfall. It was the voice of reason and the voice that lied all in one fell swoop, speaking his name. Which name is the lie, now? How could he forget that voice, resurrected after a peaceful decade by the daughter?

No, he couldn't do Marta the injustice of such a comparison. But now he knew they both saw him within the other. Now he was dead maybe they could even be friends, if she would allow it.

No. Marta was nothing like her father other than in voice.

"Oliver?"

Whether it was the President or one of his gang that muttered his name, he would never know. From his lap fell the heavy machine, to the floor between his boots. When Oliver opened his eyes the screen was still lit up, but a swift kick with his steel-toed boots remedied that in an instant. Feedback cut through his skull, and his hands blindly found the headset, flinging it across the small space. It hit the door and fell, the force having snapped it in half and ripped the cable before it even reached the ground.

He had just caught his breath when he wished he would find the laughter again. Where it came from, he didn't know, but it had been a long time coming. The caged animal had had its time on stage. Oliver had taken his final bow.

He had to get out of here.

He lifted his head from the cold headboard, sure that his convulsions had pressed bruises to his soot-stained scalp, but it was a small relief to lift the pressure and don once more the loathed oxygen tank.

But the weight of it on his back was welcome, if only for the first and last time, as he ventured into the crater once more, crowbar in hand.

He had no headlamp, but something guided him through the darkness. His feet fell heavy on the floor of the ravine, as if the very ground was lighter than his body. With each step the next one might land into thin air, and he would float away. Wouldn't that be ideal? Then he could really look the superhero part. As he stumbled in the darkness he listed in his head the names of all flightless superheroes he could remember.

Someone grabbed his shoulder. His eyes flung open, invaded by a blare of white light. How long had he been walking blind? The rockets were still fully visible in the starlight. "Dante, are you alright?"

I am Dante. Dante the saviour. The rescuer. There is no going back. Oliver is no more.

"Of course."

Dante, the hero, walking to earn it.

He flashed a curt smile, which was greedily received. That was what they really wanted when they saw him. That smile. It was what they worked for, lived for, the only reason he was to be trusted. If only they knew he was about to save them all. A simple smile will never compare with that.

But what if they already knew? What if their looks turned sour as soon as he turned away? He peered into the eyes of the man who'd awoken him. Angus Unstrum, 39, Cardiographer, what did he know? The eyes were the window to the soul, or so it went. They know nothing. But Marta did. Marta found out, only because she went looking. She knew, and nothing stopped her from telling them all. In fact, the opposite was true. Everything pointed her to knock him down, and kick him before he could get back.

They were all playing with him, toying with him, poking and prodding. Some twisted game. Don't play with your food. They were all waiting to pounce, counting the seconds until he let his guard down. If only they knew.

"No aliens yet. Maybe it's for the best."

"From the boy's descriptions, perhaps." Oliver pretended to shake off a shiver from his spine. "The night's young. Maybe they're nocturnal. Maybe we're early." Why are you still talking? Don't you see they need you to-

"Are you sure you're okay? It looked like you were walking with your eyes closed." Angus squinted, "Are you getting enough sleep?"

"Don't worry about me. You should get some rest." He nodded towards the biggest rocket. "Big day tomorrow."

The fellow's head bobbed in agreement, then they both spotted the two newest members of their mismatched group. Don't let them scare you. Despite this, he found himself speechless, just watching them, unsure really why he was marching toward them in the first place.

Angus was the first to speak up. "Has he really been alone for nine years?" Dante couldn't find it in himself to enlighten the man on what would be found inside the shuttle the pair were struggling to open. Encased in metal and darkness, a victim he was too late to save. He won't make that mistake again. "How did he not notice us following him?" An electric sting reached his neck.

"Well, he didn't have the expert help I did." He dug his elbow playfully into the fellow's ribs, a solicitation. Instead of laughter came a yawn.

"I'll round up the troops. You should get some rest, too. And get out of this crater." You aren't special to the ones at home. You are a number to them. Not me. I'll save you. I'll be your hero. He looked around at the caverns which spewed forth orbs of light that spun until they locked on Dante. "I wouldn't want to get trapped down here any night, but if those things come out..."

"Don't worry about them. Did you check the fuel?"

Angus nodded. "More than enough, but we should get a move on first thing tomorrow." He looked nervous at this, even in near darkness, so Dante made himself inviting, a confidante, the warmth of his wool-lined jacket always giving him broader shoulders that made him look stronger than he was. A hero.

"The- the food supply is getting pretty low." Angus's gaze fell to the American flag patch on Dante's jacket sleeve.

"Did you have dinner with the rest?"

Angus shrugged, "I gave mine to Faith. She skipped yesterday, so..."

Dante shook his head. "Nobody skips anymore. We'll get this all over with quickly." He thought for a second. "I'll be too busy tomorrow, so you should have my lunch now. Can't let it go to waste." Angus nodded. Dante held on to his arm as he was trying to leave, and looked into the glimmer of his eye. See me. "You'll see your daughter soon enough. Don't you worry."

Angus smiled, and with a slap of camaraderie to the shoulder, he was gone into the darkness behind him. Dante was alone again, walking. Alone again, thinking, like he used to do when talking was pointless or worse. Thinking never got him anywhere.

Actions are listened to.

You'll never make it back in time. They don't expect you to. You're a passing fancy of the worst kind. Once they find you out, they'll want to kill you.

"Shut up."

"What did you say?" Horace was backing away, though Dante barely regained consciousness when he was at arms' length from him. Marta emerged from behind, placing herself firmly between the two men, making a shield of herself. The light from the night sky turned her skin the colour of cold steel. The colour of the rocket. Her hair was a copper mane, not the neatly brushed bun that the nurse had spent delicate minutes combing back. Helena Mezzo, 44, Nurse. You're not a number anymore. Not to me.

He suddenly became aware of the trailing weight. He had walked all this way in the darkness, crowbar in hand, with God knows what expression on his face. They were right to cower when he approached. Dante's arm slackened, the metal hook touching his heel.

"Need any help?"

# PART 3

# SERENITY

Chapter 1

## ANY MEANS NECESSARY

They had been trying the entire time, to no avail, to pry open the door with their hands and whatever tools they could find around the makeshift campground. Turned out that Dante had disappeared with the only crowbar on the planet.

To spare Horace's already battered fingers, Marta sacrificed her own tidily filed and buffed nails, but by the time they had all been chipped and split, the door hadn't budged, still fastened closed by the rubber piping of the oxygen tank that hung out of it.

"We don't need your help." She made a fist, partly for intimidation, but also to apply pressure to her sore fingers.

Horace tugged at her elbow from behind her and she reluctantly broke his numb and sleepy gaze. Without speaking a word, Horace conveyed the many hours they could save by accepting the help of his strength and tool he offered. He made to step toward him, but Marta followed his advance, remaining fixed between the two men.

"We'd appreciate it, but-" the old man caught himself mid-sentence, unsure how to end it on a sensitive note. "You know what's on the other side, right?" Maybe he was asking himself the same thing.

Dante nodded, picking up the helmet from the floor that had cast long shadows from its white light. He reached out to Marta, helmet in outstretched hand. She took it without breaking her stare.

She hates you.

Dante didn't blame her.

Change her mind. She doesn't hate all of you; only the part of you that makes her remember him.

Dante turned to face the door.

You can't see them, is that wise?

He lifted the hooked end of the crowbar to his free hand and, in the darkness of his own shadow, found the tip, lodging it halfway up the metal hatch, about elbow-height. He tossed his shoulders back, feigning some type of strong form.

Suddenly he felt so foolish, like he was trying to impress an audience that wouldn't bat an eye at such a display.

His fingers tightened around the dark metal, knuckles turning white, looking blue in the darkness. Blue as death. He started to push from his elbows, then his shoulders, shifting one leg back and leaving a long smear in the earth where his foot slid.

It didn't give.

Stop pretending.

His shoulders fell, and as they did the jacket shifted loosely down his elbows. Knees slackened, fingers loosened and re-arranged around the handle. The foot came back and the other slid forward, knee held tight against the surface just outside the edge of the door.

He pulled from his upper back this time, feeling the tendons shift beneath his oxygen tank and jacket, shoulder-blades rearranging to make space, make movement. Strain and release.

A muffled groan erupted from below his wrists and the door gave in to his pressure. He let the breath out through his mouth and let his body relax. The cloth of his trousers had caught the door before it swung open, and he held it as the knee fell to the floor.

Look inside. You know you want to.

He dropped the crowbar, and it jumped a step back toward Marta. She could feel it throw dust onto her shoe, but still held the helmet with both hands, the elbow she had reached out as a barrier between the two men came back towards her body as she stepped over the hooked metal, eyes fixed not on Dante but the cavern he had just uncovered.

With newly free fingers, Dante gripped the edge of the door as if some invisible force would snatch it back and lock it better this time. At his feet, the loose tubing slid out under its own weight, falling limp like a dead snake, its head, the silicone mask, burying itself in the shallow dust layer. Already, some dust was whisked into it, like it had been coughed out.

The edges of the mask looked black in the darkness. Dante didn't need to disguise a grotesque shiver. He was prepared for blood as soon as he stepped over the edge of the ravine's wall.

Taking a silent breath, he urged his stationary arm to pull back, to uncover the treasures this rocket has to offer.

When he opened his eyes, another pair was staring back. His body went cold.

"Wha-"

He stumbled back, stepping over the rubber tubes, but not loosening his grip on the door. It swung open and out of his hands as he came away. At first only one step, but the force of something cold, something airy, pushed him and kept him going until the top of his body was leant back, while his legs were stuck in the same footprint.

Marta held the helmet still as he fell backwards, into the dust, and as he hit the ground she cast white light into the guts of the rocket.

It was empty.

"What did you see?" Horace pushed forward through Marta, making the light sway slightly, but she held her stance. It was difficult to see, but the inside of the rocket was not all metal and wires and buttons, as she expected. Glimmers of black made themselves known when the light had swayed, illuminating dozens of painted symbols – all the same – in the same slick black paint.

Among them, a single white eye blinked with the swaying lamplight. She focused on that, so that her eyes wouldn't fall on the shadowy figure curled up beneath it.

"Blood."

Horace stopped halfway to the mouth of the rocket, and cast a look back, then proceeded. He could see inside, where Dante hadn't had the time to let his eyes wander. He watched as Horace stepped around him, blocking his view.

The taller man's forehead met the cold metal above the door as his head slumped forward. The night was silent for a long time after that. Here she was. Arms limp by his sides, Horace came face to face with his worst fear. And there was nothing to be done. Here she was.

Here she was and yet he missed her. His shoulders rose and fell in a dry sob, hands feeling heavier, reaching lower and lower to his knees. He knelt beside the door for the first time since he had let a prayer escape his lips. Now he was silent.

Dante watched the giant crumble to the ground, shrouded in darkness, and wondered if what he had seen was real. A trick of the weak light could be to blame, but the eyes felt so real. They looked at him with such disappointment, like they were cast upon the wrong person.

A dragging of feet signalled Marta approaching from behind and Dante regained the strength to rise again. He got the feeling she wouldn't have lent a hand even if they were free. Marta was still liking in, past Horace's shoulders. She stepped closer.

With the reminder of his audience, Horace straightened. Without looking back he spoke:

"Did you see her? When you looked in?" Horace's knee bent and he knelt beside the open door as if in prayer, like the last time he was here. "Is that why you jumped back?"

His mind was still winding around what he had just seen, and any words he could conjure up got tangled on his tongue. He thought about the day that would follow. It would all be so complicated if he had this much more to think about. No distractions.

 Lips sealed shut, he stayed silent.

He shook his head. It was better than saying nothing, for now.

Never be silent again.

Oliver would have let himself be silent. Dante had a voice now. He was going to use it.

The eyes.

When Marta reached the opening, Dante saw her shoulders tense up, but Horace recoiled from the light and waved her away, like he couldn't stand to see what he held in his hands. Like it was better the horror be obscured by night than bleaching in the sun's cold mimicry. She pointed the light instead at the bloody symbols on the walls. From behind Marta, Dante could see them, but not what Horace was looking at.

"Just give me a moment with her. Leave the light."

Marta backed away, signalling for Dante to do the same, and as he did he took note of the peculiar symbols, written in blood and fingerprints. The desperate scrawls of the last seconds of another person's life.

There were many secrets he wasn't allowed in on, throughout his whole life. Even days before the mission, the other ambassadors were speaking in codes and words he'd never heard, referencing people and events that, to him, never existed.

There was a code, painted on a wall, that he wasn't meant to have seen. He had a key. It wasn't his own, but he had it then, and that was all he remembered. He used it where he wasn't meant to go, where the other ambassadors often went. The Engine Room.

A wide concrete chamber shaped like a dome, from which many exciting sounds could be heard around the compound. Sometimes, other diplomats would be brought around, and shown into this room, but never anyone who would be on the mission. Never Oliver.

So he made his own way in. There was a tour going around at the time, down on the floor of the dome, several feet below from where Oliver entered, and stood on a metal platform. Frank was working, or pretending to work, when one of the suited men approached him.

For a brief moment, he looked up at Oliver, like he knew he would be there, watching. Watch this, he seemed to be saying. He watched Frank show off, go into what he called "professional mode" where he used big words that often meant nothing, partly to look smart, which he was, and partly to avoid all the really important details. "The things that ordinary people don't need to know, or wouldn't understand anyway." Frank saw diplomats as ordinary people.

That was when Oliver saw her.

One of the so-called ordinary people, who were going on the mission, who shouldn't have been in The Engine Room. But neither should he, so he said nothing again. She had come in through the lower entrance, and was looking up at the wall of the dome, where there was a grid of symbol pained on the curved grey surface.

He looked back down. Frank's tour was approaching her. He wanted to shout, and warn her, but that would give everyone away. Frank stopped just out of her sight, but they could now both hear him.

"...will ensure the mission will be long and prosperous. It's a safety measure above all." The diplomats all nodded wisely, and Oliver watched the girl shrink back through the door she emerged from. "The last thing we'll need is bad publicity." The crowd that was following suddenly halted, and each stole a knowing glance at each other. Frank was none the wiser, but Oliver saw. From where he was, he could see everything, including the painted words beside each symbol.

Why couldn't Dante remember what Oliver saw?

The only other person he could have asked was dead and cold beneath the watchful eye of the secret of both their trespasses.

It was a ghost.

No - it was just the hallucination of a tired and overwhelmed and out of breath person who shouldn't be exerting himself as much as he did. Yeah, that was it. It was the plague of memories shared, unspoken. It was a ghost. You saw it.

"I didn't see anything."

"I didn't ask." Marta had overtaken him and spoke back at him.

"Sorry."

"Why do you say this?" She stopped again and he almost stumbled into her back. She spun around; soft wisps of her wild hair ticked the underside of his chin. "You don't mean it, or anything." She realised how close she was to him, and stepped away, almost in disgust. Her eyes flashed to his jacket and back up again.

"What do you mean?" Dante tried not to take offence at the gesture.

"I hear you and I hear him. You can say sorry a thousand times and I will not listen a thousand times."

"I hear him in you as well."

They were at a standstill, a stalemate, steps apart, but separated from each-other only by the empty air, and while they were almost the same height, she commanded the very night that blanketed them.

The resemblance really was uncanny. It was painful even to look her in the eyes.

"I won't listen to you." But Marta didn't turn away.

"Then don't listen to 'sorry,' but please listen. I am not him. You hate me for the same reason I do because I let him lie to me. Loneliness made me ignorant." Marta was trying her hardest not to listen, or to pretend not to understand. "Now I see whatever friendship I thought I found was fake." His gaze fell, as if a decade of shame had just been exposed before her. "I let him use me, thinking I had a guardian, I even almost enabled his legacy. He occupied my mind because it was hollow. I don't blame you for seeing him in me, maybe part of him is still there-"

"Is there?" There were few times that Dante knew someone was on the proverbial warpath. After the man in the suit visited his home for the first time, everywhere his mother looked, she glared as if she was trying to start a fire with her eyes. She dug at her garden for hours on end, and he watched from the back door, how her elbow arched before plunging into the black underground. She was confined, in a sense, to the order that she wanted in life, that she couldn't have. Chasing an endless goal of perfection, she burned herself up inside. "Is there?"

Marta was on the warpath, but her eyes, which found kindling in Dante's own, weren't trying to burn him. They were searching for the remainder of their common villain. Dante looked for him as well.

"No," he spoke at last. "No, he's gone." Dead and buried. Misburg, Hanover.

Marta had already turned and continued walking. "Please stay." She stopped at arms' length, but he didn't dare reach out for her arm. That's what Frank would have done. "I will make everything better. I owe you- them as much." He tread around her carefully, as if any wrong shift of the dust beneath his feet would startle her like a wild animal. "You gave me a chance, let me carry it through to the end."

The flames in her eyes sparked a shiver down his spine. In the darkness she was still, but beneath that mask she breathed heavily, he could see the anger inside her little frame, threatening to boil over.

"We all have lost a lot. More than we thought we had, or could lose in a lifetime." He held out his hand, but she looked as if through his body. "Don't let me lose this last chance. Please." He tried to smile, but was unsure if she could see it behind his mask. It could have looked like he was squinting. "We won't even have to be friends. I just to deserve your forgiveness."

A gust of wind threatened to knock him over, but she stayed firm, finally meeting his eyes one final time. Her hand crawled its way up, and grasped his. "Forget that I was his daughter. Forget that you were his friend. Neither was ever true." There was the same firmness in her voice as in her feet, and in the handshake that left his fingers numb. She shook hands like a man, like the man Oliver used to pretend he was. The man Dante was going to be.

As she released his hand he was frozen. Over his shoulder he saw the figure illuminated by the light that swung from his hip. The helmet fastened to his belt flashed in their eyes with every step, and with every step he flashed a bit closer, like an old movie reel being shown frame by frame.

There was something shiny dangling from her neck.

Here came the giant. Here he came carrying the girl in his hands. Here came the father with the sleeping daughter, her head cradled, hair falling over her face. His back was straight, but his square shoulders slumped under her weight.

Marta met him in the middle, but as she approached she made a wide circle around the girl's legs, stumbling to unhook the light from his hip as they both moved. He muttered something to her, and she waved Dante over. "Here's your chance," she seemed to say, though her mouth was clamped shut.

Horace was walking faster, and as Dante approached and the light sat still in Marta's steady hands he saw how the old man's knees were buckling.

Go on. Take her.

"Take her, please." He gasped, his wild eyes straining at keeping her up, as if, now that his legs had stopped, his arms might give in as well. "Quickly."

Dante slid his hands under Horace's old ones, skin against skin, until her whole weight was resting on him. One hand under her back, one under both of her thin knees, he carried the girl to the edge of the ravine. Her head had lolled back, but he didn't look down. The glimmer at her neck dazzled as it caught flashes of light both from ahead and behind. Horace gasped and coughed against Marta's shoulder as they followed close behind, nearing the steep climb.

The coughing had roused from sleep those in the nearest caravans, or stirred from rest those on night watch, hoping to get a glimpse of any aliens that might decide to slip into view. They gathered around, watching from above, peering down with vulture eyes, waiting to snap him up at the first sign of weakness.

Marta's light stretched his shadow almost to the top of the hill, though it now danced with a dozen others. This one was the boldest, the darkest, reached furthest. His head could almost touch their feet, yet none thought to come down to help him.

This is a test. To see if you're real.

"I'm not real. Not in the way they think."

Then you better fake it well.

The more he walked, and the higher he climbed, the lighter she got. Was it only the sight of the giant struggling that added imaginary weight to the burden?

With more and more lights finding their ways into his eyes he wasn't once tempted to look down, not when a gust of wind blew her hair out of her sleeping face, and not when he got near enough to the top to hear their gasps and hushed remarks about "is that blood?" and, "she looks asleep, not dead," or "if it weren't for the blood, she would look so peaceful."

"Look at that scar."

Look at her.

He tipped his chin up as he made the last few strides to the top.

Look at her. She's so light.

Hands found his shoulders and pulled him over the top.

So light, but he couldn't carry her. He asked for your help.

He lost track of where the other two were behind him, having been swallowed up in a crowd of lights. Cheers and prescribed smiles and slaps on the back, but everyone kept clear of the body.

Look at her, his weakness.

He looked down.

You have nothing to be scared of. Look at her, the feeble thing, all scarred and dead, how she downed the giant without a breath of life within her. It's all a game, a play-act of strength.

"So am I."

You don't have one of these.

Where did these come from? These voices, their origins untraceable, echoing in his skull as if they were of his own creation. He ought to be careful. He checked himself, straightened up. Where Oliver allowed others' voices to fill gaps in his conscience, the space must be occupied by himself.

But this voice wasn't the same. It was his own. It was encouraging, guiding, like he finally held the reins of his own story.

You have what you've built all this time, and nobody ruin it.

"I don't deserve it yet."

You will. Soon.

Someone took the girl form his arms, but they stayed in place, hovering in the air as the rest of them crowded around her, mesmerised by the image of a sleep never to end. He wondered what they saw in the cold unmoving face, the marbled skin and closed eyes. For once he wasn't the centre of attention around them. The breaths captured just below his nose felt lighter. He felt invisible, and never more relaxed.

They wanted so bad to be as alive as she looked in death. He looked deeper into one of their faces. It was the same look they always gave to him.

"I know what I have to do now."

They will follow you.

Chapter 2

# LAST THREAD

True to his prediction, nobody was sleeping through this night.

Horace dusted off his hands in the semi-darkness, the helmet's beam illuminating his handiwork. He'd had to get Marta's help with calculating the Earth date, but other than that brief intermission, he'd done the job totally alone. As it all started.

Lucille "Layla" Monique Smithe
August 21$^{st}$, 1959
October 1$^{st}$, 1987

He'd thought for near an hour if he should inscribe a message into the brittle stone, found on the rim of the crater, far from the campsite. As he carved with the screwdriver, he felt eyes searching for him in the darkness, but not the eyes he wanted. There was a large space below the dates where he thought his words would fill it, where he could have carved some emotion into the emotionless stone, but it just stared back, a blank, flat void.

In a way, this was better. This was what Layla would have wanted. Blankness, she would have said, is more poetic than a scroll of rhymes. She always had something prepared like that.

God, how he missed her.

He felt like he should pray, if only to fill the silence, newly discomforting. He wanted to speak but had no words. No words to speak and none to carve on the desolate headstone that would likely be gone by next week's storm. It was the poetry that counted.

*****

It wasn't poetry anymore. She begged them to stop, or to say something else, but all they said was the same agonising name over and over to the full air, full of her name. "Layla."

"Who is this? Who's calling me? Tell me!"

Their sweet perfume turned sickly as it mingled with the sound. The sun wouldn't set. This was not her heaven, after all.

She couldn't sleep, she couldn't dream, no matter how she hated it before. Before what? Where was she? No matter how she fought, the roots wound and wound and never released her heart and lungs. She really was trapped, just waiting but not sure what for. Anchored to her life, death evaded her.

She used to feel her face, thumbing over the soft skin of her scar. She used to lick at the end of it that curved into her lip. Now there was nothing. She felt like nothing.

"Nothing can be made out of nothing," she remembered. "Speak again."

"What am I forgetting?" She beat at her head and felt nothing, but loosed a shower of petals from her hair. The scent taunted her nose and she cringed at the sugary cascade that snowed her vision.

She closed her eyes and shook the white blindness off.

It was cold.

There was someone else's breathing.

*****

Someone was behind him. He smiled. "Back so soon?" He laughed. "Gave me a fright."

"Sorry," she gasped, and found she could breathe. The vacuum where her lungs had been felt so… normal. Until now. Her voice sounded different, untainted by silicone obstacles. She spoke again, just to hear it. "I didn't mean to. Again."

Horace squared his shoulders. "Don't worry about it. Can't exactly blame you." They were silent for a long time. Layla not knowing what to say, and Horace not wanting this moment to pass. "Though it does mean I broke my promise." He had her again. Couldn't see her, or hold her, but he had her.

"Sorry."

Horace's head fell forward, but she could see the edge of a smile behind his wispy silver beard. "Oh, kid. What are we going to do now?"

"There's always something to do." She looked over his shoulder. "Is that…"

He nodded. "I don't have your way with words, but I remembered you saying something about blank spaces-"

"More poetic than a scroll of rhymes. You remembered that." It wasn't a question. She crept closer to read the words, but stopped when he recoiled. She realised she was colder to him than this world was to her, after so long in the sun. "Sorry." She sat down behind him.

The hair son his neck were raised. "Don't come too close. I might be tempted to look back."

"Am I Eurydice?"

"It would seem so." He said. "I think I understand now why my old headmaster drew those pictures for me."

"The ones on the glass?" He nodded again. "Why?"

"To get my attention. So he could be released. There must have been a nameplate or something in that room, holding him back. The last thread to this world, and he wanted me to sever it."

"That's why I'm here." The name in the stone. The name on the metal plate over his heart. She saw his shoulder move and then his hand holding it out. It glinted in the darkness. "Oh."

"This is your last thread. Just tell me when you want me to cut it."

"Not yet." She gasped. "Let's just… sit here a while."

"All right." His shoulders fell and the metal struck his chest. "Let's just talk."

Neither of them spoke. A gust of wind tossed Horace's hair to the side, and blew through his thinning clothes, but Layla felt none of it. "Are you cold?" He asked.

Layla thought for a second. The sensation of coldness she had initially felt had vanished, and she wondered if it was only the feeling of not belonging, of being out of place in this world that was left over.

"Layla?"

"I'm still here."

"Okay."

"No, I'm not cold."

"Okay."

What now? He was so close, but to reach out would mean the end of this – forever. So now they were both trapped. She looked around instead. There must be something on this infinite plane of existence she could do. Somewhere to go.

"I guess you believe in ghosts for real now," Horace said.

"Yeah, well... When you've seen enough death it's kinda hard to deny it. I only wish I could have been the one to tell the world." Horace stayed silent. To his right, the rockets' tired noses pointed to the absent stars like steeples. "I can see where I died." He turned his head into the ravine, and she moved left, only catching the corner of his eye.

"I... can't see. It's too dark." He blinked and squinted to no avail. The moonless nights were unforgiving to the lonely, he could remember as much from the war. Staring out and finding only void was effective in making the world feel infinitely small, and infinitely big all at once. A world saturated in blackness was a solitary one. "What else can you see?"

Layla was static, by her own choice. After locating the rocket, remembering how she tried so hard to remain, to find him... She wouldn't let herself leave so quickly. She turned in place and found she didn't need to move at all.

"I see... everything. I can see everything."

"Everything?"

"Yes, as if it's right in front of me. I see you and – and the man who released me."

"Oliver?"

"I don't think so. He's trying to sleep now, but I don't think he's having any luck. I can see everyone at the campsite. I can also see... I can see you but – but from before."

The void was closing in on Horace. He sensed his time was nearing an end. "How do you see me?"

"At the rocket, when I was trapped inside. You were… kneeling."

Horace closed his eyes, and from the darkness to the back of his eyelids there was hardly a difference.

"You were praying for me." It felt like an accusation.

"What else can you see?"

She looked far, across the planet, and found much of the same thing. "I can see everywhere we've been, and us as well."

"Can you look into the ground?"

She turned her eyes do the ground.

"Layla?"

"Yes."

"What do you see?"

"Do you remember the boy's letter?"

"Can you see the aliens?"

"I can see them leaving."

"What?" Horace wanted to jump up, but the darkness encased him like a cocoon.

"They're all retreating." She looked to the cluster of rockets once more. "I think they know what's coming."

"Oh, yeah." He gave a desperate half-laugh, like he was struggling to evoke anything. "I forgot about that."

"How could you forget?"

He pretended not to hear. "Tell me what else you see."

"Don't ignore me. Please." Horace bowed his head. It hurt to hear her like this. It hurt to remember her, and to have her so near without her being really there. "Please, I've had nothing else for so long." In the cold, the tear that was swelling in his eye felt scalding. "Don't let me go yet."

"Oh, how could I ever let you go?" He tossed his head to the stars. "Layla, you're the only person that has made me cry twice." The time was nearing. "From the start, it was just me, against one world. Then I found you, and it was us against this one. I broke my promise when I let you die, and I'm alone again but I'll never let you go."

"You need to get home. This is what we've been working to for over a decade. Don't let go of this."

"I never had a home, Layla, and to find one after I promised to bring you home wouldn't be… it wouldn't be f-fair, now would it?" He choked out those last words.

"Horace?"

"I have to let you go. Neither of us belong in this place."

"Horace, wait-" She stood up, frantically evading his gaze, but the pull had begun again. She counted the seconds she had left. She wasn't ready to leave him again, so much of what was on her mind would remain there – and what of the warning? Surely they must have seen it. She put both her hands on his shoulders.

"Let's stay here. It doesn't have to end yet, we – we have the rest of the night!" The laugh she forced out came out in a sob. Her hands couldn't feel the cloth of his clothes. "We can just talk… think of the memories we've made."

"Thanks, kid. For the memories. For everything. We'll have plenty of time to talk about them soon enough."

She bent her head down, and her head connected with the back of his neck. "Don't leave me here alone again. Please, you're my only friend."

"You won't be alone," Horace said, and this time he would keep the promise. "You'll never be alone again." The tear that rolled down his cheek burned a path in it and got lost in the prickly hairs of his beard, but he had already turned around. It was too late to care.

*****

It was warm again. And bright. And silent, for the first time.

Chapter 3
---

# THE BRIGHTEST SUNRISE YET

How ironic that a hospital car would be Horace's last glimpse of what life on Earth used to be. Here he was again, dead friends and dried tears on a hospital bed. At least this time he could breathe clearly. He felt the end nearing either way, but just like all those years ago, he hated it would have to be in a bed. Dying in sleep was not the most artistic way to go out, but he figured it was the lucky way.

Nonetheless, there would be no sleep for him, and he wasn't trying, but he could tell Marta was: tossing and turning her red curls on the bed she had carried in from her own caravan. Elbows dug into the thin mattress, bumping the floor through layers of fluff. "No luck?" he asked.

She flailed one last time and laid face up. "No." She answered, defeated. "You?" They had been checking in on each-other like this since Horace came in by himself a few hours ago. Marta could tell without asking that he knew his time was nearing an end. Maybe that was why she wanted to be here with him. The darkness alone on this last night was surely worse than darkness with someone else. At least she wouldn't be talking to herself.

Plus, it wasn't like he was wheezing at every word. Tired, of course, but clear, was their conversation, every time they decided to begin one. Meaningless little snippets of them, but they filled time and space and were a welcome change form the endless hum of shifting engines outside. Yes, nobody was sleeping that night.

"Stopped trying." The buzz of chatter from the people outside reminded him of the city. He couldn't tell which city. It couldn't be New York. There were not nearly enough motors or yells, or elevators whirring on the other side of the Hospital building. The loud ding chasing you down the packed hallways, the nurses chattering over coffees in the next room. A baby crying somewhere. Everyone unsure whether to rejoice or mourn tonight.

"Did you... let her go?"

Horace opened his eyes, expecting more darkness, but the flicker of white lights on the walls from outside were a cruel reminder of where he was. Where he would never leave.

"I did."

To see the moon again – what an idea!

"Do you want to talk about her?"

He smiled at the ceiling. "How did you know?"

"You only had each-other for a long time. It is hard to talk about someone to themselves. You must have a lot of memories together."

"Are you the same? With your brother I mean. Do you have a lot of memories?"

He heard her shuffle below. "No." He tried to decode her tone. "We didn't talk a lot. You and Layla managed a life here. We just survived." She buried her shoulders under this thin blanket. "He was always so far away, even when he was right next to me."

Horace's cold hands were folded as if in prayer. If he did live then, it was because of Layla and his duty to her.

But it was more than just duty, wasn't it? There were real memories, real emotions that came out of it. There was no point denying it. He thought for the last decade that he was there to watch over her, to keep her alive. The truth was that she was doing the same thing even if she didn't realise.

She would have called it a dynamic, but there was nothing dynamic about it. They lived. They were happy.

"If I start talking, I couldn't stop 'til I was dead."

"How about until you sleep instead?"

"Wouldn't know where to start." He felt something prick the corners of his eyes. It might have been fatigue because he was all out of tears.

"Start at the end."

An explosion of noise, both from himself and from the storm hurtling around him, invaded his memory. "The end?"

He could still feel the warm blood drying on his fingernails as he drove away, Layla and the wind behind him. In his mind he imagined the Earth's Moon shedding light on his path as he drove, but the artificial was all that he could afford. He wondered where the photographs he had taken all those years ago ended up. Layla must have been in at least one.

"How did you do it?" Marta asked in a hush. "Let her go. Was it easy?"

A Moon that followed him everywhere he went on Earth. He was never really alone there. The Moon that frosted every dewy rose in cool light. The folds of the petals impossibly beautiful in their icy fabrications. When he lost the Moon he found her, then he was never alone again.

"I have never felt such pain." His eyes remained dry, but still stung. "Imagine letting go of the Moon, or the stars, or to joy itself." He turned on his back, his bony shoulder blades piercing the pillow. "It's unfathomable until it happens, whether you want it to, or not. So it's better to do it in your own time, otherwise you forget, which is worse." He was quieter now, and Marta thought he was falling asleep, or worse. She turned over, unsure what now to do, when he startled her by speaking again.

"You remind me of her," Horace said. "So quiet."

Finally, they were reaching the point she wanted, the conversation she knew he wanted to have, but was too locked up with grief to initiate. It burned up like sparks waiting for kindling. But she never expected that comparison. She was again speechless.

Horace laughed, and Marta thought it was at her.

"Of course, that didn't last long." He was lost in memory. "The first few weeks at the compound, you could hardly get a word in, no matter who you talked to, and no matter how many times the same conversations were repeated. Everyone wanted to talk about themselves, to as many people as possible.

Obviously, nobody considered they might have the next eleven years to get to know each other."

These pauses he was having were getting more frequent, and longer. A coldness brewed between each phrase, like he was piecing together fragments of a memory that kept derailing.

"Layla was always on the edges of these conversations. Sat far away at tables or meetings. I saw her observing, but never taking the step through the door. Honestly, I was starting to hate everyone, before I even heard them speak, but she looked so lost, so tired. I heard footsteps outside in the hallways at night and found her. I thought she was sleepwalking…"

Marta had only ever known her dead, but she could imagine the young girl, unscarred and colourful, pacing the cold compound floor in government-issue pyjamas, barefoot. It was something she'd done on countless nights.

"I showed her the way to the gardens…" Here he trailed off. Marta knew why he hesitated to share this memory, torn between preserving it or preserving a part of himself that was buried deep in it. "We became good friends soon enough, and even sooner she stopped being so quiet." Marta heard the smile on his lips through his words.

"When you're alone for so long, you become quiet, because there's nobody to talk to. And when you've got nobody, you forget yourself."

Marta brought one hand up to her hair, and combed the dry curls in the dark. "You miss her?"

"I do now. It didn't feel real to me until now. When she fell quiet for the last time, all I could think of was how, eleven years ago, I found her like that – sleepless, quiet. And I was losing her the same way."

He sniffed loudly. Marta imagined him holding back tears, but she knew it had already been too long a night for there to be any tears remaining.

"Soon enough, though, I'll join her. I'm lucky like that. We won't be apart for so long, unlike most others. I've always been lucky, haven't I…?" She let him drift off, leaving her adrift in the silence that grew between them, but it didn't linger, as he suddenly sat up on his elbows, casting a dark shadow over Marta's half-closed eyelids. They snapped open.

"You'll have to swear to me, before I go, you'll never forget." His tone alone was sobering: it channelled an urgency akin to nightfall, like something – an unsure something – impending, that she would have to face alone. It was sobering against the unrelenting drowsiness that wouldn't give in to sleep. She was fully awake again, mind racing to catch up with his words.

"What if you do want to?" She asked. "What if… I wanted to let go, and forget?"

Horace fell back on the hard mattress. It almost knocked the air from his chest. The ceiling stared at them both. "Is this about your bother again?"

"No, not Markus." The silence turned the air icy. "We parted ways long before he died."

"If not Markus… then, him?"

She folded her hands over her chest, tensing fingers into fists under each elbow. "Maybe."

"I thought you hated him?"

"I do hate him. But I never got to let him go. He left when I was so young. He was only… an idea. A ghost." She remembered her mother's scolds as the edges of the picture darkened into the flames. "I grew up thinking I was a rebel for missing him. It was forbidden. He was a monster."

"You were just a child."

"He was just a soldier. Just a man." She sighed. "When he wasn't there, I built him in my head. Then there was more of the fake than the real."

Horace remembered an idea from over a decade ago: the promise of a new life, new beginnings, no attachments, or debts – escape. This was the one dream that nobody wrote on a poster, or in a contract or certificate, but it was universal. Over time the idea faded for everyone. Marta was severing the last tie on the eve of her return.

"You must have been so disappointed."

"There is no word for what I felt." She turned away from him. "Unfathomable, like you said. But Oliver had him for longer than I did. He thought he had a friend."

"Do you feel sorry for him?" Outside, someone slammed a door. There was momentary silence that broke the illusion again.

"To lose a friend... it is worse than losing a father. His pain is greater than mine." Her hand flexed under her pillow. She told him to forget. Not a father, but a friend. They shook hands over it, and she became a hypocrite, telling someone to do the very thing she couldn't. "Oliver has lost himself."

"Do you hear that?" They listened closely, letting the night wrap around them, with its ambiance. The outside was louder, but they didn't let it in. A door slammed, then nothing else. Within seconds it was as if nothing happened, and they were back in only each-other's company.

"I think I was wrong about him."

"Yeah?"

"What you said, about being alone, living quietly." Marta felt this night had changed a lot in her. "It hasn't been quiet since I got here. And I don't think it has for anyone else."

"You're saying Oliver actually saved these people?"

"All I'm saying is... I'm glad I was found. I'm glad everyone found each-other. Through him."

"You found me," Horace said.

There were voices again, calling out. All calling out the same. Dante!

"What's happening?" Horace pushed himself off of his bed with newfound vigour, and stood between Marta and the glass double doors. A shadow approached – quickly.

Oliver hoisted his sleepless body up the shallow steps and through both of the doors in the blink of an eye, leaving both doors swinging behind him. He was maskless, and huffing, full-chested, the glimmering pearls of sweat trailing his pale brow, that gleamed deep blue like inky bruises smearing his complexion.

"Medicine." He gasped.

Marta sprung from her bed. "Door," she said, pointing behind him. Horace backed away to give her room. As if pulled from a daze, Oliver spun around and closed the two doors, shielding them from earshot of the dozen or so people that had followed him. Their lights illuminating Marta's desperate fingers flicking through vial after vial. She grasped one and pulled it form the shelf. "Is this-"

"Brown. Yes." Oliver's cold and trembling hands enveloped hers as she pulled the stopper. He'd never looked so cold. She realised he wasn't wearing his jacket.

He guided her hands to his dry lips, and she eased him into the same chair as before as he choked the medicine down, holding his nose with his free hand. "Where is your jacket?"

Horace slid past them and pulled the curtain over the inner door, muffling the only light source, but sensing Oliver wouldn't want to be seen in this compromising state. It was enough of a risk to wander across the camp without a tank. He really must have been desperate.

Oliver released his nostrils and gasped for air. "Thank you." They let him catch his breath before speaking. "I threw it out. I couldn't look at it."

Horace squinted to look at his face. Were his red eyes a sign of strain or sleeplessness?

"Have you slept?"

"Tried." He coughed into his shoulder, arms still limp and trembling on top of his knees. When he caught his breath, he wheezed out a weak, "You?" His neck was bent, head fallen forward as if too heavy.

Marta held his wrists. She mouthed to Horace. Kalt. He nodded, taking the cover from his own bed and draping it around his shoulders. Only his hands visibly trembled, but grazing the skin of his neck, Horace felt as if he were draping a pall over a sitting corpse. Oliver didn't see his movements though his eyes were open. He jumped at the touch, but Marta's heavy hand kept him in place. It was oddly comforting.

Don't let your guard down.

The blanket joined under his neck. It was soft. Warm. Oliver giggled with closed and sore eyes. "Like a cape."

"Will you be better tomorrow?" Marta asked, pressing his palms together and miming to rub them together like a child.

He did as instructed, but his palms barely made contact before falling apart. "Of course I will." Now his breath was caught, the tremor reached his voice. "I will." He looked to the door, where the orbs of light had become distant. "Can I stay here for a bit... until I..."

"Of course." Horace sat back on his bed and put on his shoes. No use laying down again. "Take all the time you need." What to do with him? Just a day ago he was standing over the poor boy, chest puffed out.

Yesterday seemed an age away. But that would make Layla even further away.

Oliver laughed. "I need more time than I have, my friend-" He winced and recovered as if by instinct. "But thank you. It means more than you know."

No friends.

"Of course."

"Truth is... I was meaning to speak with you before morning came." He coughed again, and Horace felt a tickle in his own throat, but suppressed it. "I did see something when I opened the door and I- I wanted to apologise for lying."

"Oh," Horace straightened up. "Thank you?"

"I just wanted you to know – if I have the right to say – there's no hostility between us." He looked to Marta, whose eyes were wide, as if taking in as much as she could at once. "And to you, I want to thank you for giving me a second chance. Whether I deserve it or not."

"You need sleep." Marta said impatiently. "Find your jacket, keep warm." He brushed her off, then looked back, wide-eyed with regret.

"One more thing." Horace interjected. Oliver looked up at him. "Did you see... the symbols?"

Oliver stifled a breathless cough. "The-The blood?" Horace nodded.

Ancient runes, a secret language. Decode it to solve the mystery...

"You saw them too?" Marta asked. "I didn't imagine them..."

"Do you know what they mean, by any chance?"

Oliver shook his head. "I remember seeing them, at the compound. But there were hundreds of symbols to learn, and it's been years-"

His eyes were pulled magnetically down, and his hands tightened the sheet to his chest. "I'm truly sorry."

"It's okay, really, don't worry." Horace saw the redness returning to his cheeks. To his forehead and neck as well, beneath the white sheet. He mouthed to Marta. Fever. "You should really sleep. At least try."

"Yes. Thank you." He pulled the sheet off one shoulder, then paused, stiffening. He dropped the other side and let the sheet gather on the chair behind him, eyes still glued to the floor as he stood up. In a single step he was at the door.

"Will you be fine ki-" He caught himself. "Oliver?"

"Of course." There was an air of determination around him as he set his shoulders back before placing his hand on the handle. "Of course I will," and it sounded like he was convincing himself more then them. He pushed through the doors and left them swinging again. Marta sighed, getting up to close them again.

"Do you worry about him?" Horace retrieved the sheet from the chair. "He's been… erratic since he used the radio." The sheet itself had been drained of warmth. "Have you looked in on his caravan?"

"Hmm." He had looked in on his way back from Layla's grave. The floor, though darkened, was littered with mechanical debris, wires and smashed glass screen. The headset hung limp off the inner door handle and the door was ajar, no doubt all the oxygen was drained from the room. What a waste.

"I don't think we need to listen in to know what he heard." He handed her the sheet. "Take this and fold it up. It'll make your bed softer. The ground is too cold to rest on."

"What about you?" She took the sheet, still holding some fever-warmth.

"I'm going to make sure he gets to a bed." He opened the inner door and took his oxygen tank. The metal nameplate escaped his shirt as he leant down and spun in the light from the next caravan over. "Bad things happen when insomniacs get around rockets. I'll be back soon."

He closed the door behind him, and Marta sighed. Sleep had evaded her so far tonight, and it seemed she wasn't the only victim.

Perhaps pretending could help. What was it Markus used to do? For someone who slept half the day and most of the night away, he was certainly secretive about his tactics.

Maybe it was the lack of prospects that eased him into slumber. Believing that tomorrow would bring the same disappointment and the same reminder that there really was nothing to do, sleep became a menial task to hasten the menial turning of the clock. There was no future to Markus.

She closed her eyes and imagined she was camping. The summer science camp had really been a fun time, though looking back she should have spotted the American secret service agents terribly disguised as camp technicians. Markus had fun, at least.

There hadn't been a lot of bugs, surprisingly, and the views from their campsite was unparalleled. Sprawling hills and trees, and so much water. Glassy lakes with swans and frogs and lush green algae. A distant waterfall lulled her to sleep at night and greeted her with a fine cold crawling mist that flooded the valley every morning. A procession of ghosts retreating with the rising of the sun in the blue sky. And how could she forget the sky? Always bright and cloudless and so blue. Blue like she had never before seen blue, and certainly not any blue she could find here.

When she used to read at home, instead of diligently following the illustrious imagery and descriptions on the page, she would picture the stories being set right here.

But it was the sunrise that was to die for. Marta would rise early every morning and make the short walk up to the cliff's edge just to watch it. The sky would be painted all shades of gold and pink by then, and any cloud that dared break the colour would be caught ablaze in orange as if the heavens themselves were burning up.

Such a sunrise was all she looked forward to returning to. She could almost hear the camp counsellors calling for morning showers, or breakfast. She would hold out until the last shade of pink faded from the horizon before descending again to rouse her brother from rest, which was always the first challenge of the day.

If Marta could have slept, she surely would have dreamt of the camp. Instead, half-slumber kept her drowsy but restless all night.

The light of day was already piercing her eyelids, and it felt like less than an hour ago Horace had followed Oliver out the double doors. She rubbed her eyes. The morning hadn't warmed yet, but she couldn't pretend it had ever warmed her.

The walls were painted a shade of orange that was a stranger to the Martian palette. As she let her eyes adjust, still seeing stars from rubbing them, the light from the brightest sunrise began moving, swimming around the walls of the caravan, over shelves of glass bottles, vials, and pill boxes. It morphed into a crawling blaze that ebbed and flowed over the cold interior, somewhat hypnotically.

The waterfall of her dreams had roared, drowning out the sound of screams, but as it subsided a new roar replaced it.

Fire.

## Chapter 4

# STILL BURNING?

The light had all but dimmed before Marta had stumbled out the second glass door, her oxygen tank in hand and mask held to her face with the other, but the heat still rippled past her when she opened the door. As she emerged from the dark inside, she closed one eye and squinted with the other as she turned to face the ravine.

There were people running out of caravans, in a similar fashion, and shielding their eyes with their palms, but with mouths gaping open. Others who were closer to the ravine were mere silhouettes against the flaming backdrop. A choking kind of grunt escaped her lips and as she lurched forward, head spinning, she looked for Horace. She couldn't find breath in her chest to yell out his name, and wasn't sure if her voice would be heard above the commotion. A broken buzz of shrieks chorused against the deep rumble of either the fire's chilling roar, or the crumbling earth beneath them.

A stampede proceeded to the outer edge of the crater, where the blaze was already receding behind the rocky lip, but the noise that accompanied it did not muffle, just went down, down, down, retreating while at full power.

Each crack, each groan of metal and rock, each explosive burst of noise echoed and rebounded in the crater's terrible throat. Every ripple of stones clashing below the crust sent a tremor through the ground and made Marta's knees buckle.

Somehow she found her footing before being sent running prematurely by a great surge from below. It felt like something was crawling through the air, an invisible force tearing at the ground and wind alike and shaking the very fabric of the night. For it was still night. The brightest sunrise yet had been merely a mirage.

The light from the crater came with a great blazing plume of smoke, a pillar of fire enveloped in a giant cloud that dove out from beneath the surface of the planet and blended in with the clouds above, the very top plumes being whisked away by high winds as the flames with their refreshing heat haunted underground.

"Marta!"

She heard her name before being swarmed on all sides with people that rushed past as if running through her.

"Marta! Get away from the edge!"

A new shock wave sent her to her knees again, and the tremor in the earth renewed. A stampede of knees and feet landed and scraped her back and thighs as the crowd changed directions. A strong fist grabbed her by the arm and hoisted her to her feet just as she spotted a fissure stretching along her line of sight. The hand pulled her along away from the ravine with surprising strength as the earth ahead of her split and pulled away. She watched as the slab of solid ground she was just on top of slid into the ravine, disappearing into the void of smoke and fire within seconds.

She remembered to breathe. She closed her mouth and took long drags of air through her nose. Smoke coated her nostrils, and she felt her mask was loose, but it was too late. Tears already filled her eyes, and a bout of coughing overtook her.

The hand loosened on her shoulder, falling to her upper back just as the final crack was heard, and the nearest caravan to the edge had vanished inside the cloud. They all heard it falling, crashing half a dozen times on the way down, then it fell silent, sunk into nothingness.

The smoke remained long after the sounds stopped. It plumed, regenerated and spun, weaving itself into the patchwork of colours with its unnatural light.

"Are you all right?" Horace asked after a long time. Everyone had gathered at the edge of the top of the ravine, steering clear of the inner drop, which every so often crumbled under its own weight, and sent another wave of pebbles and slated ground into a burning abyss. Nobody was talking.

She tore her teary eyes from the smoking column that stared down on them all. Horace's eyes were red. His beard was dusted with ash. His skin was red as if sunburnt.

She nodded, for she found she no longer had a voice. If she did, there would have been no words she could have said to convey the numbness within her.

Everything – gone.

The trucks had all but been emptied. The camp that had been set up, not even a night ago, was now burning at the bottom of a burning put, along with all of the rockets, their passage home.

Timidly, and one by one, they gathered around the inner rim of the ravine. On the other side, Horace saw, Layla's grave was untouched.

"What happened?"

"What got into him?"

"I saw him run into the ravine-"

"-No oxygen tank."

"He went mad!"

Among this new noise, resentment couldn't be heard for Dante. Nobody wanted to say it, but everyone was wondering what would have become of them if he had waited until the morning, and everyone would have been in the rockets, all setting off all at once.

Nobody wanted to say it, but they had been saved, even if there was now nothing to give them hope for home. This, the rockets, Dante, would now live on only in their memories, just like the Orchard, and Odyssey, the cursed city. They all felt cursed.

Marta picked up a smashed headlight that had come free of a helmet. It didn't turn on. Or maybe the sunrise had made its own light overbearing. There could be light in this broken thing still.

"Marta, come look." She watched the top of the pillar of smoke dissolve into the air, scattering ash for miles overhead until the true sun came under threat. If it rose even a few more hours its light would be drowned out. The blanket of grey was only waiting, like a blindfold, to stopper it up.

"Look down, on the edges." Horace was almost whispering.

The outer layer of the smoking pillar had blown away and dissolved into the sun-swept air, clearing away the haze that obscured the new perimeter of the crater. Below them all, the ground made sounds like heaving breaths as it spewed forth spurts of fire that momentarily lit up the caves that dotted around the wall.

"Are those-" Giant, writhing creatures had poked their heads out to test the damage done, but with the blasts of light and heat, turned and burrowed back into their caverns. "There they are." A hush fell upon the crowd. All talk of Dante, of home and distraught was silenced.

Only the crater's groaning breaths could be heard as the final traces of the alien creatures was sealed up behind them, each secreting their slime to wall up the entrances to their caverns as they took a final lingering look around.

"They're all gone."

Every so often, a distant explosion, presumed to be a rocket's engine, could be heard, shaking the ground for a second before subsiding. There had still been rocket fuel within their reserves. Everyone listened in horror as another exploded beneath their feet.

A long hour passed with the rising sun and the smoking pillar had all but blended its ash with the burnt fields of Mars. Someone leaned over the edge at last, held back by two others and with careful footing, approached the mouth that had by then uttered its final words. He stood hundreds of feet from the throat of the thing, but the heat still singed his grey hairs.

Marta recognised the man as the same one that had come into the hospital caravan after her first talk with Dante, opening the door wide as she clapped a hand over her mouth. His face was now obscured with his own mask. Her oxygen tank felt light on her back.

There was a fire still burning in the planet's lungs.

*****

Humans are naturally inquisitive creatures, willing to jeopardise their own safety, or even risk their lives, for the sake of curiosity. In this case, it was fear of the dark that drove them into the ravine.

Nobody was a stranger to the uncertainty that came with the fall of night, but when the sun dimmed before reaching the middle of the sky, a new kind of fear, the likes of which the surviving Pompeians would have felt, was instilled in the survivors. The fear of darkness in the daytime.

Nevertheless they spent the first day talking. How human, thought Horace, to talk when you think you're about to die.

Someone brought up Oxygen. Everyone shifted uncomfortably, like for the first time, the weight on their backs would be more than missed. Horace cast his mind back a few days, retracing his steps. He looked around. A few trucks that had been left behind at the bottom of the hill on the outside were dusted with ash among the usual red dusting of Mars.

Marta saw the cogs turning in his head and was already halfway down the hill, the brown jacket, thrown down the hill by Oliver, almost calling to her.

He hated taking charge. He hated having to stand up and give orders, knowing that everyone was in this precarious situation because of his mind and his pencils, all those decades ago. Even worse, his maps were all gone. "There is one dispenser left. It is nearly full, but we'll have to search for it."

All of the trucks departed that same hour, and agreed to drive out in each direction, and return before sunset.

Three returned. By then, plans had been made to venture into the ravine, with sideways glances every few minutes, to see if the fire truly was still burning. If it went out, then the oxygen would have run out. If it stayed burning, even weakly, that meant there was a source, and a steady flow. One which could be accessed.

They watched with anticipation as the sun dipped below the planet's surface once again. If their pride hadn't survived the fire, many of them would have asked to hold each-other's hand. Alas, there was no need for that.

A motor was heard before they saw the driver. She waved the tarp above her head as she sped toward the hill. A cheer erupted, full-chested like there was nothing stopping them from taking hearty gulps of air between hoots of laughter. Horace sat down. For now, they were at least able to breathe with moderate comfort.

The next morning they started the steady climb down. It didn't take long to reach the first uncovered cavern. It seemed the aliens had left some of them free of their luminescent walls, or perhaps it was on purpose, a generous taking of pity upon their misfortune invaders.

In single file, with Marta leading them, cracked headlight in hand.

*****

Eleven years.

It had been eleven years since the first landing. Eleven years since Odyssey and nine since their death warrants had been signed and dangled in front of their faces, and now they find a paradise hidden beneath their feet. An Oasis.

The cave they found ran spiral into the inner wall of the ravine, which they followed into its warm depths. The fire at the bottom raged on, but as they followed its distant rumble, some thought they heard another sound join it.

Enticed by the sound, they followed, the distant rumours of salvation, the masses came down one by one, tracking the cave by ear. The light of the fire had been snuffed days before, no longer dancing behind them on the cave walls, but some glowing slime had withstood the test of scorching heat. However, they could have found their way blind, following that sweet and promising sound.

At last they turned a final corner. Marta had turned out her light long ago, realising it added nothing in terms of finding her way. Before her stood a final exit. The fire above had gone silent, and now the new sound overwhelmed her ears. She stood motionless on the lip of the cave, looking out, as others met her back and looked over her shoulder.

What they found was an Oasis. A real one, not a glass dome with feeble trees and no grass. This was a true hidden paradise, unblemished by a shattered crystal canopy or the fabrication of a world, hand-crafted to imitate nature. It was not a juxtaposition - it was authentic.

This giant chamber they uncovered was furnished wall to giant wall with greenery of all foreign shapes. Orchards hung from the ceiling and vines traipsed luscious fruit across the mouths of the caverns left by the old inhabitants. Every new shrub they spied dangled a new vibrant discovery before their famished eyes and hands. At the same time they rediscovered hunger.

The lush, mossy carpet cushioned their footsteps and didn't scatter a cloud of dust with each kick. Instead it folded and sprung back beneath their feet.

There was real humidity, real warmth in the air that replenished their skin, soaked into their pores and wet their cracked lips and tongues.

But the centrepiece of all their attention, the sight that none could tear their eyes from, was the waterfall.

Strong and loud, fresh water poured from a crevice high in the wall of the giant chamber, which spanned the width of a wild valley through which a river ran, enriching the soil and air with its life-giving ebb and flow. The ceiling of the chamber was unseen beneath the dangling white cloud of warm mist that crawled ghostly above them.

Horace stepped away from the gaping crowd, breaking ranks and crossing the rich earth towards the river that formed at the base of the waterfall and disappeared into the other side of the great chamber, trailing into another dark crevice on the floor. The clear, roaring river tore at his ears, whose mist tossed his hair back and left droplets dripping from his beard before his hands had even reached down to cup the water in his hands. The crystal stream housed a living carpet of aquatic plants that swayed in the rushing water as a scarf in the wind.

The cold water spread a tingle over his skin as he drew his hands towards his face, and with trembling and dry lips he closed the space, and took the crystal liquid into his mouth. The tender kiss of sweet water to weak lips spread a warmth of life through his body – his vessel. The old man knelt in the river and let the cold water shock him to the thighs and stomach, leaning back in the heavy current as the water soaked through to his flesh. Submitting to the tidal onslaught that gently rocked him. He let it weigh him down, saturate his clothes and skin alike. He spread his palms and sprawled his fingers in the oncoming waves, grabbing at the fresh sensation like he could grasp it, like it was running away from, not toward, him.

Throughout all this there was a droplet of guilt trickling down his neck.

You would have loved this. I can't stay here.

*****

Layla was laid on her bed, across the room from a sleepless Horace busy at whatever he was doing that carried over from the day. It was a rare event when neither of them could sleep, and Layla couldn't help but worry. The company, at least, was a nice change. For hours they seemed to be just talking. About everything and nothing, and it all came down to words. It always came down to words.

"Regnant," Layla murmured.

"Regal," Horace tossed back.

She dangled one leg over the side of the bed and swung it lightly. She thought of a grandfather clock. "Pendulum."

"That's a nice one."

"It's good," she said. "Not a favourite."

Horace waited. Usually when favourite things came up she would start listing them without being urged. This time she was silent. "Can I guess?" She was silent again and he thought she might have dozed off, but when he turned around she was still swinging her leg below her. The discarded recorder laid beside her on the pillow, the both of them voiceless.

Her eyes were open, fixed on him. She gave a slight, unsure nod.

"Token." He began listing his own favourites. "Mutual." She shook her head. "Ascend. Caricature. Train. Digit." She rejected all of them. Half-lidded eyes trailed away, and he felt he had failed. After a minute he turned back to his silent work.

"Cinnamon. Hope. Holiday." She said at last. His pencil halted mid-calculation. Without looking up he grunted in approval. "My favourite words are things I've never had."

"Cinnamon is good," Horace said.

"I bet it is."

Chapter 5: Serenity

Horace had chosen to wait out the oxygen levels on the rim of the crater, leaning against Layla's gravestone as he watched the others seal the entrance to Serenity using metal sheets they had retrieved from the destroyed rockets. "Odyssey II" was offered up first, but Serenity had a nice ring to it. For them, it meant peace, and a home at last, even if it wasn't the one they were looking for. It was the one they had found, and would grow to love, and would grow with them.

Marta among them had taken the upper hand in leading the construction efforts. She was the first to toss aside her oxygen tank and leap into the river after Horace, the others followed after. It seemed this was how it would be, for a short while at least. Marta would make sure it didn't last.

She gave the wool of the jacket a good wash, but the wool would never be white again. She felt she was washing Oliver out of it, but as the brown leather shone, now clear of Mars' characteristic dust, he felt more present than ever. Perhaps it wasn't such a bad thing.

Oliver had made his decision. He wanted to be a hero. He wanted to bring people home. And he did. Now that things were settling down, it was up to Marta to lead them to unlearn Dante.

His real name would be at the top of the memorial, the one in the centre of Serenity, at the noisy base of the waterfall, built using the metal plates from Layla's box, as well as all the others that people had saved. From their friends, colleagues, even strangers. Serenity brought the living and the dead together under the waterfall.

There, the names could be a part of everything. Both man-made and bizarrely natural. This new world would take getting used to, especially the nature. There were living things again – tissue, mass – of colours and textures new, or previously forgotten. Everything was coated with colour, even the boulders upon which giant fungi were suspended, or the undersides of the "trees" that grew on the cavernous walls, their canopies crowned with lush fruit that were sweet to taste and filling to eat.

This was a real Eden, but nobody said it, afraid they would lose it in the same way.

"Ready to go? We want to seal the top before night." Marta wiped the sweat from her brow and took another swig of water. She had refused to put back the mask after taking it off, and as a result, all the remaining tanks, masks, and the last oxygen station had been left in a cluster just outside the entrance to Serenity.

"Do you want more time?"

Horace glanced at the level on his tank, threateningly low, then to Layla's grave.

"I want more time than I can have, Marta. I went all my life thinking there was no place for me to call home. Turns out I was looking for the wrong thing." His eyes gleamed. "A place." He shook his head and smiled, tracing a hand over the roughly inscribed name. "This new home is a gift, but not for me."

"So you are not scared."

He shook his head. "When I first knew I would lose her, that was when I felt fear for the very last time. I'm not scared this time."

Marta pushed herself to her knees on the flat top, and untangled the strap of the flask from her hair. She held it out to the old man, and he took it gladly, though he would have never gotten used to the sweetness.

"Final chance."

She nodded to the entrance.

He wiped his mouth with the back of his hand. "It wouldn't be fair for her." He gave a friendly elbow to the solitary gravestone and handed back the flask. "Enjoy Serenity. I'm already home."

Marta stretched out her hand to take the flask, then captured his before he could take it back. Horace thought she would try to drag him down, tear him away from the desolate sky and lonely landscape, but she only tensed her fingers into a firm handshake.

His eyes snapped up. She said nothing, only smiled as she turned on her heels, sending up a final puff of dust. In the hand with the flask Horace had slid the pictures he had taken eleven years ago.

The impossible might not have been achieved, but his view from his final day was good enough.

He closed his eyes and listened to the swish of boots, sliding down the dusty wall of the ravine, for the last time. The sunset burned the horizon behind his eyelids, but the cold stone engraved Layla's name into his back.

On this little planet that smelled of blood, he was already home.

L - #0179 - 141222 - C0 - 210/148/13 [15] - CB - DID3449228